Praise for the first edition

'Whoever he is, this author likes conic sections.' *Archimedes*

'Whoever he is, this author likes syllogisms.' *Aristotle*

'Sets a new standard for historical accuracy.' *Herodotus*

'Medical themes well explored and up-to-date.' *Hippocrates*

'A work of deep piety ... liturgical seriousness ... [deserving of]
the gratitude of clergy for its exposure of cant.' *St Ignorius*

To Three Women

My son.

God created Man, I say. For why would Man, who is rational, create the God who has power over him, demanding obeisance as I do?

O Lord.

Man is more deceiving than rational, I say. Man created God not to have power over him, but to have power over others.

Leonardo di Boccardo
Conversaziones e Silenzio

FOREWORD

When it was suggested by Dr Darian that I provide some prefatory remarks for his latest work, I confess to having reservations. For a start, I knew very little of the culture and contemporary geopolitics of the Ferendes, and even less about its evidently unique ecology and natural history. Indeed, my abiding qualification regarding the South China Sea is that once I fell into it, fully frocked.

Another difficulty was a shameful, life-long reading indolence, especially around fiction. For weeks I plotted how to introduce this volume persuasively without actually opening it.

Then, last Sunday, in one of those freakish accidents that are surely sent to repair the incorrigible in our souls, I dropped the manuscript and it fell open on my study floor. I saw endnotes. There was an index. There were citations. There were names: Newton, Shannon, Markov, Machiavelli, Darwin—all real people. And real places: Cambridge, Perth, Madregalo. This wasn't fiction at all! I was enticed. I began to read.

Now, the perfectly understandable expectation was that my contribution should draw the reader in. (I must here give assurance that neither author nor publisher exerted undue pressure. I was tasked only to inform the reader, as seductively as I am able, that throughout the work all angles are in radians.) Even so, I am bound to be honest. I will say that here, partly, is a text of philosophical preoccupations, foremost perhaps being the issue of truth; especially truth constructed and relativized within what I can only suppose is simulated fiction.

There are also informative expositions, drawing on multiple sources and levelled at the non-specialist, on belief, evidence, dreams, conscience, the individual in a causal world, the social ratification of personal identity, and practical perpetracide. The last comes with helpful advice on the Prussica gunsight, hydrogen cyanide, incapacitating bewilderment, and the universal law of gravitation.

My personal favourite is Dr Darian's exploration of modern linguistic themes, including generalized translation theory — I promise you no better explanation of Thortelmann equivalence exists in all of English than can be found in these pages. And if you are affected by what you learn of the mute man, or the industry of silence explained by Barbara Bokardo, then you will find the nexus of language and destiny at work in the story of the Syllabines heart-wrenching.

Though serious and scholarly, I can assure the reader there is no academic sterility here; on the contrary, the text is light and accessible. So quite apart from those with a professional interest in conjecture, language, and authenticity, and students of civilization more generally, here is a work that would suit reflective readers of all ages.

As if this were not enough, there is also much to engender, and satisfy, our curiosity on matters ranging from advanced balloon craft engineering to the metaphysics of glass to the haematology of the swint. And to all those who engage in commercial air travel, I urge that you commit to memory the Reckles principles of survival science; they might well save your life one day.

But the greatest audience for this book may prove to be those who would inform themselves of developments in South-East Asia, and the criminal organizations connecting that region with Australia. Were it not for the intelligence and retiring heroism of people like Edvard Tøssentern, Richard Worse and Emily Misgivingston, and the professionalism of law officers like Victor Spoiling, the ruthless activities of those secret societies would impact more obviously on our lives. This book is, beyond all else, a graphic documentary of the odiousness of one such enterprise, Feng Tong, and the fitting dispatch of its principals.

Finally, and very much to my liking, Dr Darian has provided a compelling history and travelogue that is factual and entertaining, ideal for those who would immerse themselves in the romance of the South China Sea without the ignominy of near-drowning.

Magdalena Letterby
Perth

1. THE WEAVER FISH

Within the opaquely threaded dialects of the Ferendes, and in all the languages of all the coasts that share their latitude, there must be ten thousand distinct words for weaver fish. More words than reported sightings. More words than actual fish by now, possibly. And more words than the number of fishermen who have use of them.

The latter is logically, if speculatively, explained by Thomas MacAkerman's observation that each person uniquely owns a private, talismanic name, as well as sharing the communal vocabulary, itself vast. Since MacAkerman's time, the accumulated effort of a distinguished rollcall of anthropologists, sociologists, and linguists has generated no more plausible a theory.

More surprisingly, modern oceanography and marine biology, for all their sophistication, seem to have advanced our knowledge of the fish itself not at all. Except, of course, to amplify its mystique and elusiveness. No specimen having been caught and dissected, there is yet no scientific nomenclature, no genus, no species. *Acarcerata textor* might serve, when the need arises.

MacAkerman was a physician and amateur naturalist, of catholic interests and impressive breadth of scholarship, who accompanied Captain Joseph on HMS *King of Kent* for two voyages, in 1816 and 1819. An enthusiast of the new sciences, he was apparently a brilliant popularist and quite famous for his public lectures. These, unfortunately, were never edited for publication, though their quality can be inferred from the comments of contemporary diarists. He did author several papers and monographs on varied subjects, but in respect of the weaver fish only two primary sources survive. One is a short entry, bearing his initials, in the first (and only) edition of the *New Scottish Encyclopaedia*. The second is a letter in the *Transactions of the Philosophical Society of Edinburgh*, of April 1823. MacAkerman there describes how, shortly after sunrise on Greater Ferende, he was exploring the littoral for crab species when he 'occasioned' on a large sea-pool, sequestered from the receding tide by a sandbar, and

about a half-fathom in depth at its most. My attention being focused in pursuit of the crustaceans, their size and colour and actions, I did not at first see something altogether more interesting, which I took then to be some optical phenomenon of the sand and water. I walked the circumference of the pool, to see it vary in place and intensity, and with light in front and behind. It took many minutes to discern, and then only in half belief, that I was seeing fish swimming, many hundreds of them, and of the most transparent substance imaginable, except for small eyes, themselves faint, so that what I had witnessed was the movement of eyes, and a changing refraction of the pool sand of great subtleness. My interest in crabs for the moment set aside, I watched for perhaps a half hour, then something impelled me to throw dry bread into the centre, expecting I don't know what, but I hoped for some intensification of visible movement. What did follow I could not have expected, for I could not wildly invent the sight, nor would I wish to, for it recurs to me in most distressing images and waking dreams these last seven years. The bread floated for some moments in several pieces, without noticeable disturbance, nor any interest of the fish. Then a solitary gull, to whose aerial squawks I had been only half attuned, plunged at the feast, and rather than plucking one bit in flight, settled on the water, intending, I fancy, to enjoy the multiplicity. Then followed an event I would wish on no man's conscience, and I am sorely in need to expunge from mine. In an instant the water rose in symmetry around the gull, but it was not water, but a mass of fish stacked high, as well as I could see from the disposition of their eyes and the faintness of their bodies, in intercrossing alignments of great discipline that was surely not accidental. The wretched bird attempted flight, but to nought avail, as its legs seemed bound in a viscous gel. Then the fish trap (I should call it) rose higher to the full measure of its hapless victim, which soon became lifeless, appearing I thought as encased in ice fully a half foot above the water surface. The orchestration of the trap was now more evident, fish bodies tightly woven crisscross, like warp and weft, but layered, as a solid tapestry might be made, and quite still. And before my eyes, the gull dissolved. I repeat, the beast dissolved in minutes to skeleton alone, but for a strange purple colouration (which I would name Tyrian) surrounding it. Then abruptly, as if on some regimental bugle call, the whole edifice unweaved, the pool returning to its former state but for the gull bone sinking unimpeded at its centre, not five yards from where I stood.

I confess then to great perturbation in my heart. Where previously I had thought lightly of entering the water for the better inspection, I was now repelled, I should say fearful, and stepped back from its edge. For if they could rise so deliberately above its surface, could they not breach its boundary also? After some minutes of composure, and my anxieties abated, I resolved to learn more, and taking from my wares a fine pole net I set about straining the shallows from a discreet distance. To my delight I soon scooped one, a half yard in length as they had all appeared, and held it up for transport to the sand. But to my astonishment and sore disappointment this triumph was quickly reversed. For the fish, which made no movement throughout, took on the purple hue that I had noted earlier, though more intensely, seeming to secrete or gurgitate a slime that I can only guess was some digestive acid of the greatest potency, for almost in a second the fabric of my net was burnt and through its deficiency so effected my captive escaped, falling to the water where it was instantly invisible. Standing there, with my net made useless for its purpose, I admit to the strangest feeling of defeat and perplexity, which in all my years of collecting God's creatures has no equal before or since.

MacAkerman goes on to describe further unsuccessful attempts to ensnare a specimen, but his efforts were eventually frustrated by the returning tide. It is difficult now to judge how this account was received. It was a time of a growing culture of wonder at the natural world, with a proliferation of gentleman scholarship that was rarely challenged. The last vigorous debate was on infinitesimals, and the next would be evolution. The modern critical discourse of science was in its infancy. Thus there was no subsequent correspondence on the topic in the *Transactions* or any other journal. None of this, of course, should be taken to impugn the accuracy of MacAkerman's report. He was, from all the evidence, a man of unimpeachable integrity and intellectual rigour whose contribution to the sciences has few parallels in his era. Only many years later, and then only in the practice of medicine, was his judgement disordered by the cruel and tormenting decline of his final illness.

There is no doubt that MacAkerman's discovery had a profound influence on him. In a public lecture series of 1824 (abstracted by the canal engineer James Lypton in his *Journal* of that year), he explained his motivation for the second voyage in 1819 as 'to further my researches in the natural history of the weaver fish' (the exact wording may be Lypton's). As it turned out, he never did acquire the specimen for which the Old World museums would have bid dearly; indeed he reported no further observations with any confidence.

But that is not to say the voyage was a failure, and at least two major achievements can be ascribed to 1819. First, he completed the collection that would form the basis of his definitive work on tidal crab speciation (long before Darwin's ideas were published), and secondly, he conducted what we would now call field ethnography among indigenous fishing communities, centred on language and folklore pertaining to the weaver fish. The latter is a fragmented opus surviving only in notebooks, journals, and many secondary sources, and greatly deserves the attention of modern scholarship. From these studies, we learn that the majority of names for the weaver fish have roots in native words for death, water (that is, a fish made of water), invisibility, the colour purple and, of course, a woven cloth or matting. These meanings were so concordant with MacAkerman's own observation that he was persuaded that similar sightings must not have been infrequent, though obtaining witness testimony proved more problematic. In any event, MacAkerman first employed the term 'weaver' in 1816, apparently quite independently of any native tradition, and never varied from its use. Paradoxically then, whilst no synonyms exist in English, he has left us with a monumental foreign lexicology far exceeding that of any other single referent.

In 1916, exactly one hundred years after MacAkerman's seminal observation, a fisherman named Josef Ta'Salmoud, from the village of Madregalo on Greater Ferende, saw weaver fish. Ta'Salmoud himself gave only a brief description of his experience, and was never persuaded to repeat or enlarge upon it. But there are many eyewitness accounts, from villagers on the shore, which are fully corroborative of what he described. Some of those present were still alive in 1996, and were interviewed by this author during a Language Diversity Initiative field trip. It should be said in this regard that more research is needed using newer validation tools applied to both linguistic and thematic elements. Authentication studies also require a good understanding of cultural specifics in oral tradition, which can be very localized and idiosyncratic. This work is continuing as part of a wider LDI programme.

On days following severe night storms the fishing grounds of the Ferendes could be deceptively treacherous. It was customary for the chieftain of fishermen to enter the water first and, having ascertained conditions in the bay, signal to those on shore that they should remain there or join him. One morning, Ta'Salmoud set forth on this task. As was normal, his progress was observed closely by those on the beach. When he was about fifty yards from shore he stopped paddling and stood in his canoe, facing the villagers. To this point, nothing seemed unusual, and they next expected his signal. None came.

The bay was rough with a big sea swell and a bad current. I stood in my canoe to give the signal: do not come out, I am returning. I thought, be careful, Ta'Salmoud, stand safely, these are the times—rough days making the signal—when my ancestors have drowned. But when I got up, suddenly the bay was calm and my canoe became still. I could have stood on one foot. I thought, I have been wrong, the bay is smooth. Then I saw water in my canoe, with little holes in the hide, and purple colour near my feet. When I saw the purple I knew it was the kenijo before I saw the kenijo themselves. The water came up to my canoe side, but it was the kenijo weaving, but water from the sea was inside, on my feet. I was thinking, I must give the signal to save my fisherman brothers, but I don't know if I did. I was so full of fear. Then my canoe was full of water, but not sinking because I think the kenijo kept it there. For as far as I could see there was the weaving, like a thick mat on the top of the sea, and I thought, Ta'Salmoud, you must run for your life and even though I thought I would die I stepped from the canoe onto the weaving fish mat and it seemed very strong. My feet sank only a little and my good balance from standing in my little boat kept me from falling. I took another step, and another, then I started to run. I knew that if I stumbled I would be eaten but I kept running. Every place that my feet touched there was a purple mark, and my feet hurt but I hardly looked down. I was looking at my village and my people. They said later that I was crying out my word all this time but I don't remember that. To me it is like a terrible dream, until I see my feet.

From the village beach, these events must have appeared truly astonishing.

It was very strange. When Ta'Salmoud stood up the rough water became smooth. Not like wind stopping but as if it was made into glass, all in a second. I thought, what signal will he give? Then his canoe sank and he just stepped onto the water and ran to us. The whole village was quiet. Poor Ta'Salmoud, he was saying over and over his word, not shouting, but very softly but we could all hear it. We all knew it was the fish. I did not breathe until he was safe, and then I did not breathe when I saw his feet. I don't know when I breathed again.

Not even the sight of a man running on the surface of the sea prepared the villagers for what they next saw.

When Ta'Salmoud was close to the shore he stopped running, I think as he felt the sand under his feet. He was still saying the word, and we could see his face was very frightened. He came from the water and was bending over like an old man. We were too frightened to go to him, and all of us stayed quiet. I could not look away from his feet but I could not look at them also. Then Maria [Ta'Salmoud's wife] stepped forward and took his hands, but she was looking downwards too. I think Ta'Salmoud then stopped the word and started crying, and I thought his face is not fear but pain. But we still stayed back, and Maria held him closer. He seemed in much pain and then he looked down, at his feet. From his ankles down there was no flesh, just bones and sinew, all purple stained. Poor Ta'Salmoud cried out and fell to the sand, in Maria's arms. He was half man, half rinlin. Purple rinlin.

The last word translates (somewhat inadequately) as skeleton, which is surely exaggerated. Presumably, the digestive secretions of the weaver fish had destroyed the skin and much of the soft tissues of his feet. There is no doubt that the foot bones below the ankle joint were exposed, but we must suppose that sufficient blood supply and other attachments were preserved to maintain rudimentary function. Sensory innervation was clearly compromised, for he was not in constant agony as we would otherwise expect. Only when his feet became dry did he suffer pain, and this was quickly assuaged by immersion in seawater. Almost certainly, the cleansing action of the latter practice minimized the bacterial contamination that in these circumstances would ordinarily lead to suppuration, fasciitis and fatal septicaemia.

It is said that as Ta'Salmoud collapsed on the beach, the calm in the bay vanished, replaced in a moment by the most frightening storm the villagers had seen. For Ta'Salmoud, then, the weaver fish was not an agent of disfigurement and pain, but of salvation, providing safe deliverance from the temper of the sea.

Not surprisingly, the news of a fisherman who apparently calmed the sea, walked upon water, and suffered uncomplaining an unspeakable injury attracted the attention of the Church. In 1921, papal envoys visited the Ferendes to investigate the claims and determine a recommendation of sainthood. They declared in the negative on the grounds that, though the events truly occurred, they were not miraculous but explained by natural causes, namely the weaver fish.

There is one known photograph of Ta'Salmoud, taken during that visit, and protected under *lex Vaticani* (it may be viewed but not reproduced). He is at the centre of a small group, standing on the beach with the village behind. The others are bowed, but Ta'Salmoud's head is high, looking not at the camera but into the distance beyond. Almost certainly, he is staring at the sea. The photographer was clearly not a scientist, for what we would like to have had recorded is an image of Ta'Salmoud's feet. But the manners of the time, or ineptitude of the nuncio, have forever denied us this evidence. While his companions' feet are all on view, Ta'Salmoud's are hidden by the tub in which he stands, presumably immersed in his anodyne seawater.

Ta'Salmoud died, from all accounts peacefully, in the following year, 1922. He had never fished again, nor ventured into the bay. All the stories attest to him being treated with the greatest reverence, and after his death his word, *kenijo*, became the main word, the most precious word, and the most protective one, for all his descendants. There is something poignant about a great fisherman who had walked on the sea, thereafter to be made forever to stand in it, in pots and pans and ignominious tubs, or at the water's edge, half in half out. Half man, half *rinlin*.

This is an edited version of an illustrated address entitled 'Thomas MacAkerman to Josef Ta'Salmoud: A Century of the Weaver Fish', given to the Lindenblüten Society in Nazarene College, Cambridge, by **Dr E O M Tøssentern**, Fellow. The Advocacies referred to can be perused in *Edictum MCMXXI Iesus Solus*—Only Jesus (Walks on Water).

2. ORIEL GARDENS

To a casual observer crossing New Latin Square, the modest apartment tower at Number 7 would not rate a second glance, unless the eye found pleasure in distinctive drabness. Or unless some private resonance piqued the interest: not for the first time might those paired windows evoke two sorrowful eyes, their feature lintels heavy brows, and the grey, brooding fabric the face of human melancholy returning a stare.

But Oriel Gardens was not always so easily passed over. Sixty years ago, we might encounter a gaggle of excitable spectators, looking, pointing, declaring this and that, approving or disapproving — but whatever the case, opinionated. For a year or so, it was probably the most discussed and photographed building in London.

It is usual to attribute the building design to Howard Prescott, then of the partnership Knight Prescott, but this is an error. For it is this very issue of attribution, indeed of what constitutes a building no less, that placed Oriel Gardens at the centre of a storm. Prescott, the city's most revered architect and shortly to receive a knighthood, accepted the commission under a Royal Assent, a prestigious appointment even for him. He designed the fabric, then unceremoniously passed the project to a junior partner: 'You do the internals, Enright. I've finished the building.'

Today, that sounds culpably patronizing; we can only imagine Enright's dismay. But that was Prescott's view of the world. Architecture was transformation of the landscape, a building was designed to exist amongst other buildings, to please on an urban scale, and to be admired from the outside.

Fortunately, Lawrence Enright had an interest in the design of 'internals', and to his credit produced workable plans within four weeks. These were so innovative and adaptable that half a century later the apartments remain works in transformation, a fusion of the continually modern and the period gracious. This capacity for renewal within the fixed structural constraints set by Prescott was a triumph of the imagination, not widely recognized at the time. Enright later established a new practice, more to his philosophic liking, with Rosalind Fitzwilliam, became president of the Institute, and received a peerage after refitting the Royal Yacht. He never criticized Prescott, and was not a party to the acrimonious debates that centred partly on his work, on the two architectures of a building, the inside and the outside of Oriel Gardens.

Most publicly, the antagonists in this controversy were Prescott and Julian Kaldor. Kaldor was not an architect, but an artist and photographer who lived well off private means — evidently power generation in Hungary — and exhibited for pleasure rather than profit. His connection to the debate seems to be his passionate beliefs in the functionality of good design, the pre-eminence of human experience in parametrizing space for work and living, and a temperamental impatience with Prescott's pomposity.

Prescott, accustomed to the respect and admiration of professional colleagues, must have been taken aback at the directness and impertinence of an outsider's criticism. But beneath the superior manners of the knight-to-be was a ready pugilist. Kaldor once described Prescott's architecture as 'skin deep'. Back came Kaldor's artistry as 'paper thin' with an informing intellect 'emulsion thick'. He gave as well as he got.

The dispute can be dated from what should have been a perfectly uneventful dedication ceremony held in late May, 1954, when the building was approaching completion. Proceedings took place in the foyer and the adjoining garden entry, which are easily seen from the main gate. Prescott had given an address of thinly veiled self-adulation, and was about to resume his seat when Kaldor, who was present by reason of being well connected, and had prior knowledge of Enright's contribution, asked loudly about the principles governing the living space design, and when these were clearly articulated, did the result not naturally subsume the building fabric as a logical determination? Indeed, was not a building's exterior wholly derivative, and was not Mr Enright's solution a work of genius?

A heated exchange ensued, which clearly had the normally sleepy court-circular reporter agog. Then, spectacularly, in the midst of the growing fracas, at their feet in the garden, arrived Miguel Pájaro Lorca, prone and with limbs outstretched in a bizarre caricature of failed flight.

Poor Lorca. A roof carpenter who was known to have demons in his head was instructed by his foreman to 'try Crome' (a trade sealant of the time). For want of any other explanation, it was conjectured that, in a state of mental imbalance, he heard 'fly home'. His fate put close to the architecture debate on the day, but hostilities quickly reignited in the press, in professional journals, in the civil courts, and in galleries (Kaldor staged an influential and rather defamatory exhibition entitled 'Integuments', of apocalyptic, damaged building shells, some echoing quite unambiguously the stare of Oriel Gardens).

By 1963, the *cause célèbre* was all but forgotten. The liberal tide had swept away much of authority, guild mentality and prescriptive aesthetics; individualism, modernity, and the Kaldor 'statements' were in ascension. Architecture was about people, not buildings. Prescott had begun his slow, choleric retirement. Kaldor was a celebrity *Quartier Latin* stylist, in vogue with the daring as a portraitist, and was about to found FotoZeit, destined to become the foremost European school of photojournalism for a generation. And Oriel Gardens had retreated to a maturing sedateness.

Enter Mingle Lane and walk along the services access passing to the rear of Number 7. From here you obtain a more proportioned view of the building, set in a well-maintained terraced garden, and the windows, rather spooky from the streetscape, look almost charming. You are now standing on the exact spot where began the short notoriety of Mrs Lydia Chalmers and her dog Mordax.

Late one evening in October, 1963, the two were walking along this lane when Mordax broke free of his lead and ran across the terraces to the building, jumping and barking inconsolably. The elderly Mrs Chalmers followed and in the gloom thought she could see 'a big parcel' hanging from a window, this being the cause of her dog's excitement. (From where you are standing it is the left-most window on the fourth floor.) The general commotion attracted residents and passers-by alike, and it was soon established by better eyes than Mrs Chalmers' that the parcel was in fact the lifeless body of a junior attaché to the Soviet Embassy, clad only in a twisted bed sheet tied around his ankles and by which he was suspended from the window.

The police were quickly summoned, and forced their entry into the apartment. There were found the bodies of Tory moralist Sir Roger Tealady MP, and society heiress Miss Lucy Montague-Tiese, whose property it was. All three were bound together at the ankles by bed linen, being otherwise clothed in rich layers of decaying yoghurt.

Because of the Soviet connection, a joint inquest was conducted with State secrecy, and its finding was cursorily published as deaths by misadventure. Misadventure! How the snigger press loved that. 'Attaché' was briefly defined to mean connected by the ankles with bed linen. But there was more. Run your eye up to the top-floor window directly above. Across its lintel there still exists a rusty cable, which can be traced over the roof and up the edge of the closest chimney. It was a crude short-wave radio aerial; the top apartment turned out to be a hastily evacuated Russian safe house and monitoring post. Misadventure in the Safe House, they sniggered. But there was more. The name of the hapless aide who misadventured from the window? Yuri Groynyich Kondomov. They should never have sent him to London.

Oriel Gardens has managed to keep out of the news for some decades now. Captain Kondomov is no longer a risqué cocktail, and yoghurt is boldly purchased by any English lady without a trace of self-consciousness. The building has properly reclaimed its place in the history of architecture, rather than of scandal. For a few years during the 1980s a ground-floor apartment was periodically opened for students and academics with an interest in design history.

In the mid-1990s the entire property was acquired by the Bokardo Trust, renamed Clement House, and extensively refurbished under the supervision of the Enright–Fitzwilliam architectural practice. The ground and first floors were remodelled into professional suites for medical specialists, with a new dedicated entry off Mingle Lane. Residents still access the upper floors using the original grand entrance and foyer off the square.

To see inside these days, you will need to befriend a resident or represent yourself as an interested party when an apartment is contracted for lease. Alternatively, you may wish to make an appointment with one of the several psychiatrists who keep rooms in its lower floors.

There is a small plaque commemorating **Lorca** in the foyer. Though appearing to be soundly fixed to masonry there is a tradition that, from time to time, it falls to the ground.

In an odd parallel, **Prescott** also fell to his death, from a barn roof in Surrey.

Apart from pre-eminence in architecture, **Lord Enright** is an accomplished illustrator, linguist, and historian. His two-volume *Runic Alphabetology* is definitive. Most recently, his poetic translation (with **E Knielsen**) of the Norse epic *The Slaying of the Brothers Orsifal by the Brothers Parsifal* is the most accessible account in English of the invention of dynastic murder.

The author is indebted to the publishers of *FootNotes: A Walking Guide to Unpedestrian London* (Walk No 17) for much of the information given here.

3. FROM *AVIATION REVIEWS*

HANGING ON, UP HIGH ... WALTER RECKLES IS NOT A HOUSEHOLD NAME, AND AERONAUTICAL ENGINEERING DOESN'T RATE AMONG THE WINNING CONVERSATION STARTERS AT A DINNER PARTY. ALL THAT MAY BE ABOUT TO CHANGE WITH THE PUBLICATION NEXT FALL OF *HOW TO WALK AWAY FROM A MIDAIR COLLISION*. *AR* SPECIAL CORRESPONDENT ANNA CAMENES FOUND THE AUTHOR AT HIS DESK IN A CONVERTED HANGAR OUT OF WHITE SANDS, NEW MEXICO.

I don't think that I have ever seen such an improbable contrast, and felt such an unsettling disjunction, between the inside and the outside of a building. That two vastly different worlds — two realities almost — could co-exist separated only by a thin boundary of pressed steel seemed to defy the Second Law, or something.

Outside, Building B1 looked like any other abandoned, derelict hangar at any other abandoned, derelict airstrip. Dented, rusting, flapping sheet metal, roughly musical, competed with dying long grass and pitted bitumen to advertise the desolation. A cracked concrete plinth with corroded tie bolts that once secured some prized exhibit was now itself a testament to extinction. Closer to the building, near its left-hand end, was an antique gasoline bowser that belonged in an industrial museum as much as in this scene of relics. As we approached, I just made out the designation B1 inside a faded decal high up on the wall. Were it not for that, I would have thought I was being led to the wrong place.

The strange thing is, I can't remember the point of actually entering or leaving the building, the phase transition, as it were. I just remember being outside and being inside.

And the inside, as they say, was something different. I was guided by a helper called Rory to the centre of about an acre of open-plan offices, some made barely private by low glass partitions. Everywhere were men, women, and not a few teenagers sitting at computer terminals, some with racks of accessory test gear housing flashing oscilloscopes, spectrum analysers, and so on. Here and there, two or three would be huddled over a desk or a screen, animated yet hardly noisy. That was a surprising thing: it seemed very quiet for so many people.

And right there, in the centre, in an office like any other, I was introduced to the man I had come to interview: Walter Reckles, President and Chief Executive of all this, as well as the author of a controversial book on disaster survival that had somehow generated a critical industry of its own before being actually published.

As I approached, Reckles was facing away, watching a large screen with a graphic of, I suppose, an aerofoil—though it might equally have been a long section through a chilli. The image was to form a slightly insistent, visually seductive background to our interaction. Several columns of numbers were streaming up the right side of the screen, while the figure to left progressively changed in shape, occasionally drastically. I guessed that some kind of optimization was proceeding, but I didn't ask.

Rory hesitated, mesmerized it seemed, by the screen. I expect everyone there thought that the most interesting, the most important, the most fantastic design work on the whole floor would begin its life on that monitor. Then he said, 'Dr Reckles, this is Dr Camenes. She has an appointment.'

Reckles almost jumped out of his chair, turning awkwardly in the confined space. It was a complex welcoming gesture combining splayed arms and a large smile, as well as, I suspect, a recovery of balance manoeuvre. He responded warmly, 'I know. I know.'

It was a broad, beautiful Southern accent. We shook hands, and he gestured me to a chair, at the same time swivelling his own to face me, and moving it to my left. The effect, I came to see, was that he could turn his head from time to time to glance at the unfolding numerical drama behind him; for me it was just a little distracting.

I would have to say that Walter Reckles, on first impression, is a likeable man. He was tall and clean-shaven, dressed in tee-shirt and jeans, with a certain elegance of speech, accentuated by an intensity of gaze from disconcertingly pale green eyes. I was soon to form the impression that his mind was busy on several channels of concurrent activity, yet his attention to me was almost impeccable. His age was difficult to place, probably mid-thirties. Even so, from some conservatism of manner, some slight formality, I decided at once that he was to be Dr Reckles, not Wal. I knew I was going to be Miss; I almost expected Honey.

You're here to talk about the book.
THE BOOK, AND ITS AUTHOR.
What would you like to know about the book?
WELL, THERE'S NOT MUCH RELIABLE PREPUBLICATION MATERIAL AVAILABLE, BUT I GATHER THAT YOU MAKE A CASE, BASED ON YOUR AERONAUTICAL EXPERTISE, THAT AIRLINE PASSENGERS COULD SAVE THEMSELVES IN A MIDAIR CATASTROPHE BY PILOTING AIRCRAFT FRAGMENTS, PARTICULARLY A WING, SAFELY BACK TO EARTH. IS THAT THE ESSENCE OF YOUR BOOK?
It is. What you need to understand is that every piece of debris is a potential airfoil, some good, some bad. The wing, of course, is a natural. That's the piece to hang on to.
WHAT ABOUT THE TEMPERATURE, THE ATMOSPHERIC PRESSURE AND SO FORTH AT THOSE ALTITUDES?
Right. The physiology. There are issues. You need some preparation. I deal with all that in the book. At length, I might say. Look, I'm not claiming it'll work every time. It depends on a lot of variables, rotational moments at separation, intrinsic damage to the wing, engine power, lots of variables. But we should be designing our airplanes with these contingencies built-in.

SO THAT A WING CAN FLY ON ITS OWN?

Sure. That would happen already. Just go through the math in my book. You'll see that, once separated, the wing takes possession, so to speak, of its own eigenvalues. It flies, solo.

EIGENVALUES?

They're just numbers—solutions to what we call a characteristic, equation. Their location in the complex plane determines the stability of an object in flight. Planes have them. You have them, I have them.

I KNOW.

Reckles looked at me with what was surely respect, either for the depth of my understanding or the magnitude of my lie.

Anyway, on the wing, the only control you have is moving mass.

BY SHIFTING YOUR WEIGHT?

Sure. Jettisoning some freight as well.

YOU MEAN OTHER PASSENGERS?

Start with the lightweights, women and children. Build up a feel for the change. It's subtle. But remember, managing the mass distribution, that's critical.

I tried to glare the message: I am a woman. I think it worked, because he invited my interests into the explanation.

What was your last flight? What plane?

A 7T7.

Right. You need Row 13, 14. Window seat, stay belted. First sign of trouble, borrow a necktie from the nearest businessman and strap your ankles to the bar under your seat. Believe it or not, you're only two locking screws, a titanium rivet plate and three strong welds from the principal wing strut. You can fly home. All the other seats—they're just sitting pretty on some damn thin fuselage lining. Tinfoil rating.

From where I was sitting I guessed I could see perhaps two hundred computer screens. Triple, say, that estimate for units obscured from view and I was in the midst of a major enterprise.

TELL ME SOMETHING ABOUT YOUR COMPANY.
Sure. Martin and I set up eight years ago in an internet café in the Albuquerque badlands. We got hounded every day for blocking the terminals. Now I own thousands of screens and the café's gone under. Funny, isn't it?

I agreed it was funny, but I hadn't encountered the name Martin in my pre-reading.

MARTIN?
Martin Reckleson. Co-founder. We were room-mates at MIT.

Reckles, Reckleson. I wasn't getting less confused.

RECKLES, RECKLESON. THEY ALMOST SOUND RELATED.
Yeah. Not kinship of course. Related by common interests. Aerodynamics and sisters. I married his and he married mine. That was a nice symmetry.

He looked momentarily lost—I'm sure it was sadness—and glanced again at the screen behind.

We nearly called ourselves Reckles 'N' Reckleson, but somehow Flight Control got registered.

There was another pause.

Martin's passed on now, of course.

Passed on, I later discovered, meant being thrust across the lab at high subsonic speed when a wind tunnel malfunctioned.

Left half his interest to the Sisters over on Charity Fields. Now we work three quarters for a living and a quarter for God, and I can tell you, it shows in the results. Anyway, as I was saying, we started off just two guys with running costs of fifteen dollars an hour at the café. Now we employ about one hundred fifty engineers, dozens of math grads, material science folk, machinists, technicians, you name it. Over at the tunnels—they're down the way—

He gestured over the same shoulder as if the facility were within reach, or at least within sight.

—there'd be another forty anytime we run tests.

I was genuinely impressed, and said so. I was then invited to visit the wind tunnels (they operate a supersonic one as well) set up in an old Proving Ground laboratory, but my schedule prohibited this.

HOW DID YOUR COMPANY GROW SO LARGE? WHAT WAS YOUR FIRST BREAK?
Actually, we started off in roofs, not planes.

I was so surprised, I uttered redundantly:

ROOFS?
Yeah. It's not so surprising. There was this big shopping mall chain across the South with its own branded gas stations. Called Wingsters, funnily enough. They're gone now. Anyway, some executive thought it would be a good idea to put this fancy distinctive roof over the gas station lots. They used a kid out of design school who came up with this great-looking gull wing-type shape. Anywhere flat, you could see it for miles. Great promotion, great commercially. They built two hundred before one took off in a windstorm. Flew like a kite then flipped upside down onto the food hall.

NOT GOOD FOR BUSINESS.

Yeah, custom was crushed. Then about a week later a tornado took seven in one day. The company panicked. They were ordered to take them down and couldn't comply fast enough. That shape, visible for miles remember, suddenly became advertising poison. Well, Martin and I were thinking, they just need to understand their shape better, its aerodynamics. We drove to the nearest mall and photographed the roof from all angles—I can tell you we got some bad-tempered hustle for that—then came back to our room and reconstructed the form. I did the computations and Martin made models that he tested in a tunnel rigged up from a cola carton and a bedroom fan. We figured out a pretty simple mod that basically inverted the lift—forced it down in wind rather than up. Forty-eight hours later we took a proposal to Wingsters. If the mod failed, we would pay. If it worked, they'd pay. That's when we registered our company and put some patent papers together.

Well, we started on the mall down in South Stormfield and what should happen? Tornado struck the next Sunday, flattened the whole area matchstick style minus one thing left standing. Our roof. Overnight, we were famous—small-town famous, that is. Wingsters couldn't pay us enough, for the patent, for consultancy, for supervising the rebuilds, for public relations appearances, reassuring folk and explaining a bit how it all worked. So the roof got back its magic, people even congregated there in storms for safety. Only now it didn't just advertise Wingsters. It was good publicity for Flight Control as well.

SO THAT'S WHEN THE AERONAUTICAL BUSINESS STARTED? Not so fast. We did submarines first.

Again, I was so surprised that I barely repressed an inane 'Submarines?' But Reckles stayed quiet, evidently needing a prompt. I capitulated.

SUBMARINES?

Sure.

AND AERONAUTICS?

Sure. Think of a submarine as flying under water. You have buoyancy, power, lift, drag, stubby wings even; currents like wind, vortices. It's fluid dynamics. Same physics. The Navy did all their development with simulation, tank testing and ocean trials. Not bad, but we showed them extra value from wind tunnel studies. No one had thought of it before.

SUBMARINES. IN A WIND TUNNEL?

You'd be surprised what goes into a wind tunnel, Miss.

GETTING BACK TO YOUR BOOK, DR RECKLES, SOME OF THE PREVIEW COMMENTARY HAS QUESTIONED ... BEEN ANALYTICAL ABOUT ... ITS VERACITY. ITS SERIOUSNESS. ITS WRYNESS. WHETHER IT'S FICTION, EVEN. IS IT A SERIOUS BOOK?

Very serious. Look, that misunderstanding, that confusion, probably arises from the book being a bit technical for the average reader, but I'm not apologizing for that. It's a guide for survival. Survival.

I was silenced by the unexpected emphasis here, almost an impassioning. Then he added:

Remember, the average reader would pretty much equate to the average airline passenger.

I was further silenced, examining what I thought were *non sequitur* properties of this assertion. And somehow, in that state of absorption, I became inexplicably and, I knew, unwisely, emboldened.

SO YOU REALLY SEE SOMEONE RIDING THIS WING DOWN 30,000 FEET FROM A DISINTEGRATING JETLINER, HALF THE TIME FROZEN, OXYGEN STARVED, DECOMPRESSED AND BLACKED OUT, THEN GLIDING SMOOTHLY INTO SOME

ABANDONED PARKING LOT AND WALKING TO THE NEAREST
PAYPHONE TO CALL A CAB?
I really see it. You just need the knowledge, the science.
Survival science, and the good math, that's what my
book is about.

Well, I had come here to discover what the book was about, and
now this man with the multi-channel mind and the green-eyed
gaze had told me. It was the good math. With, I suspect, a bit of
the good Lord too.

I thought then about the building I had entered. About inside
and outside, and the containment of opposites by a millimetre of
paradox. About extremes of altitude and two forces of insistent
violation, each of the other, stopped dead in a thin wall of metal.
I said:

DR RECKLES, KNOWING WHAT YOU KNOW, ABOUT AIRCRAFT
AND EIGENVALUES AND TINFOIL, DO YOU ENJOY FLYING?
Sure I do.
WHAT IS YOUR FAVOURITE PLANE?
Well, I'd have to say the newest, fastest, highest, toughest
one there is.
AND THAT WOULD BE?

He tilted his head slightly, directing my attention once more over
his shoulder to the busy CAD screen behind.

And that would be on the drawing board, Honey. There's
where I like to fly.

Anna Camenes was Founding Editor of *Altimeter* magazine. She flies Row 14.

4. SUBSCRIPTION OFFER

Take out a 2 year subscription before end May and we will ship you a genuine Reckles® Texan hat! Uses special aerodynamic 'NegLift' patent brim design! Proven in wind tunnels! This hat won't blow off even in a tornado! Used by leading twister-chasers, mine ore blasters, skydivers, and more! Suitable for swimming! Go chic scuba diving! Cowboys: walk, ride, hogtie, sleep in the unlosable hat! Approved for space travel! One size fits all!
(Advise head circumference when subscribing.)

5. OBITUARY

The Norwegian-British logician, linguist and dream theorist Edvard Tøssentern is unaccounted for, and presumed to have died when the research balloon *Abel* disappeared during a severe storm over the South China Sea.

A man who seemed to inhabit fully three or four careers at the one time, he contributed to applied logic, led both theoretical and field research programmes in linguistics, and became simultaneously revered and reviled for demolishing the bogus foundations of dream analysis, finally closing the chapter on a century of Freudian and Jungian psychologies.

In logic, Tøssentern was best known for the invention of structures called inductive graphs, which serve to formalize the transitivity of a very general class of epistemic relations. They have proved to be a powerful tool of symbolic reasoning with particular utility in causation analysis. In certain circles, and this delighted him, the technique has gained a reputation as the enemy of political rhetoric — many a suspect argument being fatally dispatched by its application. Recently, using a probabilistic formulation, Tøssentern had increased the generality of inductive graph methods, with intriguing implications for game theory, machine intelligence and automated translation.

In the early 1990s, Tøssentern headed a campaign which resulted in the formation of the Cambridge-based Language Diversity Initiative. This is now a major programme with conservation operations throughout the world. Tøssentern personally brought to public notice the forgotten linguistics of the Ferendes (Friendship Islands), and the intimate connection between daily language and the folklore of the mysterious weaver fish. This, in fact, became a subject of special interest to him, and he was known to be editing the collected papers of Thomas MacAkerman, who first described the weaver fish and its curious place in language in 1816. Following the Indian Ocean tsunami of late 2004, when seafloor seismic shocks and disturbances to benthic ecology were conducted well beyond the Ferendes, Tøssentern became aware of unsubstantiated claims to weaver fish sightings. It was his desire to investigate these reports that drew him back to the South China Sea, and to the small LDI research station whence he disappeared.

Of all his contributions to intellectual life, however, probably the most far-reaching was a new theory of dreams. Interestingly, though he was foremost a scientist and published normally in the refereed literature, Tøssentern viewed this work as belonging to *belles-lettres* as much as to scientific discourse. For the matters in question, he valued the informed judgement of a greater interested audience more than fanciful theorizing and the flawed empirical methodologies available to dream research. There was as well, he observed ruefully, an almost unassailable academic bias in favour of theories that powered the psychoanalytic industry.

As was often the case, Tøssentern began his enquiries with a simple question and a surprising proposition. Observing the proportion of animal life spent sleeping, he asked: Why has this state of extreme vulnerability (to predation) so prospered in natural selection? And: Dreaming is not incidental to sleep, but its very purpose. The puzzle of sleep thereby became the puzzle of dreaming, and why this activity should be so evolutionarily advantageous.

In essence, Tøssentern proposed that the dream was instructional: a highly evolved but pre-lingual, pictorial mechanism by which knowledge benefiting survival was communicated from one generation to the next, so that, for example, what we term instinctual behaviour in animals is learned from exemplary imagery in the dream. In the sleeping animal, we observe the autonomic and motor rehearsals for complex survival behaviours. In the case of human dreaming, its utility is subsumed by the development of language; the normative codes of socialization, survival and reproductive behaviour are instructed verbally. Therefore, in humans, the machinery subserving the translation of wakeful experience into dream, its reproduction during sleep, and its inheritance, is in a state of advancing atrophy. This degeneracy, and the lack of a natural grammar of visual scene description, explain the fragmentation and apparent irrationality that typify our dreams. The characteristic amnesia for dreams is illusory, but also fundamental; it serves to disambiguate the lesson world from the lived world. Tøssentern believed that the obsession with symbolism in dream analysis was a mistake. The content of a dream was a portrayal of reality distorted by information loss and neural processing error, and its interpretation was consequently a problem of image restoration. In any event, much of the ancestral content (the earliest of which is characteristically non-verbal and non-graphical) no longer analogized coherently into a rapidly evolved human culture, and was further contaminated by recent, personal (and, of course, defective) dream invention.

With one idea, Tøssentern provided a new ontology and a theory of phenomenology and semantic content for dreaming. He viewed symbolic theories as interesting but over-determined; they should be reconceptualized only as attempts to translate pre-lingual, disordered imagery into language, and be cleansed accordingly—particularly of mysticism. Using arguments that we cannot reproduce here, he also systematically dismissed other contemporary neuropsychological and neurocognitive theories, being especially (though politely) contemptuous of the idea that dreams are not actually or vestigially purposive but are epiphenomenal to a nightly clearing of memory, or even more fatuously, result from random nerve firing.

Edvard Oliver Montague Tøssentern was born mid-Atlantic, aboard MV *Okeanos* en route to New York, on the night of 28 February, 1953. His mother, Henrietta (née Montague), was travelling to join her husband Henrik Tøssentern, who had sailed three months earlier to take up a professorship in mathematical logic. She was accompanied by thirteen-year-old Lucy from her previous marriage to the cellist Pierre Tiese, a union that was dissolved amicably in 1942. Edvard was to become deeply attached to his stepsister, and her scandalous death in the Oriel Gardens affair of 1963 caused him permanent grief.

Henrik Tøssentern had occupied, with equal facility, academic posts in musicology and mathematics in both Oslo and London. During the war he was active in a Norwegian Resistance cell devoted to signal interception and decryption. His contribution was noted by the British Admiralty, which drafted him to Bletchley Park in 1942. It was there that he met Henrietta, a linguist seconded from the Foreign Office, and they were married in 1945. The eponymous Tøssentern transform (referred to by him as K^N transformation), now indispensable in quantum cryptography, belongs to Henrik.

The family remained in the United States until Edvard was eight, moving then to Oslo, London, Paris and Oxford. While still at school in Paris, he published a paper on problems in the translation of subjective terms, illustrated extensively with the vocabulary of pain. His graduate studies were at Cambridge, which he made his lifelong home, and where he became a Fellow of Nazarene College.

His home in Chaucer Road was famed for relaxed hospitality and a kind of informal, salon scholarship. It also housed an enviable library that expanded adventitiously into available living space; it is said that the mathematician Rodney Thwistle thought it imprudent to continue visiting as, room after room, 'books displaced oxygen'. Nevertheless, the vitality somehow remained. In recent conversations, Tøssentern shared ideas that, typically, unified his interests. One was concerned with defining semantic coherence (he used the example of narrative sense) in terms of a suite of conserved properties (such as temporal, nominal and causal content). Another was an inductive graph-based approach to spatial reasoning and image analysis. One is tempted to speculate that some of these advances might have led to a rigorous method of dream description.

Tøssentern set out from Madregalo on Greater Ferende in fine weather on 1 April. He was an experienced navigator and was flying alone. Authorities describe *Abel* as an all-weather steerable balloon with hurricane-rated burners, fully equipped for emergencies, and provisioned for three weeks of powered flight. It carried specialized skipping traps thought suitable for the capture of weaver fish, though these were unlikely to have been deployed in very rough conditions. Final contact with *Abel* was an automatic status signal recorded by ground stations at 1543 hr GMT on 3 April, approaching midnight local time. Far Eastern news services report that an extensive air-sea search was downgraded after failing to locate any trace of the craft or its pilot. Investigations continue locally, and statutory enquiries will be conducted both by the United Kingdom and by Norway.

Tøssentern had many friends, and some will remember back a few years to a convivial evening at Chaucer Road when Edvard spoke movingly of spiritual and psychological identity, and his own sense of statelessness. Trans-cultural parenthood, birth at sea, international schooling and his being non-discriminately multilingual were the complex predicates to an indistinctness of personhood that he revealed as deeply saddening. His words were memorable in being both very exposing but also surprising, because he was a man of considerable fun, with evident certainty of self, and appeared relaxed in his many worlds. It is difficult to accept that his last experience was like his first, travelling in the night, again at sea.

Edvard Tøssentern never married. He is survived by his close companion, the psychiatrist and aviation writer Anna Camenes.

Rede Professor Wallis Pioniv contributes: The proposition that primitive dream imagery might reproduce, albeit imperfectly, the experience of one's ancestors, including their terrors, was rather too existentially charged for post-modern sensitivities, for which the meaninglessness hypothesis of memory de-junking was much more appealing. Even worse, the notion that one's own ideation, one's own monsters, or indeed oneself as a monster, might be transmitted forward to future generations threatened deeply held assumptions about the privacy of the mind and an individual's discretionary power of inviolable concealment over unedifying thoughts.

For a suggestion so injurious to universally approved beliefs about personal identity, free will and autonomy, Tøssentern was subjected to a firestorm of attacks, many *ad hominem*, and many based fallaciously on accusations of essentialism, teleologism, and Lamarckism. Nevertheless, despite a temperamental disdain for the non-rational, he responded to all his critics with practical argument, recourse to first principles, appeal to precedent, and a methodical display of the evidence. Only occasionally here did exasperation intrude on formality: in the appraisal of competing theories, he applied, along with standard measures of best fit and parsimony and the rest, a novel test of 'least silliness', which quieted whole blocs of academe indefinitely.

Tøssentern knew, of course, that from a biological point of view the outstanding problem to address was the claim of heritability. Recent decades had brought to pre-eminence the molecular genetic basis of life, and the idea that a dream synthesized from experience in the parent could be passed to offspring was stigmatized by discredited theories of acquired-trait inheritance. Tøssentern argued, however, that although the nucleotide sequence was clearly necessary for inheritance in complex organisms, it had not been proved sufficient, and to suppose otherwise was conceptually restrictive (and, he thought, an act of hubris). Indeed, it could not be so proved until the mechanism of every potentially heritable feature, including, possibly, dreams, had been explained. Though desperately unfashionable, this was strictly logical, and given the state of the art, not refutable. Most importantly, the argument dispersed a siege of intemperate orthodoxy and served to legitimize a body of serious research. It is fair to say that the Tøssentern theory is now accepted by most major schools of philosophy, psychology and cognitive science, and it remains only for mainstream biology to fully accommodate the paradigm. Extraordinarily, by the close of the twentieth century, the signs were there: evidence is accumulating of epigenetic heredity based on selective methylation of DNA segments in the genome. How obvious it now seems that Tøssentern was right to demand an open mind on the possibilities.

6. ABEL

Dear Dr Camenes

As the lead design engineer for the balloon craft about which you enquired, Dr Walter Reckles has asked me to respond on his behalf and provide you with whatever information you require. He has asked me to convey his sympathies, to which I add my own, for the loss of your friend in such tragic circumstances. Dr Reckles will also be writing to you separately.

We presume that your primary interest is in those design and performance characteristics that might be of relevance to optimum search planning. At the current time, we are unable to explain why mayday/GPS signals were not transmitted.

The craft is non-traditional in design and I expect you are not familiar with many of its features. I therefore give a brief overview, with more detailed design and test data in attached files. We have, of course, extensive flight simulation software for the craft, and you are most welcome to access this. The problem is that, at this stage, we don't have sufficiently detailed meteorology for that location. Aside from navigational error and freak weather stresses, we have to consider the possibility of some catastrophic structural failure, including due to fire. Dr Reckles has given this matter the highest priority, and we are doing our utmost to determine what might have happened. I should mention that British authorities have contacted Flight Control for assistance also.

The L-99 craft, of which *Abel* was a slightly modified example, is of hybrid type, having a sealed outer envelope containing helium, and an inner hot air compartment serviced by dead-baffled butane burners. The helium provides approximate neutral buoyancy on station, adjustable as explained below. The burners fine-tune elevation and provide emergency lift.

Unlike conventional balloons, the L-99 is conformable, incorporating gas piston telescopic struts. This allows two things. First, the volume of the balloon, and therefore its density, can be altered, compensating for local thermal and barometric variations. Secondly, the shape of the balloon can be altered, specifically its horizontal-plane radial symmetry. The standard circular profile reconfigures to sigmoid, presenting a subtle convex–concave surface to the airstream. The effect of this is that the balloon will rotate in wind, rather like a turbine roof vent. Then, instead of the craft being propelled resistively at near wind velocity, much of the linear wind force is dissipated in rotational energy. In this way, down-wind ground speed can be reduced more than seventy per cent. This option rather complicates predicting the balloon's position, even if we had detailed weather data.

The gondola is a sealed cabin constructed of space-rated composites, and accommodates a crew of two. It will float if ditched. There are three hatches: the main one at side and emergency ones above and below. The whole assembly is stabilized gyroscopically using torque from the balloon controlled through an electric clutched gimbal transmission. The cabin is longitudinal and has airfoil curvature which generates a horizontal 'lift', allowing the craft to tack across wind quite effectively. This also complicates prediction.

The main modification was to do with the fish trap mechanism, which was designed and fitted by another company (Custom X Engineering, 1010 Cambridge Technology Park, UK). They consulted us regarding mass, power, and structural strength constraints, but we never sighted the final design. Their concept was to operate the lines through the floor hatch; induction motor winches were snugged into the co-pilot's space. We recommended adding a photovoltaic membrane to the balloon fabric to ensure power needs were met. We also insisted that the hatch seal was not compromised. All modifications were supervised by the client, and we had no further input. We believe that there would be a small, but not hazardous, effect of trap deployment on the balloon performance. Custom X was obliged to perform flight trials to document this, but they reported to the client directly, and we suggest that you approach that company for more information.

In order to tighten error bounds on our structural and dynamical estimates under typhoon stresses we are urgently embarking on more comprehensive wind tunnel analyses using L-99 scale models. We will forward to you results of these and other investigations as they become available. In the meantime, please feel free to contact me, or Dr Reckles, at any time.

Sincerely
Linda Feckles PhD

7. THE ASIATIC CONDOR

CONDORASIATICUS FUGAX. THIS MAGNIFICENT BUT RARELY SIGHTED CREATURE IS NATIVE TO THE FERENDES. REPORTS INDICATE A WINGSPAN OF UP TO SIX FEET, AND ALTHOUGH OTHERWISE ANATOMICALLY SIMILAR TO AMERICAN SPECIES, IT HAS PLUMAGE OF A UNIFORM IRIDESCENT BLACK, LACKING A WHITE FRILL. FERENDE TRADITION HAS IT THAT THE CONDOR NESTS AT SEA, HALCYON-LIKE, AND RETURNS TO THE SEA WHEN DYING. WHATEVER THE TRUTH IN THIS, ITS HABITAT IS CERTAINLY ONE OF EXTREME REMOTENESS, FOR NO NEST HAS BEEN DISCOVERED, MUCH LESS APPROACHED FOR A STUDY OF THE YOUNG.

IN 1906, A RESEARCH PARTY LED BY MAJOR TERRENCE, UNDER THE AUSPICES OF THE ROYAL ORNITHOLOGICAL SOCIETY AND WITH INSTRUCTIONS TO CAPTURE OR OTHERWISE OBTAIN A SPECIMEN, PENETRATED DEEP INTO THE JUNGLE OF THE JOSEPH PLATEAU. THEY REPORTED THREE DEFINITE AND SEVEN PROBABLE SIGHTINGS. LARGE NETTING TRAPS PROVED INEFFECTUAL. ON ONE OCCASION, A SHOT WAS AIMED AT NEAR RANGE BY AN ACCOMPLISHED MARKSMAN, WHEREUPON THE BIRD WAS SAID TO 'VANISH IN FLIGHT' AND, DESPITE AN EXACTING GROUND SEARCH, NEITHER CORPSE NOR STRICKEN CREATURE COULD BE FOUND. THE EXPEDITION DID, HOWEVER, RETURN WITH AN IMPORTANT COLLECTION OF AVIAN SKELETAL FINDS WHICH MAJOR TERRENCE BELIEVES INCLUDE CONDOR REMAINS. THESE ARE CURATED AT THE SOCIETY'S MINGLE LANE MUSEUM.

SINCE 1918 THE CONDOR HAS BEEN PROTECTED UNDER ROYAL CHARTER, AND IS CELEBRATED IN THE COAT OF ARMS OF THE PROTECTORATE OF THE FERENDES.

Cambridge World Index of Birds (1922)

LDI Station
South Joseph Plateau
Greater Ferende

Paulo Cinnamonte straightened in his chair, interlaced his fingers with palms outward, and stretched his arms whilst yawning. When his eyes opened they were focused precisely as before, on a smudge in the final frames of a video segment. Without shifting gaze he leaned forward and again clicked Replay. In the course of seven seconds the great bird arched in the sky, one wing momentarily occulting the full moon, before accelerating downward into the forest canopy. In the very second of the video finishing, that indistinct form appeared perhaps a hundred metres further along, but whether it was the same or another bird was impossible to know.

Next to his computer, a water bottle rested on a stack of papers, and he absently reached for it. The papers, relieved of weight, rustled slightly in the air current from the cooling fan. Paulo noticed, as if their agitation were sentient, seeking attention. Sympathetically, he took the uppermost document and read it through, though he had seen it many times before. It was a scanned copy of an historical note on the native condor.

In the seconds of reverie that followed, it began to rain. The first sign was not sound on the iron roof, not droplets on a window, not even the characteristic tropical smell. It was a subtle shift in the musical note of the air conditioner; a machine, mused Paulo, with the acuity of a forest animal.

He replaced the sheet, resilencing the stack with the water bottle. By now, the computer display was dimmed, the image of bird even less discernable. With a touch of the mouse, he re-livened the screen and opened a previously suppressed page. Research Progress Report. He left it displayed as he walked to the door; perhaps, foregrounded in machine consciousness, it might become written for him.

The rain was heavier now, collecting in tyre ruts outside his hut. The main clearing was mostly gravelled and drained well; it glistened, mica-like. The forest edge had lost some definition, darkened and suffused with mist.

Paulo thought of his visitor, somewhere on her crazy, uncomfortable journey from Madregalo. He knew she was a special friend to Edvard Tøssentern, and had been pivotal in the politics and organization of the search operation. She was also a trustee of Language Diversity Initiative, and he had hoped to have the research report completed for her arrival. But the weeks since the storm and Edvard's death had been just too difficult, too exhausting. Still, there was a publication in press, which would be mitigating. He glanced back at his computer; the screen was dark. No progress there, then.

Leaving the door open, the rain intruding just slightly, he walked over to a second desk. It was Edvard's workspace, and he presumed Dr Camenes would settle there. She would also wish to see something of Edvard's LDI life, and Paulo's efforts to tidy the area had been dissipated by ambivalence. He missed his supervisor, his advice, their conversation, the shared enjoyment of speculation and rigour and iconoclasm that made this modest hut in the wilderness an exciting place to work.

The rain had moderated, and he could now hear voices from the canteen. Folding a light anorak under one arm, and putting on a peaked cap to protect his spectacles from the rain, he set off across the clearing.

The Land Rover laboured upwards, its slow diesel throb and racing whine sounding mixed resolve and complaint. For two hours they had followed the coast through dozens of fishing villages, each a few huts, public spaces, a water tank, canoes on racks in varied states of construction or repair, and silent souls, observing them. Only startled fowl and protective dogs had reacted to their passing. Now, on the long ascent to the plateau, the vehicle slid this way and that in mud, its tyres finding purchase on rock or tree roots to propel it forward, into more mud.

Anna was feeling sick from a combination of lurching ride, engine fumes, anti-malarials and insomnia. Beside her, clasping the wheel tightly, her driver was hunched forward, watching intently, as if every slide and thrust came of calculated steering. His name was Nicholas, and out of Madregalo they chatted easily. But as the road worsened, he had fallen silent.

Silence suited her. From time to time the track hardened and edged close to the escarpment, affording glimpses south to the Bergamot Sea. She imagined floating serenely above it a great silver and white balloon craft; it was *Abel* coming into view, emerging brightly from a private sojourn in the clouds and oblivious to earthly concerns. She would scold him: *Edvard, we thought you were dead!* So vivid was the mental narrative that, even in the wishful hypothetical, she felt the physicality of emotions. She wiped beginning-tears beneath her eyes and then the make-believe was broken. A displacing imagery of night and storm, of danger and disappearance, was the new, recurring encounter with her friend. She turned to view the way ahead.

Almost another hour had passed when, unexpectedly, Nicholas braked hard at a turn in the track. The Land Rover slid to a stop.

'Sorry', he said. 'There's something I need to look at.'

He forced the gearstick into reverse and backed up several metres, again sliding to a halt. Anna followed his gaze off to the right. Leading into the forest, almost concealed by the low, dense understorey, were recent tyre tracks. Without turning to face her, he said, 'Loggers. Illegal. I'll need to take a look. You might like to stretch your legs as well.'

He opened his door and jumped out, leaving the engine idling. Within a few seconds he was out of sight. Anna also got out, pleased that she had the foresight to wear walking boots. Just as suddenly, Nicholas reappeared, holding in one hand a camera, in the other a large exotic-looking pink fruit.

'I photographed the tyre tracks', he offered, as Anna looked inquisitively, and he replaced the camera in a deep pocket of his chinos.

'And this,' he continued, as her curiosity seemed undiminished, 'is seki fruit. I thought you might like to try some. Tea?'

That simple word seemed providential in this place. Nicholas looked into the luggage tray and lifted out a battered ammunition box, the inside of which was a renovated picnic case. He set it up on the bonnet, serving tea from a thermos, then reached through the driver's window to switch off the engine.

'See what we can hear,' he said without elaboration. Anna warmed to the mystery, and the harmless contradiction of this.

The seki fruit had been sitting at the front of the bonnet, mascot-like. Nicholas took it up, and turning the base into view, ran a finger around the stem.

'If it is brown here, don't eat it. They ferment inside. Send you crazy.'

'Drunk?'

'Insane.'

Anna concealed slight bemusement. But by now Nicholas was peeling its skin, using a serrated knife from the hamper. Underneath, the flesh was a darker pink colour. He placed it on a cutting board and sliced a segment, meticulously guided it to the edge of the board, then lifted it toward her. This was done, Anna thought, with surprising solemnity. As she reached for it, he said, 'Take it slowly.'

He said 'slowly', she knew, but she heard 'respectfully'. Raising it to her lips, her eyes were drawn to Nicholas. But in her mind she saw the Bishop of Bilbao at her first Communion, and this forest bread as long-abandoned Host.

Nicholas watched her, saying nothing. Anna could feel his interest; she closed her eyes in protection of her other senses, of the exquisiteness of the moment, and in search of language. '*Sacramento*,' she finally pronounced, softly. Nicholas smiled.

Paulo was back in his office when he heard the vehicle. The weather had cleared and two hours of light remained. He hurried outside to find Nicholas pulling up in front of the accommodation huts. He had never met Anna Camenes but they had corresponded frequently by email since Edvard's disappearance. They introduced themselves while Nicholas unloaded her bags, and Paulo led the way up some timber steps, pushing open a door to show Anna her living space.

'Would you like me to come back in an hour or so to show you around?' Paulo expected she would like some privacy to unpack and clean up.

'I'd like you to show me around now,' she said.

Paulo was surprised, but also pleased. His slight apprehension about their meeting was quickly easing. Nicholas had moved the Land Rover to a large open hut and was unloading some stores from Madregalo. Paulo pointed.

'That's the canteen. We all eat together. Seven o'clock.' He checked his watch. 'No one dresses up. Come and I'll introduce you to people.'

They walked around the edge of the gravel clearing.

'Paulo, was that Edvard's room, where I am staying?'

'Yes.'

She stopped. 'Before the canteen, can you show me where he worked?'

'Of course.'

Paulo changed direction to cross the clearing, heading for the hut with a large aerial and a satellite dish on its roof. He pushed open the door.

'You won't find many things locked around here,' he said.

As they entered, Anna looked around, identifying Edvard's desk. 'This is it, isn't it?'

'Yes. We shared the room. This is my lot.' He gestured to a desk piled with papers.

'May I use Edvard's space while I'm here?'

'I expected that you would. I tidied it, a little,' he added.

Anna smiled. She looked at a framed photograph of Edvard and herself taken at Chaucer Road.

'Yes, I can see you must have. I'll set myself up tomorrow. Shall we continue our tour?'

When he had pulled the door shut, Paulo looked at her directly. 'I was wondering if you would like to walk to the Edge before dinner. It's beautiful in the evening. One of the great sights of the Ferendes. We often do it.'

'Yes,' said Anna, supposing that 'we' had included Edvard.

'Nicholas is interesting, a nice man.' She expressed the appreciation without warning.

'He is a very nice man,' said Paulo. 'What did you learn about him?'

'He's quite a linguist. He's been here three years. He does odd jobs. Fetches groceries, maintains the computers as best he can, helps with the language recording. Parents elderly; a sister in England.'

Paulo laughed. 'I ask because you never discover much about Nicholas from Nicholas. We've all learnt that here.'

'What do you mean?'

'Well, he doesn't just look after our computers; he's a mathematician and the proverbial IT genius. All the linguistic analysis and statistical inference we do, he's developed or improved most of it. He came three years ago as a volunteer.'

'What's his surname?' interrupted Anna.

'Misgivingston.'

She immediately made the connection to the author list on several LDI publications.

'I didn't realize.'

'No, he wouldn't have said. Every morning he works four hours solid on the net. Financial models, risk evaluation, derivative costing, net security, amazing stuff; he consults for banks and brokers all over the world. That's how he's been able to stay on here, and help out so much. They must pay him well, but he's frugal personally. He's much more generous with the rest of us than with himself.'

'What do you mean?' she repeated.

'He's funded all our new computing hardware, lots of camera equipment that I'll show you tomorrow. That Land Rover you came up in, and a second one, he bought. I once went with him into Banco Ferende in the centre of Madregalo and he was treated like a rock star. He was embarrassed. I thought there was an identity mix-up, but it was because he has all these big London–New York–type fees being deposited and not much to spend them on. By the way, he financed most of the search, made wheels turn locally. He won't want you to know that. Some other big project costs, too.'

Anna had always puzzled about the finances of this LDI station. As a trustee she saw all the statements, and read them responsibly. It always seemed that Edvard managed to run a mysteriously sophisticated, expensively idiosyncratic research programme on a very modest, essentially charitable budget. She wondered now what other quiet philanthropy might be occurring.

The track widened into open space and they reached the plateau edge. Here was the docking station for *Abel*; tall steel columns rising from the ground, and from their summits nylon mesh and flaccid tethers falling back. On its forest perimeter were some lean-to shelters, with helium cylinders and other equipment on view. Paulo walked across to one where half a dozen canvas director's chairs were stored against a support. He unfolded two, setting them up facing the ocean, and Anna and he sat down.

They hadn't spoken for several minutes; her thoughts had turned to Edvard, and not left him. She looked across the Abbott Plain to the Bergamot Sea. Daylight was beginning to leave the sky, and the water was much darker than she had glimpsed earlier in the day. Somewhere out there, it merged into the amorphous, treacherous South China Sea. And somewhere out there was the wreckage of a passionate experiment, and the remains of her friend.

'I want to thank you for everything you did to find Edvard,' Anna said unexpectedly. In many respects, she had come all this way to make that statement, personally.

Paulo moved his head slightly in acknowledgement, still looking at the sea. That time had been unbearable.

'What are your plans, Paulo?'

'I hope to stay on. There's really interesting material to study still.'

Once spoken, his reply seemed more perfunctory, and rather facile, than he intended. He made no attempt to improve it. All the staff, all the volunteers, were wondering about the future, whether LDI would remain in the Ferendes.

Anna was pleased to hear his reply. The station would need a new director, and Paulo was the obvious candidate. She kept that thought to herself.

'I read your paper on criticality conditions for diphthong fission — Edvard sent me a pre-print. Very impressive.'

Paulo's face lightened. 'Thank you. Actually, most of that work was Edvard's.'

Anna smiled. She knew if Edvard were sitting there he would be saying most of that work was Paulo's.

Paulo stood up. 'We should get back for dinner.' Anna looked again at the sea, noticeably darker now.

The next morning, Anna didn't join them for breakfast, and Paulo thought she must be catching up on sleep. When he entered the office, he was surprised to find her at Edvard's desk.

'Good morning.' She was cheerful but did not look up. 'Email.'

He had brought for himself a coffee from the canteen, and offered to get her one.

'No, thank you. I'm nearly done here. Then can we meet for an update on the programme?'

'At your disposal.'

After a few minutes, Anna swung in her chair and said, 'Would now be a good time?'

Paulo turned from his computer. 'Yes, of course.' He reached for a two-sheet document from his desk. Beneath it lay exposed the *Cambridge World Index* extract. 'I've prepared a brief research-in-progress report for you.' He passed it to Anna and she read it through.

'It's very good. I think the governors will be pleased with this, and the publication record.'

Paulo was relieved. Anna placed the report on her desk, then looked at Paulo.

'Paulo. I know that Edvard was interested in lots of things that could be viewed as, let's say, tangential, to the linguistic research. Like the weaver fish, for example. But I want you to know that anything he was interested in, I am interested in; whatever he valued, I value. So I would like you to tell me about those interests. For one thing, it might help me make sense of all this.' She waved at the papers on Edvard's desk. 'Also, I could possibly sort matters from the LDI point of view.'

To Paulo, there was something angelic about these words. He decided to place his trust, fully, in this friend of Edvard.

'Well, the really big thing, as you know, was the weaver fish. Out of that he became amazingly involved in aeronautics, getting the balloon design perfected, because he knew that was the best transport for studying them without disturbing the water. There were a few patentable ideas in *Abel* apparently. He corresponded a lot with an engineer in the States.'

'Walter Reckles?'

'You know about him?'

'I met him on an unrelated matter. We also communicated about the crash. What else?'

'The Chinese problem was really worrying him. And the rest of us.'

'What's the Chinese problem?' asked Anna, imagining it was language related.

'They've effectively colonized the north, ripping down the forests and shipping the timber out.'

'Nicholas mentioned illegal logging on the drive up here. Is that the Chinese?'

'Yes. Of course, they would claim that it's legal, that they have an agreement with the Administration in Madregalo, and that they pay large concession fees. According to Nicholas's informants in town, the agreement involved a hastily expanded Chinese legation and a few corrupt civil servants, and the so-called royalties are bribes and hush money. No one down there is aware of the scale of deforestation. The northern plain is virtually inaccessible. The Chinese have established a beachhead for their operation; it's very military. No one from the Madregalo government goes there. There's no monitoring. No controls.' He paused. His voice had become emotional.

'Do you literally mean "military"?' asked Anna after a few seconds.

'Definitely. It's a nasty standover profit-making venture by the armed forces to enrich the generals. It happens all over, condoned racketeering; it's the new hegemony.'

'How do you know it's so bad?'

'We've been there and seen it. It's about four hours by four-wheel drive. There are villages on the way where we do regular language studies, anyway. We first took a look in November last year. Since then, we have tried to get back monthly to audit the destruction. Nicholas takes serial photographs from a reference point on the plateau, and along with data from a laser range finder and GPS and some old topographical maps, he's been able to create a program that accurately calculates the acreage of clearing. It's bad. We're putting together a dossier, but how best to use it I don't yet know.'

Paulo glanced at the files on his desk. 'There was something else Edvard was interested in. There's a local bird, a condor, native to the Ferendes. It has a sort of mythological significance but is actually very real. Have you heard of Rep'husela?'

'No.'

'She was the virgin queen who brought these islands out of the darkness, and ruled for a thousand years. Her chariot was harnessed to a flock of condors. Anyway, there've been more condor sightings in recent months, reports from villagers mainly. I think Edvard was wondering if that was related to the clearing in the north. He had started a literature search on it, though all the material is historical and anecdotal. He also caught one on video from *Abel* last January; just a few seconds, unfortunately. Something about it intrigued him and he asked me for my thoughts. I confess I've looked at it a hundred times and I'm not sure I have any thoughts at all yet. I'll show you.' Paulo turned back to his computer and ran the video.

Anna watched and said, 'Again.' It ran again, and again. 'Can I have a copy on my machine?'

'Sure. There'll be one there already. I'll find it for you.'

'Before you do that, Paulo, when are you planning to drive north next?'

'We should really check the situation in the next few days.'

'I'd like to join you, if that would be all right.'

At the end of the track, Nicholas turned the vehicle so that it faced back the way they had come, and switched off the motor. Paulo handed Anna a pair of binoculars, and the three walked the few metres to the edge of the plateau, still well concealed by the thinning forest. At this point the land fell sharply away, and they had an unconstrained vista of the forest plain about two hundred metres below. In the distance, five kilometres north, was the glistening water of Lunulate Bay.

Paulo raised his binoculars, motioning to Anna to do the same, and began a systematic description of what he could see. 'Five ships, two naval, three freighters, larger than last time. Several landing vessels on the shore. Huge transport centre, maybe twenty logging trucks, tractors, dozers, cranes.'

He lowered the glasses to look at Nicholas. 'The skids have been doubled at least. The log stacks are much bigger. They seem to have built some kind of wharf or jetty. Look how much the clearing's advanced.' He passed the binoculars to Nicholas, who had been positioning a camera tripod over a previously placed survey peg.

'That big covered structure is a mill, Anna,' explained Paulo, 'and the smoke you can see just east of it is from burning offcuts.'

As far as Anna could see, the plain before them was criss-crossed with tracks connecting large areas of forest clearing. Many of these were now swampy wasteland, acres of marsh water reflecting dirtily the clear sky.

'They push through to the best timber—that's mostly over here where there's run-off from the escarpment. That closest patch is new,' continued Paulo.

Directly below them was an enormous clearing with a logging track leading straight back towards the mill, though in many places it was obscured by uncut forest.

Paulo spoke again to Anna. 'Last January, Edvard and I camped over for three nights to monitor the shipping activity. The mill works through the night. They seemed to load a freighter in two days.'

'If that's a deep-water jetty they're building it will be much faster than using tenders.' Nicholas had returned the binoculars to Paulo and was studying the scene through a telephoto lens. 'The whole northern plain could be marshland in five years.' There was a quiet indignation in his voice.

Paulo had resumed surveying the scene. 'I see a vehicle coming towards us, Nicholas. About halfway between this clearing and the next.'

Nicholas redirected his telephoto lens. 'I have it. Not logging. Army. Personnel carrier, maybe.'

'Not after us, I hope', said Anna.

Paulo was reassuring. 'We're too well hidden for them to see. Anyway, they can't get up here in that.' He was still looking through binoculars, and suddenly pointed below them. 'Anna! See the condor!'

'Fantastic!' She picked it up flying low over a swamp, first seeing its reflection. Then it gained height effortlessly, almost to their level, the famed iridescence of its feathers giving coloured scintillations in the sunlight.

'There are some more. Five. Amazing.' Paulo was excited.

'They must have taken off from the cliffs beneath us,' said Nicholas. 'I wonder if all this habitat destruction is leaving them exposed and displaced. Angry, too, I would think.'

Angry. Anna watched anew. Yes, they were beautiful, they were graceful. But from the propitious to the sinister was a small step of imagination.

'Do they attack people?'

Nicholas looked at her, shocked. 'No, no. Rodents, small mammals, other birds.'

The military vehicle entered the clearing and continued a further quarter kilometre, bucking wildly as its six-wheel drive tyres splashed in the uneven, poorly drained ground. It stopped at a point where the track was essentially a raised causeway between two large swamps. A door opened and two men, dressed in sailors' kit, jumped out. Both were carrying rifles. One walked forward about ten metres, the second falling behind, staying closer to the vehicle. They were looking upwards.

'What are they up to?' asked Anna.

'I would guess their commanding officer requires something special for the table,' said Nicholas bitterly.

'Heraldic stew,' murmured Paulo.

The condors had grouped above the sailors, circling. Both men raised their rifles and fired several rounds rapidly. The birds seemed unperturbed. One had been flying more slowly, drifting downwards in a diminishing spiral. The subtle loss of altitude would not have been evident to the men below, but from the perspective of the cliff top it was obvious. Suddenly, it dived sharply, not directly at either man, but between them. A few metres above the ground it levelled out with astonishing agility, beating its muscular wings quickly to launch at the furthest man. It flew directly into his chest, knocking him off balance. He stumbled backward, dropping the rifle, his arms flailing defensively. Enormous wings spread open, seeming to wrap around him, and he collapsed to the ground, buried in plumage. A brief, convulsive movement in that iridescent surface of embracing blackness was the only sign of struggle.

The second man ran a few metres toward his comrade but stopped short, staring. Then, throwing his rifle to the ground, he turned and fled for the vehicle, grabbing at what was probably a radio on his belt. But before he was halfway to safety another condor attacked, also knocking him over with force of impact, great wings reaching around, enfolding him.

For those witnessing this from above, the sight was sickening.

'My God,' whispered Anna, 'My God.'

It seemed profane to watch. She turned away and sat down, lightly holding the tripod for support. The others looked at her, expressionless. Then, as if physically weakened by what they had seen, they also sat.

'What happened there? How do they kill?'

The two men were quiet, observing her emptily. Eventually Paulo spoke.

'Talons, beak. Suffocation maybe.'

Somehow this elementary rationality served to distance the grotesqueness, and Nicholas nodded without conviction.

'I'll get us some water,' he said, rising to walk to the Land Rover.

'Actually, I've never heard of condors attacking people, except mythologically,' said Paulo when Nicholas was gone.

'It was pretty unequivocal.' Anna spoke with unintentional dryness. In both their minds was the strangeness of sentiment. Before, seeing the depredation of the forest, watching the hunting of the birds, only villainy attached to the Chinese. No consequence seemed too severe. But the vengeance they had seen, so extreme and merciless, unsettled their sympathies. It also unsettled their fears.

'There's nothing we can do. We can't get down there.'

Paulo might have been speaking to himself. Nicholas was handing them bottles, looking out. He took up binoculars and quickly scanned the plain.

'Those condors have gone. The men look dead. I think we might have a new visitor. Helicopter above the deck. They got a mayday through.'

He crouched down, and the others moved forward, keeping low.

The aircraft came directly at them. When it reached the scene it banked, hovered at about twenty metres, slowly turning as the pilot studied the terrain. It was army camouflaged, loaded with armaments. It put down on the track, forward of the first victim and facing back. The pilot stayed in place, keeping the rotors spinning, while two figures jumped out through a sliding door in the hull. Each was carrying a rescue pack. They ran to the nearest man and knelt briefly beside. One looked toward the pilot and signalled with his hands. The pilot acknowledged through an open flight deck window. Then they ran on to the other body, repeating the exchange. This one they rolled onto a stretcher and hurried to the aircraft, returning quickly for the first. They clambered back on board as the revolutions picked up. The whole operation was over inside three minutes.

From above, they heard the characteristic thwacking as power was increased abruptly, and saw small clouds of dust raised from the drier parts of the track. The aircraft lifted, quickly reaching half their height, and they could see into the cockpit through the raking roof shield.

Then, just as the pilot pulled the nose round and dipped on course for the ship, three large condors appeared from nowhere. They dived below the rotor and streaked upwards, two through the side door, one into the flight deck. Instantly, the cockpit turned solid black. The machine lurched to port, made a little height, then the nose dropped and it fell like a dead weight. The main rotor touched the surface of the swamp and sprayed a great arc of water as the forward half of the fuselage disappeared into the mud, tail rotor still spinning until residual torque flipped it sideways into the water. Before the side door fully submerged, three condors sped out and up, heading for the cliff.

They watched until the turbulence settled. Each wanted some remission of the horror, a crewman to emerge, gasp for air, swim to the bank, walk clear. But only a spreading oil slick remained; it diffracted sunlight beautifully, like the iridescence of the condor itself.

'We should move out,' said Paulo. 'The Chinese won't understand what happened. They'll think sabotage, terrorism. All hell could unleash. If they have another 'copter they'll be scoping the plateau. They'll easily sight us under cover with sensors.'

Nicholas was already folding the tripod. They collected the rest of their gear, covered the datum peg with brushwood, and ran to the Land Rover. Nicholas drove. The first village was fifteen kilometres in; they would be safe there. Wherever the forest thinned, Paulo looked anxiously upward, hoping not to see pursuing aircraft. So did Anna, hoping not to see a condor.

8. ANNA CAMENES

Over the following week, Anna joined in the activities of the station, as well as maintaining daily contact with her colleagues at the Compton Institute, where she ran a research programme in psychiatry. Nicholas had set up excellent communications and she was able to participate in teleconferences with, it seemed, fewer technical problems than occurred in Cambridge. She found herself adapting easily to the minor privations that were part of remote station life, and discovered new and surprising appreciations of the country's beauty and climate.

At least daily, she would walk to the Edge, usually alone. There was always a point in the path, depending on the atmospherics of the moment, where the sound of the camp generator became fully attenuated by the forest. By some odd alertness of her senses, this fact of silence always presented itself, forcing her attention to ideas about isolation and loss. They were often painful. In a way this walk became a visit to Edvard, and as the forest broke to a view of the sea she was sometimes tearful. Sitting there on the canvas chair, looking out, that would have been a perfect place for conversation.

She liked the society of the LDI team, and admired their commitment, their intellectual integrity, and the ethos of the whole station community. Sharing an office with Paulo, she had enjoyed many stimulating discussions about his work. And although an initial impression was that Edvard had cultivated research interests sometimes only tenuously related to language studies, it became clear to her that, in fact, and in proper accordance with the LDI charter, it truly was linguistics that held centre in the whole, dedicated enterprise. She learnt more why the Ferent language family was particularly fascinating to researchers, having unique features of grammar and no discernible ancestry in all of East Asia. Much of Paulo's current work, and Nicholas's statistical modelling, was concerned with identifying elements of a proposed protolanguage.

A favourite project was the school. This was held in a large, open-sided tent, and provided for about fifty village children each day. It was staffed by volunteers, but Paulo was making a case to the educational authorities in Madregalo that there should be government recognition and a contribution of state teachers and materials. Anna had read his submission, partly to ascertain the legal implications for the Trustees, and been impressed; they were awaiting a response. Sometimes, she joined in with the classes, and noticed that while the children were given the benefit of education, LDI also had much to learn from them.

Naturally, the subjects of the Chinese logging and the condor occupied much of their thinking. According to Paulo, Edvard had somehow related the two. For them also, if only by chance, they were intimately connected in the bizarre, repellent events of that single day.

As a doctor, Anna had wondered about the provision of health and medical emergency services in the station, and once spent a few minutes fossicking around in a large first aid cupboard that she noticed in the canteen. She had not given any priority to the subject in her discussions with Paulo. In one reflective moment at the Edge she had imagined changing her life completely: resign her chair in Cambridge and start a clinic here, provide health care, become a volunteer, study linguistics.

And so the meagre content of the first aid cupboard was what came to mind when Anna was told that a sick man was being brought to the station. The school bus had found him staggering and wildly waving his arms on the track just south of Copio, picked him up, and radioed ahead. The driver, a local volunteer, said the man had spoken incoherently only one word, over and over. He couldn't understand it but thought the accent was western Ferent, which indicated, in the plateau scale of distance, that his passenger was a long way from home.

Paulo and Anna waited in the canteen, which had the best facilities for receiving the patient. The volunteer kitchen staff had cleared one of the refectory tables of breakfast remnants, and covered it with a thick layer of blankets. On another table were organized the total health resources of the station. Nicholas had fuelled the long-wheelbase Land Rover and converted it to a makeshift ambulance with a mattress in the rear, ready for a drive to Madregalo if required.

It was about an hour from the first message when the bus appeared, crossing the clearing with uncharacteristic speed to stop outside the canteen. Anna saw the man slumped sideways in the passenger seat, leaning against the driver. The twenty or so children on the bus burst into loud, excited chatter, and a teacher herded them away through the rear exit. Anna ran around the front of the bus and opened the door. She was shocked. She turned to Paulo, immediately behind.

'We're going to need help.'

'We can all help.'

'I mean major help. Intensive care help.'

She was matter-of-fact. Paulo looked past her and wondered how she could reach that judgement after a glance. But he called out: 'Nicholas. Get Madregalo Hospital. Tell them we have an emergency. Find out about intensive care.'

A number of men helped carry the patient to the canteen table. He was unresponsive, breathing rapidly. Someone placed a pillow under his head, and Anna quickly intervened to ensure his airway was clear. He was roughly bearded, and grossly oedematous, with swollen neck, hands and feet. She had difficulty retracting the puffy eyelids to examine his pupils. His clothing was in tatters, much of it caked with mud. Grabbing an old stethoscope, Anna tore his shirt open, exposing large areas of cutaneous haemorrhage in the chest wall. As she leaned forward to listen she spoke loudly.

'Everyone who's touched him, wash your hands. How is it going, Nicholas?'

'Still being connected through.'

'Stress the urgency,' she said.

A volunteer had been charged, after quick tuition, with keeping a time record of events. Anna called out some vital signs.

When she had completed a physical examination she looked at hands, arms and feet for venous access. The gross oedema made it impossible. She went back to examine the neck, and called for the table to be tilted head down. Two kitchen staff lifted the end and supported it on upturned saucepans. There was a suggestion of an external jugular.

Amongst the first aid supplies was some intravenous equipment, old cannulae and two packs of Hartmann's solution past their shelf life. Anna primed a giving set, then scrubbed the patient's neck with antiseptic. Using a syringe she searched carefully and was rewarded with a flashback; the cannula fed without difficulty, and she attached the Hartmann's, securing the site with dressing tape.

'Flatten the table.'

'Anna, I've got a Dr Tersley on the line. He's an anaesthetist with a field surgical team working out of Madregalo. Can you speak?'

She nodded and quickly washed her hands, taking the mobile extension.

'Anna Camenes.'

'Philip Tersley. How can we help?'

'They found a man delirious on a track into here, about two hours ago. Hard to age — fifty, maybe. Race indeterminate. He's critical. Septic, shut down, heart rate 130, rapid, shallow respiration, GCS 8, no lateralizing signs, no neck stiffness, generalized oedema. He's got petechial haemorrhages, ecchymoses all over. Lost a lot of blood, conjunctiva almost white. I've got a short line in his neck, crystalloid running, but we don't have much of anything here. No oxygen, no airway gear. No BP cuff even.'

'What's your transport situation?'

'He needs retrieval, Philip.' Again, the tone was matter-of-fact.

'Hold on.'

Anna had walked back toward the patient as she described the clinical picture. Her eye was caught by something previously noted but forgotten. A watch on his left wrist was almost completely concealed by oedema.

'Someone get that watch off or he'll lose his hand.'

'Anna?'

'Yes, Philip.'

'The colonel wants a word.' There was a short delay.

'Colonel Barker. And this is?'

'Dr Camenes.'

'Situation report?'

It seemed a waste of time. 'We have a critically ill man; septic shock, major blood loss, coagulopathy, respiratory failure. We don't have a diagnosis. He needs resuscitation. He needs intensive care. He needs air retrieval. We haven't got hours.'

There was a long silence, followed by 'Standby'.

Philip's voice came on. 'Jesus. What did you say to the colonel? He looked like he was having a stroke.'

'I just said we needed medical evacuation, as soon as possible.'

'Yeah. Hold on.'

He was back in a minute. 'LDI station, South Joseph, right?'

'Yes.'

'There's a good clearing?'

'Yes.'

'Inside an hour. Me, nurse, technician, pilot. We'll have O-neg. I'm passing you over to a signals guy. See you shortly.'

He was gone before Anna could respond. She handed the phone back to Nicholas, guessing that it was about an in-flight communication link, and said loudly, 'Under an hour, everybody.'

There was palpable relief. She moved around to the patient's head, and felt for the carotid pulse. It was slightly slower, and stronger. She called out the rate, and turned to collect the second bag of Hartmann's from the adjacent table. Someone had placed the watch there. It looked familiar. She picked it up and turned it over. Inscribed on the case was 'Edvard Tøssentern'. Anna recalled Edvard's last letter: his watch, a gift from his parents, had been mislaid. She looked at the comatose man, viewing him from the top of the table. *How did you get this? Who gave you this? What can you tell us about Edvard?*

Suddenly the whole stressful situation was fused incomprehensibly with that other pain. She moved to his side to examine the hand that had been badly tourniqueted; she still couldn't feel a pulse, but there was capillary return. She glanced at his face, unshaven, dirty, bruised, swollen beyond recognition.

Beyond recognition. She stared, trying to resist the mad, impossible thought.

'Edvard,' she whispered. Then, louder and urgently, 'It's Edvard.'

Paulo turned from what he was doing. He didn't look at the man. He looked only at Anna, his face showing acute concern for her state of mind.

'Anna,' he said gently. He briefly caught Nicholas's eye, conveying his anxiety. Nicholas came across, still holding the mobile.

'Anna,' repeated Paulo. 'How can it be Edvard?'

'I don't know. Maybe he made it to land. Maybe he even crashed on land. We don't have a clue which way the balloon went in the storm.' She felt a falseness in her heart, creating hope out of nothing, but added, 'That's his watch.'

Nicholas had positioned himself at the man's right hand, staring quietly at his face. 'You could be right, Anna.'

Anna looked at Nicholas, seeking confirmation of her sanity as much as her judgement.

'It's possible, Paulo,' Nicholas said.

Paulo shifted his stare from Anna to Nicholas, then, at last, to the man. 'I'm not sure I see it,' he said.

Several kitchen staff had heard Edvard's name and crowded around, murmuring their views. Anna pulled up a refectory stool and sat down, holding the man's hand.

She stayed there until they heard the helicopter coming in. She only half watched as three figures emerged, bent over, carrying large cases. Paulo and Nicholas met them on the gravel and led them in. They introduced Anna. Philip shook hands quickly, saying, 'This is Max and Kelly,' gesturing at his companions but looking at the patient.

'Fuck,' he said very quietly as he took in the scene. The others were setting up their gear on the adjacent table.

'Max,' he called, 'give three.'

Max nodded and walked quickly to where he had full view of the aircraft, hand signalling a message. They heard the pilot power down.

Philip started a quick physical examination, just as Anna had.

At the same time he asked, 'How's he been since we spoke?'

'No change in conscious state; his heart rate has come down a little. We've kept an obs chart.'

Philip didn't reply, raising a stethoscope to his ears. The others had already set up oxygen by mask, and attached an ear probe oximeter. Kelly was now applying ECG dots. They functioned superbly as a team. An automatic sphygmomanometer had been put on the right arm.

'Can't get a BP, Phil,' said Kelly, turning to look.

Philip acknowledged. There was an oximetry trace. He took the obs chart and glanced at it, passing it to Kelly who had started a resuscitation record. Max had opened a fold-out mobile lab and was testing a blood sample from a finger prick.

'BSL OK, Hb 50.'

Philip was reading an ECG strip. He nodded and said, 'Blood,' adding, 'Sinus, no ischaemia; 12-lead when you're able, please Kelly.'

Kelly had taken a pack of blood from an insulated cool-box and was setting it up on Anna's drip; by now the second Hartmann's was fully run through. Philip leaned across to examine the infusion site.

'Jesus, you did well to get that in,' he said admiringly.

'I wish I could have done more,' said Anna, looking at their equipment.

Philip glanced at her neutrally. All doctors wish they could do more.

'We'll look at the heart.'

Max was already preparing a portable echo machine, handing a probe and a large tube of ultrasound gel to Philip.

'You were right about volume,' he said to Anna a minute later. 'We need more access. Prep both groins, vein and artery.'

Max cut down each trouser leg to the cuff, folding them down for exposure. It occurred to Anna that they hadn't thought of checking his pockets for clues to identity. Kelly opened a sterile pack and Philip gloved. He searched for vessels using ultrasound. By now, Anna and the others, aware that they were not needed, had retired some distance.

The two lines took about ten minutes to place. They then had an intra-arterial pressure trace displayed on the cardiac monitor. Philip drew a blood sample, which Max took to the lab. Kelly had primed a pump set which she connected to the new IV access and ran more units of blood. With the lines sutured in, Philip straightened up and removed his gloves into a large disposals bag. He stared at the monitor. The heart rate was still coming down, blood pressure low but not critical. Kelly was repeating neurological obs and said, 'No change.' Still watching the monitor, Philip reached up to the pump and squeezed blood through for a minute. Kelly put up another pack, and changed the neck line to saline.

'Bloods for culture, coags, cross match, please Kelly, then antibiotics. 'Did you examine his back?' he asked Anna.

'Yes. Skin haemorrhage but no obvious injury.'

'What do you make of this oedema?'

'I was wondering if it might be anaphylactoid.'

Philip showed interest. 'Kelly, let's set up adrenaline.'

He was still pumping, still looking at the monitor. 'I wonder where he lost all that blood.'

He palpated the abdomen again. The skin was oedematous but the belly was soft. Max handed him a small printout of blood gas and biochemistry results.

'Acidotic, renal failure, not surprisingly.' He stared at the man's head. 'We should secure the airway before transfer.'

There was a note of ambivalence; with the grossly swollen neck it didn't look easy. Max already had an intubation tray prepared, and began to draw up the drugs. A few minutes later, an endotracheal tube was in place, and Philip was adjusting the settings on a portable ventilator.

'Ready to go,' he said.

Max nodded and hurried to where he had previously signalled the pilot. A moment later they heard the rotors begin turning. Max continued on, returning shortly with a folding trolley.

'Do you mind if we look through his pockets for ID?' said Anna.

'Of course,' said Philip, and immediately Kelly examined them thoroughly, but found nothing.

'Unknown male from Copio, then.' That was to be his medical identity.

'Where will you take him, exactly?' It was Paulo who asked.

'Madregalo General Hospital, ICU. We'll decide tonight if we need to ship him on. I'll update you this evening. Our team is here for another two weeks.'

They were transferring the patient to the transport trolley.

'By the way, Anna, the colonel sends his best.' Not knowing exactly what this signified, Anna ignored it.

Kelly and Max positioned the ventilator, monitor and syringe pumps on the trolley, and each took one end. Philip walked beside it. Paulo and Nicholas helped by carrying the other cases. Within a few minutes, the aircraft lifted off and headed in the direction of the Edge.

Anna walked back to the canteen. Staff were tidying up the makeshift emergency area. The schoolchildren had been given meals in their classroom and were now well into afternoon lessons. Some volunteers were beginning a delayed lunch. She found Edvard's watch, briefly polished it on a towel, and put it in her pocket. Then she poured a coffee and walked outside. Paulo and Nicholas were standing on the gravel, looking at her.

'Thanks for all the help you both gave. I'm sure he's in excellent hands now.' She paused to gauge their reaction. Paulo was the first to speak.

'Do you really think it is Edvard?'

'No. No, I don't, Paulo.'

In the following days, Anna spent much of her time at the Edge. Her imagination about Edvard's death was newly contaminated by contradictory threads of hope and pessimism. The fantasy of safe *Abel*, and the certain hopelessness of *Abel* destroyed, were alternately amplified and subsumed in the roar of the helicopter on its way to better patient care.

Philip Tersley had courteously kept her informed about the man's condition: he did not require transfer, his renal failure was improving without dialysis, he still needed assisted ventilation, and blood tests revealed a large titre of malaria parasites. He credited Anna with saving the patient's life. The police were told of the circumstances but no progress had been made with identification. Anna considered driving to Madregalo, but the prospect of finding him unrecognisable was too painful. She didn't share this thought with the others.

Besides, there were new concerns at the station. Condors, which were rarely reported in the South Joseph, were being sighted as close as Copio. Along with all her unwelcome preoccupations, Anna had developed a new instinctual behaviour: whenever crossing the clearing, she looked upwards. And as far as they knew, the LDI members were the only people aware of the condors' apparently newfound aggressiveness. They wondered how best to convey this information to a people for whom the creature was generally auspicious.

Nicholas's connections in Madregalo reported the arrival of an important Chinese envoy, and more military attachés, but there were no stories about the condor attacks. Paulo surmised that officials in Beijing were displeased with the unexplained losses of men and matériel. He and Nicholas were keen to return to the north to examine developments, but were waiting for news from Philip. Their expectation was that as soon as the man from Copio recovered sufficiently, he would identify himself.

9. THE RESURRECT FROM COPIO

'They're not birds, they're mosquitoes!' Edvard Tøssentern was beaming, like a man who has discovered that the Holy Grail was in his kitchen cupboard all along.

Paulo and Nicholas stared at him. Anna's look was diagnostic. She was quickly processing the more likely: a mosquito with a two-metre wingspan or that Edvard was ill.

It was three weeks after his medical evacuation and the four were in the LDI office, Edvard sitting at his desk. He sensed the misapprehension.

'No, no, not one mosquito, millions. In formation, *en bloc*, cooperating. Mimicking a great bird. I know this—I've seen one close up. No eyes, no talons, no hard beak. They instantly disaggregate and reform. That's how a bullet can pass right through without disabling them. They can look invisible in a moment; who can see an individual mosquito at ten metres? And that's how they travel so easily through a dense forest canopy, say, or into that Chinese helicopter you described, through a small cockpit window. Then back in the coalesced state they adopt the aerodynamics of a bird; it's energy conserving, using the wind, gliding.'

Anna had to interrupt. Edvard had given a short account of his crash landing in the storm, but not everything that happened subsequently.

'You've seen one close up? You were attacked by a condor?' She was not yet ready to reconceptualize the bird.

'I was attacked by a condor-shaped mass of mosquitoes, Anna,' he corrected. 'Think of the math, as Walter Reckles would say. Per insect we have about a milligram. Three, four, five million—that's a mass up to five kilos, a lot of momentum when they hit you at the speed they can achieve flying like a bird.'

'But to transfer that kinetic energy on impact they would need to be strongly cohered. How do they fit together?' It was Nicholas.

'I don't know. We need to study them. Apart from some *Anopheles*, we assume that most of the mosquitoes around here are *Phulex irritans*, but we're almost certainly dealing with a different species. We know, at least, it has some anopheline character, as an efficient malaria vector. But to answer the question, it must have, I would imagine, thoracic appendages that can interlock, affording whatever structural rigidity, force transfer and control linkages they require to fly that way.'

Anna was only half listening; she was thinking more mathematics. She knew that a mosquito could typically double its weight with gorged blood. Three million insects meant three litres, more than half the adult human blood volume. That accounted for shock and anaemia. The coagulopathy, allergic oedema, infection and parasitic load were explained by the volume of total salivary injectate. She looked at Edvard. He was talking excitedly about the new research project, so characteristically removed from linguistics.

'We don't capture a condor, we catch *Phulex*. Breed them in tanks, watch their development, study the integration mechanics. We'll get Walter's help with the flight science. Who's an entomologist?'

No one answered immediately, but there was no dissent. Then Nicholas spoke.

'I suggest we do the project but keep it secret for now. We'll warn the villagers to use mosquito protection and insect repellent more carefully, just saying there is a worsening malaria problem. We won't mention the condor. So if the Chinese can't figure out what's happening to them and sustain more losses, they may scale down the logging and eventually leave. After all, the more swamp they create, the more condors they breed.'

Again, there was no dissent. Edvard looked delighted. It felt conspiratorial.

'In that way,' continued Nicholas, 'our condors may save the northern plain.'

Tøssentern looked at the office clock, calculating aloud the time zone in North America. Then he phoned Walter Reckles in New Mexico.

Reckles was on the first available flights, arriving at the LDI station two days later by chartered helicopter from Madregalo. Tøssentern had requested he bring some microscopes and entomology gear from the US. These were in a large box that the pilot helped unload and carry into the joint office. Apart from that, Reckles seemed to be travelling light, with a backpack and a large blue duffel bag secured by laces.

Tøssentern introduced Nicholas and Paulo. Then Reckles turned back and placed his hands on Tøssentern's shoulders in a brief hug.

'My friend,' he said. 'You had me worried.'

Anna had been standing back slightly. She had had a technical correspondence with Reckles, about *Abel*'s engineering, but she wasn't sure how he would have reacted to her earlier interview piece for *Aviation Reviews*. Perhaps it had been a little too sardonic. Reckles turned to her, smiling broadly.

'It's a real pleasure to see you again ...' Anna steeled herself for Miss or Honey.

'Anna.'

That was nice. They shook hands. She decided to ask about the book, which had not yet appeared. He managed to convey his disappointment with grace.

'Yeah. The book. The publisher's getting very particular. They want corroboration now. Expect me to drop ten kilometres on a salvaged 7T7 wing jettisoned from a Globemaster. Pilot it down with my bare hands and a borrowed neck-tie. They're very literal, publishers.'

'What did you say to them?'

'I said I wasn't an experimentalist.'

His green eyes, fixed on Anna, looked sad. She understood. That book, for Reckles, was something of a crusade for aviation safety, however bizarre. Quite abruptly, he brightened, and stepped toward his luggage by the door.

'I've brought something for you all, folks.' He unlaced the duffel bag and pulled out four Reckles Texan hats.

'No need to worry, one size fits all. But Anna, this one's probably best for you.' He handed it to her, with that broad smile again, the green eyes now delighted and generous.

Anna was thrilled; she had read about these somewhere, but never actually seen one. She thanked him warmly, and put it on. Reckles politely adjusted its angle on her head.

'Like that. If it blows away, it wasn't on correctly. I hope there's wind around here.'

'We have big winds down at the Edge. That's a place we like to walk to. We could go there this evening,' said Anna.

The others were all trying on their hats, murmuring their appreciation, with Reckles providing fine adjustment. He had his own, in the bottom of the duffel. From then on, they wore them everywhere, every day. It was a token of membership of their secret *Phulex* fellowship.

The more Anna worked with Walter Reckles, the more she liked him. She had known that he was charming and clever. She had seen how he was more the theorist than pragmatist, and that certainly wasn't to be criticized. But in his time at the LDI station, she came to appreciate his infectious idealism, a tangential eclecticism for interesting things, and tireless enthusiasm for their project. Unsurprisingly, he seemed very content inhabiting the abstract world of models and simulation. He was very like Edvard in all sorts of ways.

Anna, as the only one with a biological background, had been voted entomologist. Paulo helped her set up the breeding tanks with high-speed video. They also used low magnification light microscopy to examine specimens at various grades of maturity. Edvard had guessed correctly. Transverse thoracic appendages developed which had no equivalent organ in any other recorded species. There also seemed to be serrations of the proboscis that were probably involved in linkage.

The breakthrough was capturing on video just two mosquitoes joined in parallel. They were powering flight with one outer wing each, their medial wings locked together to form a semi-rigid aerofoil. The video caught the altered flight for a few seconds, some glide, and their disengagement. Walter was delighted; even from that brief vision, he could adduce some rough parameter constraints that assisted in model development.

They hoped to witness larger aggregates, but this didn't happen. Paulo suggested that the mosquitoes might need air currents to stimulate the behaviour, and so it proved. When he built a new breeding aquarium with netted ends exposed to natural wind, aggregates of up to a hundred or so insects formed and dispersed with surprising frequency. In those numbers, they didn't take the condor form, of course, but video playback in slow motion showed their disposition within the aggregate, and clarified some of the mechanics of assembly. This confirmed Walter's expectation that any stable aggregation with a tensioned flight surface required individuals to occupy all axial degrees of freedom, and specifically, that aggregated *Phulex* obtained the required flight properties by adopting fullerene architectures as basic structural units.

The observation was an enormous boost to theory development. With a model explaining structural integrity, rigidity and flexibility, they could move on to the problem of energetics, essentially how the graceful wing movements in the aggregated form could be powered from many millions of high frequency, oscillatory insect flight muscles.

Their pace of work was frenetic, driven partly by intrinsic intellectual urgency and partly by the unstated realization that everyone had other commitments that could not be postponed indefinitely. Reckles needed to return to his company and family, Nicholas had agreed to take up a temporary consultancy with a bank in Australia, and Anna was increasingly missed at the Compton Institute. She was also concerned that Edvard was not best situated for his convalescence; he had missed two visits to Madregalo for follow-up tests, solely because the logistics of travelling there were so difficult. Looking after him would be much easier at home in Cambridge.

By the time Reckles left, four weeks after he had arrived, they had a reasonable first draft of their paper. The plan was for Paulo to visit the northern plain and obtain video of the condors in flight, which would be sent to Flight Control for analysis. Anna and Edvard left the following week, while Nicholas remained to finalize some of his LDI work before his own departure to Perth.

There exists, in a rusting filing cabinet somewhere in the South Joseph, a notarized **manuscript** authored by Tøssentern, Cinnamonte, Misgivingston, Reckles and Camenes, awaiting its timely submission to *Nature*. Modestly entitled '*Phulex allotropy*', it is the first fully scientific account of *Condorasiaticus fugax*, therein re-named *Phulex coalescens condorformis*. And when it is published, the Republic of Ferendes will find that its majestic national emblem is really a mosquito, and the heroic Queen Rep'husela was ever in danger of falling from the sky.

Historians of science should note that the special properties of fullerene geometry were exploited by *Phulex* long before the invention of the geodesic dome. Of course, the element carbon has priority over both.

10. THE SPOKER LECTURE

Anna looked across the table at her friend. Having rustled impatiently through the newspaper for several minutes, he was suddenly concentrated in his reading. She waited.

Tøssentern folded the broadsheet neatly into quarto. 'Apparently, there was an interesting lecture in our town last night. Quite dramatic, by the sound of it—at least, the *Tribune* sent their theatre critic to write an account of it.'

He resumed reading for some seconds, while Anna watched. They were sitting in their newly refurbished conservatory, extended into a rear garden that provided both privacy and natural light. Since the balloon crash in the Ferendes he was spending more time at home, and renovations at Chaucer Road seemed part of some instinctual re-domestication that Anna hoped would promote his recovery.

'Read it to me.' Anna reached out for her tea.

'It's by Simon Vestry, headed "Speechless, Eloquent and Very Personal".'

The spirits-in-residence of departed undergraduates would surely have found last night's lecture at the Old Chemistry Theatre, in Cambridge, more entertaining than diminuendo echoes of carbon bonds and ester hydrolysis. For into those venerable walls and *trace humaine* was delivered rare quickening in the extraordinary presence of Dr Sidney Spoker.

I say lecture, but might well add performance, or even theatre, as will become clear. Spoker, many will know, was a professor in ethics at the Mount Sycamore School of Business in the United States until he suffered some undisclosed, profound personal crisis and nervous breakdown, which deprived him of the power of speech. After intense therapy and rehabilitation, and now emeritus of that institution, he has embarked on an international lecture tour of which last night was the beginning. This first address was entitled 'Imprisonment and Shame' and I, along with others in my company, did not know quite what to expect.

There was no lectern. As the audience shuffled to their uncomfortable benches, Spoker was already seated mid-stage, in a high-backed office chair. In this he swivelled gently back and forth, watching impassively as the room filled. Then, following that mysterious moment when expectant audiences fall synchronously silent, he leaned forward. In that simple movement was command more powerful than a sudden shout, and for an hour I doubt one second of attention was diverted from the meaning in that room.

Then appeared our interpreter, referred to in a brief programme note only as the Speaker. A tall man wearing a dark suit, he moved efficiently to a point about three yards on Spoker's left. He would remain standing throughout, in subdued lighting, his attention fixed on the seated man.

Spoker's hands started to move, and the Speaker started to speak. These were welcoming remarks, and a brief outline of the lecture to follow. Progressively, the movements increased in range and vigour, involving arms, shoulders, neck, face, torso, legs and feet. From time to time his whole frame lifted from the seat, flailing, kicking, twisting, then collapsing back to rebound with even greater energy. The chair swivelled and swung and pitched and squeaked, at times rocking so violently that its legs left the floor and I was anxious for Spoker's safety. Along with varied effort noises we could hear other incoherent vocalizations, and all the while the sound of distressing breathlessness from the sheer athleticism of what we were seeing.

From the Speaker, the voice was clear and expressive, and rarely hesitated in delivery. Occasionally, Spoker seemed unhappy with interpretation, and would turn to the Speaker with great animation. There would follow a thesaurus of terms or phrases, ending only when satisfaction was somehow signalled from the chair. The material was broad ranging and at times quite technical, with a number of ethical 'theorems' stated and proven. A recurring idea, designated a moral law, was the conservation of ethical content, and agency, across acts that are causally connected, and how individual responsibility therefore propagates. Most assertions were illustrated by stories from history, literature, or the business world, or by ingenious thought experiments.

It is hard to convey the full experience of last night. I sensed I was not alone in my discomfort—as if sitting in a voyeurs' gallery—watching this writhing, contorted, exhausting man. But there came a point early in his lecture, when the words 'imprisonment and shame, torment and struggle will pass, as they have for me ...' were spoken so unemotionally that I felt a tension dissolve. From then on the movements of the man, exaggerated and somehow absurd as they were, seemed naturally attached to the voice, as if they were the unremarkable effort of normal phonation. And the Speaker, who not once looked at the audience, receded into invisibility and paradoxically, silence. From that point also, I became listener more than watcher, drawn into the lecture rather than the drama.

And only in that altered state of sensation could I possibly describe, with the spectacle of that fighting man before me, Spoker's closing words as a meditation. A meditation on the cycle of life and the purpose of mortality, concluding that the genius of the generational scheme of human existence was not evolutionary or even biological, but the obligate renewal of conscience.

Now for the reasonably doubting of my readers, who might well suppose that the lecture actually belonged to the Speaker and the performance of the other was part of a bizarre theatrical hoax, let me recount the following. At the conclusion of the lecture proper, questions were invited from the audience. They were not spoken aloud but written on slips of paper, passed to Spoker by an usher. At no point could the Speaker have seen their content. And were they from co-conspirators in the audience? Not the case, it seems, as Spoker, having shuffled through a half dozen or so slips, chose to address mine first.

'I thank the Reverend Barnabas Bending for his question: How best can the transitivity of ethical relations proven here inform modernization of the criminal code?'

A faultless reading. And there followed a reply so succinct, balanced and ironic that I marvel at its fast invention and find myself, just a little, apologetic for my scepticism.

When Spoker ended by thanking his audience, the Speaker quickly and unceremoniously left the stage. Before applause almost indecorous in that place, Spoker continued to sit, observing us without apparent joy. In the whole evening, these were his first moments of perfect stillness. Finally he stood, and like generations of lecturers before him, left the podium.

Tøssentern placed the paper on the breakfast table.

'What do you think?' he asked.

Anna was staring into the garden. 'Interesting. I usually enjoy Vestry's reviews. What do you make of this one, though—is he the deceiver or the deceived?' She reached for the paper and glanced at the article.

'You're unconvinced in some way?'

Anna was surprised at the circumspection in his voice.

'Of course I'm unconvinced. I'm unconvinced because it's preposterous. Starting with the name "Spoker"—what is that, past tense of speaker? Do we know if Sidney Spoker even exists? And "Barnabas Bending". That is surely satirical.'

'I wish I'd been there.' This came with a slightly rueful note.

'Assuming it actually happened, Edvard. Anyway, deception is like lust—nearness weakens the senses. You might have been manipulated along with the others.'

'What about Vestry's question?' Tøssentern sounded a little defensive.

'Yes.' She thought for a few seconds. 'Impressive if it's real. In that case I'd like to know more about the Speaker. If it is genuine, why would someone devote themselves to such supreme service?'

'I know,' said Tøssentern. 'Equally, if it's not genuine, why would they bother, when one or other seems perfectly able to produce a scholarly lecture?'

They were both looking out at the slowly moving figure of Thornton, their gardener, who was clipping an ancient hedge. Anna tried to imagine those inaudible movements conveying meaning different from the act they witnessed.

She was also thinking that Edvard's normal analytic self seemed oddly blunted, and wondered how that fitted with his general unsettledness of recent months. It had crossed her mind that he was depressed. But here, at least, was an enthusiasm to encourage, if also an uncharacteristic credulity to temper. She spoke first.

'Perhaps we should investigate—decide whether Spoker's choreography in the chair is differentiable enough to convey vocabulary and syntax, all that abstraction, and emotion. Find correlations with the text; there's the secret, surely.'

She recognized her own curiosity increasing as she spoke. Tøssentern needed no persuasion.

'I'll find out where the lecture tour is going.' He reached out to reclaim the paper.

11. A LETTER TO THE *LONDON TRIBUNE*

Sir. It has come to my attention that I am reported in your pages to have been present at a certain event in Cambridge recently. Moreover, I am said to have raised sympathetically, in a public discussion, the matter of legal reform.

I must object most strenuously to these falsehoods. I was nowhere in the vicinity of the place described. Whilst there is, indeed, an old lecture room in this village too, it has, I believe, no especial connection to chemistry. In any event, I was not there either. On the evening in question I was giving solace in the home of a parishioner who had lately lost her husband in the most distressing of circumstances, on which I shall not here elaborate except to say that it was not for the first time. I am pleased to relay that with further ministry she is making a wonderful recovery and at last bridge night was quite cheery.

Above all, I am most aggrieved to be portrayed a proponent of criminal code modernization, to which I am emphatically opposed. There are many who can attest to my good character in this regard.

On another matter, I take this opportunity to announce our upcoming programme of Postlepilty Symposia, the first to be on the subject of 'Recognizing Cant'. Enquiries are welcome and can be directed to my curate's office.

Might I conclude with a note for naturalists among your readers: the year's first swints alighted Sunday last.

Yours etc
Barnabas Bending MA
The Vicarage
Meniscus Pond Common
Postlepilty nr Ely, Cambs

Simon Vestry replies: I thank your correspondent for his illuminations. As other alert readers would also have appreciated, 'The Reverend Barnabas Bending' was a whimsical invention to meet the urgent need of anonymity in the course of a serious experiment, whilst by its nonsense giving assurance that it could not possibly attach to a real person. I congratulate the author on a most delicate titration of hyperbole into brine, and for his amusing meta-statement on existential drift, the economy of conceits and proto-Christian fictive irony. Should he care to supply a believable name and address I would be pleased to negotiate a schedule of identity sharing.

12. THORNTON

In the weeks following, their enthusiasm for investigating the Spoker event slowly dissipated, replaced by more urgent matters. Tøssentern had been invited to deliver a lecture to the Lindenblüten Society, and his publisher's deadline for the MacAkerman work was looming. And he wasn't completely well. Regular visits to Addenbrooke's Hospital for blood tests seemed to wear him down, despite the results documenting progressive recovery from the profound anaemia, protozoal attack and immune compromise his system had survived.

Anna had been busy clinically, and rather preoccupied with acute staffing problems at the Compton. She continued to keep a professional eye on Edvard's mood, with a view to referring him to a colleague. Returning from the dead, whatever expression it took, was not easy on the mind.

One thing arising out of the Spoker business that did maintain their interest was the daily correspondence in the *London Tribune* regarding the existence of a Rev Barnabas Bending. Letters came from archbishops, aldermen, parishioners, university registrars, schoolmasters, military officers and others purporting to have that name, or not, on some list, or know that person, or not, in the community. Amongst these, and by far the most ill-tempered, and increasingly shrill, were those from individuals claiming actually to be that person not present at the Spoker lecture on the night in question. Simon Vestry, after his first reply, maintained a discreet, and probably infuriating, silence.

To Anna and Edvard, the mystery became more diverting than Spoker himself, and they had spent a recent Sunday afternoon driving up to Ely in search of Postlepilty and its vicarage. They weren't successful and somehow, relaxing in a serene and charming village teashop, their quest was deflated of all urgency.

This morning they were sitting again at the breakfast table, where Tøssentern picked up the *Tribune* and, as had become his habit, opened it first at the Letters page. He hunched forward. 'Listen to this, Anna.'

> **Editor's Note.** This newspaper has received over three hundred letters regarding the disputed identity of a Rev Barnabas Bending. Many have been too laboured, too irrational, or too offensive to be considered for publication. Approximately five per cent claim to be from that person, five per cent offer support for such a claim, and ninety per cent offer refuting evidence. Given this, we concur with our columnist Simon Vestry's consistent assertion that the person is fictitious. Correspondence regarding Rev Barnabas Bending is now closed.

'Goodness,' said Anna. 'Poor man, if he's really out there. Declared non-existent by some crude plebiscite.'

'Democracy isn't perfect,' said Tøssentern. 'But now the idle will swarm to another paranoia, you'll see.'

Anna stood up from the table. At the garden door she stopped and asked, 'Edvard, you weren't the author of any of those, were you? The first, perhaps?'

'No, no, no. How could I fail to find Postlepilty if I lived there?' It was clear that no confession would be forthcoming, at least this morning, and she turned back to the door.

'I'm going to check progress in the greenhouse.'

While she was in the Ferendes, Anna had listened to many accounts of the central nervous effects of the local seki fruit, particularly its toxicity after fermentation. She naturally wondered if it might contain novel psychotropic ligands that her basic science colleagues at the Compton Institute would be pleased to research. She had sent some seki seeds back to Cambridge with a request to their gardener, Thornton, that he deal with them as best he could.

The result was startling; several vines were now at least three metres tall, straining to reach the glasshouse roof. Thornton was smart, and methodical. He had sought advice about an appropriate Latin square design, experimenting with different feeding regimes and soil chemistry, and was recording all this in a slightly grubby exercise book. Although he had the appearance, and in some ways the demeanour, of an unreformed poacher, there was formal horticultural training somewhere in his past.

When she entered the greenhouse, Thornton was high on a stepladder in front of the seki vines. Hearing her, he reached up to a roof beam to brace himself before looking down.

'Watch yourself, Miss Anna, there are glass shards up here could fall.'

Anna retreated a few steps to a workbench, consulting the logbook while she waited. This morning there was already an entry, a single neatly written word: 'Swints'.

A few minutes later, Thornton carefully descended the ladder, holding in one hand the remnants of a broken glass tile. He crossed over to Anna and held out the shards, pointing to a bright yellow stain on many of the broken edges.

'Swint blood,' he said, then placed the pieces in a bucket stored below the bench. His hands were protected by aged red-leather mittens, and he rubbed the palms together to dislodge glass splinters.

'Swints got in?'

He nodded. 'Six.'

'How did you get them out?'

Thornton had been facing away, leaning over the bucket. Now he turned to look at Anna, and she was slightly shocked to see the emotion in his eyes. His usual nature was matter-of-fact with little display even of humour, or enthusiasm. Now he looked about to cry. She had seen him like this only once, when telling him that Edvard was missing and thought to have died. He answered by gesturing toward the other end of the greenhouse, where the furnace was alight.

'They were all dead, Miss.'

He had noticed some broken glass amongst the seki pots, and stepped over to retrieve it, returning to dispose of it into the bucket. 'Fly all that way, then die here. Whole family. Very sad.'

'They broke in? Broke the glass? Was it already cracked?'

'Not cracked. They broke it, right there.'

He pointed, rather needlessly it seemed to Anna, to the defect in the roof above the stepladder. After a few seconds, she reconsidered; Thornton was never one to act needlessly. She looked at the roof again. The missing pane was directly above the highest reach of the tallest seki vine.

'Do you think the seki attracted them in some way, Mr Thornton?'

Thornton had his back to her. He was leaning over the bench measuring out a sheet of glass.

'They all had the leaf in their beaks, Miss.'

Anna felt a sudden chill. She walked around the bench in order to see Thornton's face. He glanced up for a moment, then returned to scoring the glass. Neither spoke for several minutes. Eventually Anna said, 'It can't have poisoned them, could it?'

'Couldn't say,' he replied. 'Very quick if it did.'

Using the edge of the workbench, he broke the pane along his score line.

'First one, died of bleeding, I'd thought.'

'But they all had seki leaf in their beaks?'

'I said, Miss.'

He had fitted a work belt and loaded it with some tools and a silicone extruder. At the base of the ladder he stopped, his back to Anna, looking at the floor. He stayed like that for several seconds. Then he said something barely audible. Anna repeated what she thought she heard.

'Crust?'

Thornton turned his head toward her. He still spoke quietly, but this time she understood.

'They were crossed, Miss. Placed themselves in the cross.'

Anna felt the chill again. 'Show me, please, Mr Thornton. Exactly.' She collected six assorted paint and lacquer tins from the benchtop and positioned them within his reach.

He took each singly, and placed it meticulously on the floor, below the largest seki plant. The six formed an unmistakable Christian cross. She now discerned a small yellow bloodstain where he had positioned the first.

Even Anna was moved. Thornton seemed to have lost all will and had seated himself on the floor, leaning back against the stepladder, his eyes closed. But she had to ask, 'Exactly like that?'

He shook his head, looking up, eyes red with distress. 'More perfect,' he whispered hoarsely.

Anna stared at him, at once sympathetic and disturbed. Then she looked around the greenhouse. She had always loved this miniature crystal palace of exotic scents, luxuriance, and sensory contradiction that somehow combined absurd fragility with elemental defiance. Now she was seeing only the great overbearing vines, the cross, and the flaming incinerator, its newly stigmatized warmth escaping through the broken roof.

She thought of her first taste of seki fruit with Nicholas, that almost religious advent in her being that was both surprising and familiar. And within the exquisiteness of that memory she was confronted by the mixture of truths in her own motivation; that the long, unnatural journey of the seed from the Joseph Plateau was less for science than for sensuality.

She thought of the swints, driven to fly, their blood changing during migration from dark red in the south to brilliant yellow in the north—deceiving ornithologists for centuries that they were two species rather than one. And she remembered the old traditions, hardly taken seriously, that they were always seen thriced, and whatever the privations of their flight they alighted only on property of the Church.

She looked again at Thornton, a man burdened and diminished and made solitary by his knowledge. And in the moment, being around him, her concern and caring were muted by an oppressiveness and affecting superstition that she needed to resist.

For relief, and her own reassurance, she turned to the door. Only minutes before she had entered there with delight; now she stood as interloper in a strange and inhospitable, hermetic place.

But for now, in an act of wilful desecration, she collected the paint tins and returned them to the bench, undoing their symbolism by studied rearrangement. Then she gathered a canvas chair stored beneath a potting table and unfolded it before Thornton.

'Sit here,' she said with authority, 'I'm going up to the house to bring us back some tea.'

Thornton lifted himself from the floor, grasping the ladder for support. He dragged the chair some further distance from the vines and settled into it, looking toward the door.

'Can you explain it, Miss?'

When it was realized that the two varieties of **swint** were actually one, the single species was newly designated *tinctoria*. This reflected a belief that the mechanism of blood colour change was akin to that seen in certain indicator chemicals known to be responsive to some ambient condition (such as litmus and pH). In fact, the chemical physiology is far more complex. The northern yellow blood cell (xanthocyte), which performs the same oxygen-carrying function as the southern erythrocyte, arises from a distinct cell line, and the two differ in chemistry, morphology and rheology. The molecular substrate for oxygen carriage in the xanthocyte is a heteroglobin in which the analogue of the heme moiety is also built on a (albeit radically altered) porphyrin ring but, fundamentally, this attaches gold in place of iron. As in haemoglobin, there are four metallic atoms per macromolecule, each binding one oxygen molecule cooperatively (evidenced by the shape of the oxygen–heteroglobin dissociation curve). Protein-complexed gold and iron are alternately stored and mobilized within a specialized lobule of the liver known to early anatomists (astoundingly, as it turns out) as the *bursa alchemica*. The dietary source of gold is thought to be the seki vine, which is believed to concentrate the metal in alluvial soils, and on which the swint appears to be an obligate feeder. The reason for the switch to gold heteroglobin in the northern hemisphere remains a mystery, but current conjecture focuses on whether magnetic field sensitivity might be improved in the absence of noise from circulating iron. If so, this would confer a survival advantage in navigational efficiency during migration. Unfortunately, it also conferred a disadvantage: the reader may recall an influential quasi-documentary entitled *In Gold Blood* which exposed a short-lived, despicable industry in trapping and slaughtering swints in order to harvest their gold. Had those perpetrators first consulted a numerate physiologist, they would have learned that their projected precious-metal yield was miniscule, and saved themselves much effort and the condemnation of world clergy.

Regarding the latter, incidentally, it needs to be stated that the Church has not otherwise been a selfless advocate for this creature. The identification of the swint with the Sacred dates at least to the first century, when several sources (*Book of Teachers, Iconoclastes*, the *Apostolikon*, and the *Gospel of St Ignorius*) describe three birds (a Trinity) alighting on Calvary, and bleeding gold onto the Cross. These testaments, and the iconology they invite, suffer an unrestful accommodation within the Catholic canon, being quite definitely out of favour now for nearly a millennium.

13. THE LINDENBLÜTEN SOCIETY

When Tøssentern had completed his address on Thortelmann equivalence and taken questions, he was formally thanked by the Society president, who invited members and guests to refreshments in the library cloister adjoining the Master's private garden.

Tøssentern himself was delayed in the hall by a few who came to the lectern with more technical questions, or requesting a citation list. When at last he was able to join the main party, the Master came forward to offer his appreciation, at the same time introducing a Signora Scintillini, before hastily moving away to welcome other guests. Tøssentern found himself defending an altogether minor comment he had earlier made about preservation of metre in a translation of Petrarch, realizing quickly that the suave introductions from the Master of Nazarene had been entirely tactical. When he elided the subject from metre to music to melodrama to murder, the Signora excused herself to seek out, Tøssentern was pleased to note, the company of the Master once more.

In the distance, he caught a glimpse of Anna in conversation with Penelope Loom, the new Fellow in Homeric studies, and was setting out in their direction when his mathematician friend, Rodney Thwistle, approached.

'Good lecture, Edvard. Very clear, very clear,' he said, shaking hands. 'I liked particularly the link to Shannon's Law and the two conjectures of 1980. Extraordinary that they should remain unproven. Actually, it set me thinking. One of my students is modelling semantic shift in rumour diffusion within multilingual, theocratically oppressed populations enjoying indefinite migratory flux, identity fraud, endemic mendacity, inculturated insularity, constrictive paternalism, pre-Enlightenment censoriousness, congenital absence of humour, sporadic headless mutism and conductive hearing impairment; it occurred to me that Thortelmann's ideas might be useful. Would you be happy to meet up with her and offer some advice?'

'Of course, delighted to, Rodney. I shan't ask where you would find such a study group, though,' added Tøssentern.

'Oh, all over, old chap. All over. You've been too long absent from high table, Edvard.'

Tøssentern was sincere in wanting to be helpful. He suggested that the student email him, and asked for her name. Thwistle told him as a drinks waiter appeared. They each took a glass of mineral water, and Thwistle continued.

'I've been meaning to ask you, how is our adventurer friend doing—is he still on that godforsaken plateau of yours?'

Tøssentern smiled. 'The LDI station. It's not that bad. And yes, Nicholas is still with us, except he's taken leave to advise a bank in Australia over some financial products development. It will be a relaxing few months for him in Perth, I hope.'

Thwistle looked thoughtful. 'I know some people in Perth. You may remember Hiro Wasabi from my department; he's there on sabbatical. Also a chap called Worse, a curious fellow. I've no idea what he does, but we've had correspondence on cryptography algorithms, mostly to do with the defective pixelation problem.'

Thwistle's final words were delivered with some vagueness as his attention moved briefly to the mathematics. 'Anyway, perhaps I should put them in touch, what do you think?'

'That might be nice for Nicholas,' agreed Tøssentern. As he spoke he became aware of a sudden earnestness in Thwistle's face.

'Look, Edvard, I'm so pleased you're back. Back and ... so well. It was terrible thinking you had perished. Let's make sure we see each other more, more conversations.'

For the second time he reached out to shake hands with great seriousness, causing Tøssentern some awkwardness in disposing of his water glass. Then immediately, he left.

Tøssentern felt weakened by this display of emotion in a man with whom relations had always been quite reserved. Realizing that he had no enthusiasm for the social formalities around him, he made his way to an exit, astutely avoiding further interactions on the way. In the garden he found a cushioned cedar bench some way from the main party, and sat down.

Thwistle's words, 'you're back', concealed a complexity and pain that Tøssentern was only beginning to apprehend. Yes, perhaps he was back, but not in a sense he could possibly share. His disappearance, and whatever meaning attached to it, belonged in the experience of others — his presumed death was their belief, and his improbable return was their shock. That disappearance had created a void in his name, a hiatal self rough-edged by the forces and failure of memory, metonymy, and the weakening spectral vision of those who missed him. Yes, he was back, but not to reinhabit that imperfect silhouette in a seamless return to his past. He was back, and he was a newcomer.

He had taken to reading his obituaries, especially a most generous one in the *Tribune*. At first a source of amusement, they acquired insidiously a proprietary life beyond his editorial reach. More disturbingly, he came to see them as a posthumous accounting of his total worth, destined for as many flawed interpretations as there were people who remembered him. He returned to them compulsively, even as he sensed the morbidness of this and concealed the fact from Anna. Yet at each reading, their subject became less familiar, not more. And the alienation this engendered, far from being distancing, drew him inexorably back; back to the silhouette and into those portraits of the void.

All this time he had been sitting forward, vigilant within his thoughts and straining for the mental language to form them. Now he placed his hands in his jacket pockets, reclined more comfortably and closed his eyes. But inevitably, behind this inattention came exploration of a vivid and unrestful privacy. And there, inside his inner picture world of adversities, he wanted to be discovered as much as he wanted to be alone. He didn't hear Anna approach.

'Hello Edvard, I was missing you in there.'

She seemed to judge quickly his state of mind, and without invitation sat beside him. They remained silent for several minutes, when Tøssentern sighed deeply. It was an opportunity for Anna to speak.

'What's happening, Edvard?'

'I'm tired. You know, a lecture like that, a year ago, would have been no effort. I like the material, I know the subject. I support the Society. I enjoy the people. But this has been really difficult. I think I'm just exhausted.'

'Edvard, it was a wonderfully relaxed and entertaining lecture, as yours always are. It was hugely appreciated. There was nothing but positive comment in there.' She hesitated. 'Besides the exhaustion, what else is happening?'

'I can't relax. I have these terrible images. Like nightmares. Intense and visceral and overpowering, affecting me physically, with sweating and palpitations. It always starts on *Abel*, with the fish trap dragging me down. I am saying something, over and over, but I don't understand it, I can't remember it ...'

He fell silent for a minute, and again sighed deeply. 'I can't concentrate any more, Anna. And there's so much to be done. I'm behind with MacAkerman. I need to get back to the Ferendes. I want to find the crash site. There's the Chinese problem to follow up. Even this odd business with Thornton keeps coming to mind. I'm feeling close to overwhelmed.'

'All those things can wait, Edvard. You know you can have complete confidence in Paulo to run the LDI station. It would also make sense for you not to go back until Nicholas is there as well. He's the one most acquainted with logging developments in the northern plain. And don't worry about Thornton; I'm looking after him. Actually, I told him your view that the invariable and perfectly mundane destiny of everything metaphysical is to become explained. It seemed to give him a renewed purchase on reality. He's much better.'

'I'm no longer sure whether I believe that myself.'

'Edvard, I think it would be useful for you to talk to someone about everything that's happened. You've never spoken to me about the storm or the crash or the condor attack, what it was really like for you.'

Tøssentern was quiet for a few seconds. 'I don't know how to start. I can't be sure if what I remember is real or hallucinatory. And I'm starting to think it's not about that, not even about nearly dying. It's something to do with being thought dead and coming back to reclaim my self, almost having to prove my ownership and wrest it back. And sometimes I feel I might truly have died and returned to discover I'm not sure of the man I was, or even if I like him.'

Anna placed a hand on his knee. 'You don't have to judge between the real and the imagined; you're not assigning truths. It can all be talked about equally, it's all important. And those feelings about appropriation and restoration, very few people have been through that experience, so it is uncharted. It is difficult, for you and for the people who know you.'

Tøssentern remained quiet, and she continued. 'Would you like me to make you an appointment? I have someone in mind, in London.'

'A psychiatrist? What's her name?' Neither drew attention to Tøssentern's assumption that it should be a woman.

'Yes. Barbara Bokardo. I have complete trust in her.'

Tøssentern repeated the name and asked for its spelling, as if appraising the person through the word. Then, unexpectedly, he said, 'Barnabas Bending. You know, that wasn't amusing, that wasn't entertainment. What we saw was identity construction. Or identity assertion. And, as it turned out, annihilation. It was frightening, in the end, wasn't it?'

'Identity is constantly nearly frightening, Edvard.'

'Yes.' For the first time, he looked directly at Anna. 'I mean, yes, I would appreciate your setting up an appointment with Barbara Bokardo.'

The reader may find useful this brief introduction to **Thortelmann equivalence**, the subject of Tøssentern's lecture. (The following is adapted from an example discussed in Thortelmann, A A, *J. Theor. Transl.* (1980) **11**: 1–33.) We are told that the scholar and mystic **al-Fakr'mustiq**, after many years of contemplation, concluded that the unity of all existence, the perfect oneness of all that is, amounts to ineffable absence, pure emptiness, the cipher of nothingness. So profound and surprising was this realization that he exclaimed:

$$\text{Unity is Nought!} \tag{1}$$

before entering an impenetrable trance. His disciple, the ascetic **al-Jabr**, who favoured the brevity of arithmetic over literary terms and was naturally disposed to replace 'is' with the equal sign, transcribed this pronouncement as $1 = 0$! Later, by a strict application of the symmetry property of equality, this was rewritten as

$$0! = 1. \tag{2}$$

Now a modern mathematician reads this as 'zero factorial equals one', an identity widely encountered in elementary combinatorics and easily proven by recourse to the gamma function. The metaphysical statement (1) and the mathematical statement (2) seem divergent in meaning but are definitely connected, since one is manifestly derived from the other. In this respect, they are said to be Thortelmann equivalent. (More formally, they comprise a cognate pair in a certain Thortelmann space.) Thortelmann equivalence provides a basis for analysing properties that are conserved in literary or semiotic transformations, thereby de-emphasizing conventional (and rather laboured) notions such as what is 'lost' or 'added' in translation. The theory encompasses all linguistic restatements including poetry to prose, abbreviation, paraphrasing, abstracting and, of course, foreign language translation. A little thought will convince the reader that Thortelmann equivalence is a symmetric and transitive relation. It should also be apparent that while semantic equivalence implies Thortelmann equivalence, the converse is not true.

[The following discussion may be omitted at a first reading.] We begin with the (reflexivity) proposition that an entity $S(k)$ is Thortelmann equivalent to itself. Let $S(1)$ and $S(n)$ be two (non-identical) statements that are Thortelmann equivalent. Then there exists a minimum (not necessarily unique) Thortelmann path $S(k)$, $k = 1, 2, \dots, n$, connecting the two. The $S(k)$ generate a Thortelmann set (actually, a Jubius group), the properties of which are the focus of much modern research, not only in linguistics but, for example, in progressing our understanding of creativity and the psychiatry of formal thought disorder. If qualities (say, trope content) attaching to the $S(k)$ are assigned numerical identifiers, we can define certain measures on the set which vastly simplify the path analysis. One, the HCF (so called by analogy with highest common factor), can be shown to be the minimal possible complete description of a given Thortelmann equivalence. Further treatment of the topic is beyond the scope of this book, but for more advanced students, the proof of Thortelmann-set Jubius-reducibility is left as an exercise. [HINT Assume a certain condition for arbitrary $S(k)$, hence prove that condition for $S(k + 1)$, then apply the reflexivity property on $S(1)$. What is the group operation?]

Interestingly, the assertion (2) above, and various corruptions, found brief popularity as tessellation motifs, a fact that has assisted historians in locating and dating the influence of al-Fakr'mustiq (see L Enright, *Architecture of the Sufi-Qurq*).

It is noteworthy that al-Fakr'mustiq's esteemed disciple is the same al-Jabr who figures in a work of **Satroit**. The poet responds (to a woman traveller seeking direction),

> The way through the desert is a riddle:
> Who is the man of letters but few words?

She replies,

> He is Mister al-Jabr, from the caravan of equals.
> Tonight his symbol sheets are bare.
> He wonders how few words, connected even idly,
> exchange invisibly fine, incalculable parts
> of purpose and surprise.

We, of course, should read the name as Algebra. Not obvious here is a pervading irony and subdued, sultry eroticism — these lines are not only about mathematics, but conspire deliciously with the poet's (unvoiced) meditation that

> Great journeys are from conversation to nakedness
> and returning. How rarely is the pilgrim
> properly scriptured, that she will know
> our spoken travel's distance and design.

Interested readers should consult the full text (Satroit, 'The Guardianship of the Holy Land'). For comparison, that poet's notorious but altogether less subtle 'A Suitor's Reverie', which was cited in apostasy charges and has only ever circulated underground, is made available. Notably, it lacks entirely the sensual modulation, mathematical subversiveness, and lightness, of the other work.

> In shaded blacks he colours her, and enters love's surmise
> sees ebony and unlit mouth, and wild jet-mystery eyes
> that could as well turn falling light
> to melancholy, or a comic night.
> They follow him, as now undressed
> he kisses evening on her breast
> then settles down; the rest is not
> to sleep, but breathe upon the raven spot
> a warmest whisper and the faintest touch
> that ever unsealed lips of such
> remotest secrecy — till vesper voice
> betrays the quickened parting of her joys
> with but an instant left to muse at length
> where, in her darkness, comes his strength.

14. DR BOKARDO

Tøssentern was becoming familiar with the taxi journey between King's Cross station and Mingle Lane, where Dr Bokardo had rooms. And this week, he noted, was depressingly unchanged from the four previous: even the passengers of the city, along with its sky, its roads and facades, were complexioned London grey.

When he entered the waiting room he found Barbara Bokardo sitting at the secretary's computer. She looked up and greeted him, with an explanatory wave at the untidiness around her.

'Constance is unwell. On days like this I am reminded that the work of a secretary can be harder than the practice of psychiatry.' She gestured Tøssentern toward the consulting room.

'I'm sure I can redress that imbalance for you,' he said quietly as he passed by. It was wryly spoken and, she thought, signalled an improvement in his mental state.

He settled into his now habitual corner of a comfortable leather couch. Dr Bokardo followed, closing the door. She sat on a matching armchair, some loose papers in one hand, and looked at him, gently and inquisitively. Neither spoke immediately.

Tøssentern was still thinking about his train journey from Cambridge. The weekly excursion was providing something unexpected: bearable solitude and an emptiness of thought that he found peaceful and restorative. He had even wondered if this experience of travel might be more transformative than the therapy sessions that were its purpose. Now, sitting here and suffused with idleness, he fell deeper into silence.

But somewhere in that submissive state was an emergent discomfort. His previous sessions had felt like interesting conversations; the issues in himself that he brought to therapy had been securely intellectualized. Today, with hardly a word between them, that artifice was dismantling, exposing a nebulous emotionality.

Only partly aware of his circumstances, he suddenly noticed that Dr Bokardo was looking down, writing on the notepaper, and the outward oddness of his distraction registered. His reaction was spontaneous, defensive, apologetic, and awkward.

'Notes on the silence?' he asked.

She looked up immediately. 'Is the silence noteworthy?'

Tøssentern felt slightly challenged, and hoped that his question had not been impolite. 'No. A phatic remark. I am sorry.'

As he spoke he regretted the reply; she would surely view no utterance in this setting as meaningless. Her response was still surprising.

'But a silence noteworthy enough to elicit a comment that destroyed its very object, the silence.'

There was a trace of questioning, but no tone of disagreement in her voice, and Tøssentern, easily amused by the self-referential, began to relax. The artifice strengthened, and within it the temptations of indolence returned. He imagined sitting there for the remainder of the session in contented silence. Instead, he took up her theme.

'Yes. As we might protect a species to extinction. Or declaring one's love begins love's eroding.'

He hesitated. The ideas had come with easy objectivity but, when expressed, left him unsettled. The antinomies and conundrums of existence that should provoke and entertain and illuminate seemed now imbued with pessimism.

'I suppose I was interested in why you would write, and what.' He wasn't confident of the truthfulness of this remark, and Dr Bokardo was not drawn.

'Actually, I like silences,' he continued, with greater composure. This was definitely true: he had to his name a scholarly monograph on that very subject of Parsan gaps, as they were known technically. Recalling at that point his interaction with the dreadful Signora Scintillini, he was tempted to add lightly that they were sometimes the only tolerable part of a conversation. Or that, in the humour canon of a student linguist, they translated impeccably. Dr Bokardo remained serious.

'In conversation, mutual silence begins and ends, ordinarily, with an expressed thought by one party. Do you agree?'

'Yes.'

'What happens in such a silence, for you?'

'I am listening, or re-listening, to what has been said; processing; exploring possibilities, directions; remembering; finding associations; searching; composing. Is that not the same for you?'

She ignored the question. 'Making judgements?'

'Possibly, around ethical issues, say. Privacy, relevance, the political. The other person, perhaps.' The last felt confessional, and he was aware of how it might reference into the present.

'What do you think is the nature of the conversation, during this silence?'

'I'm not sure I follow.'

'The silence begins, we agree, with something verbalized. This collocates both parties in thought. As it extends, their thinking de-correlates. So the longer the silence, the more the divergence, and therefore the more surprising to one party is the other's next expressed thought. Many would identify divergence and surprise as qualities enriching conversation.'

Tøssentern offered no response, and she added, 'On that basis, the richest, most interesting conversations are those with the longest intervals of silence. Paradoxical, isn't it?'

Tøssentern agreed, whilst weighing the speciousness of the argument.

'Of course,' she continued, 'an exception occurs if silence is systematically terminated by a comment of some fixed nature, say, on the silence itself.'

Tøssentern thought of his beginning remark, and felt slightly chastened. Dr Bokardo continued. 'That would eliminate unpredictability, and as we have agreed, richness. In the fully degenerate case we might find ourselves in a conversation consisting of long silences interspersed with comments about those long silences.'

'I can imagine two Becketts enjoying that,' offered Tøssentern.

'Would you enjoy it, Edvard?'

'As a participant, or as a spectator?'

'As participant.'

Tøssentern first imagined himself a spectator. His actors transformed with diminishing obviousness from tramps into people he recognized, staring mutely at each other with only perplexity in common. The audience leaned forward, expectantly, into this portrayal of the minimalist state, eager to witness an apotheosis of human communication. It came as music: Martin Allegorio's sublime cantata, *Wordless*, in celebration of the Syllabines.

He became aware of Dr Bokardo studying him intently, and was reminded of the given task. The music receded; the audience dissolved. The stage was the Nazarene Master's garden, and he was sitting quietly with Anna after the Lindenblüten lecture. He closed his eyes and the work of that silence returned. It was different now; the passage from exhaustion to resolve was effortless, and despair and hollowness were replaced by Anna's warmth.

But surrounding this happier vignette was a larger silence, set in this room, bonding him with Dr Bokardo. Yes, he was able to comment on silence, its length, purity, purpose, pathos. And of course he could manufacture delight and surprise. But, here and now, he had entered an experiment that seemed to immobilize him with self-consciousness. He couldn't bring himself to speak.

He opened his eyes, looking at Dr Bokardo for relief, but she said nothing. His thoughts returned to Anna, then to *Abel* in the storm, to the crash, and the hideousness of the condor attack. How he coated his body in thick mud as mosquito armour and stumbled, like some earthen clay monster, half the length of the Ferende plateau. How for weeks he survived, part-sustained, part-crazed, on seki fruit. How a strange amulet word, now forgotten, had come to him over and over until he thought of nothing else. And how on a rough jungle track he was dimly aware of human contact before succumbing to sleep. That was a long silence, ended not by some clever reflexive remark, but a confusion of ventilator sighs, monitor alarms, reassuring voices, and pain.

His eyes became moist and he touched them slowly with thumb and forefinger. He realized that throughout he had been staring absently at Dr Bokardo, and he found her looking back at him intensely. He forced himself into her presence, and dutifully to the question she had posed.

'Yes, I think I could enjoy that.' Even to him, it sounded ridiculous.

'Edvard, none of this is about the silence.' Her voice was gentle and concerned; as she spoke she leaned slightly forward as if her humanity were reaching out to touch him. 'It's not about the silence. It's about the introspection.'

Tøssentern understood in an instant. Far from offering refuge, silence was the theatre for an existential drama staged inside, lived singly and secretly in the white between the words. The insight drove him deeper into rumination, and again it was an effort to speak.

'I think I know that.' His voice was quiet and flat.

'Where did you go?' she asked softly.

'To the storm, the crash.' There was no need for explanation. In an earlier session Tøssentern had been able to give her a factual account of his experience. Dr Bokardo didn't speak. After a few minutes he continued.

'My disappearance was like a silence, wasn't it? Absence. Divergence. Judgements ... The unexpected conclusion.'

'A shocking, traumatic conclusion, Edvard, for those who knew you, joyous as it was.'

But Tøssentern's attention was on his own trauma, and his words came wrought from his own silence.

'I am thinking that I need to go back. I need to go back.' He seemed to retreat into self-absorption, and Dr Bokardo was the first to speak.

'To find *Abel*?'

Tøssentern's gaze shifted to the window and its light of London grey. He spoke slowly, as if escaping thoughts demanded ordered recognition and capture.

'*Abel*. The weaver fish. And the word I've lost; I need to go back, to remember it.'

Barbara Bokardo has an illustrious, if somewhat tarnished, ancestry. The Florentine philosopher **Leonardo di Boccardo**, known for a wit and worldliness too subversive for the papacy (his Vatican tenure as Ignorius, for two days, is often unlisted in pontifical histories), became private tutor and spiritual father to Niccolò Machiavelli. His observation that

> Every man dies before his masterpiece is born,

proved sadly prescient: he was believed poisoned while arranging for printing his *Conversaziones e Silenzio*, which is largely lost. Fragments survive, including two as attributed epigraphs; one is to be found in Pastaveleno's *Palazzo di Guerra* (here in a modern translation by Lawrence Enright):

> The methods of influence are argument, seduction and threat; appealing, respectively, to reason, vanity and fear. Of these, one is laborious, one unconscionable, but the third most efficacious.

Leonardo might well have heeded this insight in the upbringing of his protégé who, in all his writings, offers no acknowledgement of the master's self-evident priority. Indeed, Machiavelli's omissions seem intended to erase the name of di Boccardo from posterity. Some scholars argue that *The Prince* is a reworked *Conversaziones*.

The rumoured explanation for Ignorius' hasty expulsion was a perfectly unconscious but unforgivably profane solecism committed during Holy Week. Perhaps though, years later, in his own tenebrous hour, gravid with unborn masterpiece, his Sistine prayer was answered:

> *Miserere mei, Deus.* Maketh my end secular, with a woman near;

except that, in the event, the woman near had probably poisoned his penne.

Barbara Bokardo's innocuous '**Constance is unwell**' comment was a striking professional understatement. In fact, Constance suffered the affliction known discreetly to older physicians as Lady Coaxingly's Condition.

That Dr Bokardo's advice ('**It's about the introspection**') on the existential work of silence should present as an insight to Tøssentern, points to a retardative aspect of his illness. Apart from technical publications on Parsan gaps, he had co-authored (with **E Knielsen**) the deeply meditative *Nordic Silence*. By way of warning, readers attracted to this title are urged to fortify themselves with optimism before their journey into bleakness. There, in an unhorizoned world of ice and amber lakes called the Passible Tracts, three discoveries await. First, here is where moral* hesitation and remorse, linked to solitude, entered human nature. Second, in this wilderness was born inductive supposition, finding in another's death one's own *memento mori*. (Still might we look upon a gravesite frozen in prehistory and steal their people's inchoate thought: *At least I have outlived these few*.) Third, and a point to which the authors repeatedly return, there is a temperament made here for which the silence of the landscape, profound to us, is hymnal.

* According to Lord Enright, *blot* can mean both conscience and number. It remains unclear whether we are celebrating the origin of moral sentience, or the beginning of arithmetic. No wonder that the preface to *Nordic Silence* is a formless overture of two men brooding over what to say.

15. TWO PENELOPES AND THE HALFPENNY SET

For Anna, life at Chaucer Road had never recovered after the *Abel* accident. The contentment and easy companionship that sustained their separate professional lives seemed less assured. From once enjoying the spaciousness of a large house they now lived almost entirely in the new conservatory, where they had all meals and to which Edvard would bring work from his study and library. Pleasant as the space was for both of them, this radical resettlement felt eccentric and oddly impermanent, signifying to Anna withdrawal and distancing from what they had once shared.

The legacy of damage from the balloon crash was not limited to Edvard. Though her role in saving his life was universally praised, Anna regularly found herself intensely self-critical. It was not to do with her medical management. It was about the fact that she did not absolutely recognize Edvard when he was delivered so gravely ill from the jungle. It was a disappointment that some metaphysical bond had not immediately identified him against the evidence of her eyes. And it was her failure to dismiss categorically any doubt in herself and others about who that person was. She felt it as guilt, irrational and unfair to herself, and she didn't share it.

Another matter was again concerning her. On a recent visit to Mingle Lane, being a few minutes early for his appointment with Barbara Bokardo, Tøssentern had briefly visited the Ornithological Society's antiquated museum, situated only a few doors from her rooms. When he enquired of its aquiline curator about the artifacts and literature pertaining to the Asiatic condor he was met with astonishment. The reason for this was that earlier in the same week two Chinese gentlemen had sought the same material, which had otherwise lain dormant for decades. When it had proved necessary to impress upon them that items in the museum collection were not for sale at any price, they became agitated and left very uncivilly.

This intelligence aroused in Tøssentern a sense of urgency around returning to the Ferendes and prosecuting the campaign against illegal logging. He had, of course, been in regular contact with Paulo about research progress and some administrative decisions, but Paulo also had disturbing news about the Chinese problem. He had managed to visit the lookout on the northern plateau just once, but was able to report that a much longer deep-water jetty had been built, and he had photographed a very large vessel alongside. Enormous sheds had also appeared near the shoreline. The areal survey of deforestation that they had set up was no longer adequate as the extent of destruction was now well beyond the range of their optics. Arising from this, Paulo had copied Tøssentern into an email to Nicholas requesting that he organize access to satellite imagery.

The idea of Edvard returning worried Anna, partly because he seemed unsure what form an anti-logging campaign could possibly take, and also because she knew he would be keen to locate and visit the *Abel* crash site. That would involve an arduous trek with, no doubt, physical and (she was sure) psychological risks. She advised that she thought it unwise that he interrupt his therapy programme. She argued again that it would be sensible to wait until Nicholas had completed his consultancy in Perth and returned to the LDI station. And privately, she was wondering whether she should take extended leave from the Compton to go as well.

Despite the Ferende preoccupation returning, Anna did have a sense that Edvard's moods were improving. His morbid silences were fewer, he seemed more focused on his research and happy to be writing again. There was some return of lightness and humour in their idle conversation. These changes she ascribed, as did he, to therapy. She started to accept more the peculiar confinement of their lives to the conservatory.

It was pleasing then, given that they had not entertained friends for months, when Edvard suggested they invite to dinner Penelope Loom, the recently appointed Fellow in Homeric studies at Nazarene, who was new not just to the college but to

Cambridge itself. Anna remembered enjoying her company at Edvard's Lindenblüten lecture. This was more like the old days, when they habitually were host to new Fellows, visiting scholars and graduate students. She immediately contacted Penelope and secured a date.

They decided to include Rodney Thwistle, a long-time bachelor friend and also a Fellow of Nazarene. Edvard telephoned him and explained the dinner's purpose.

'Well, I'll bring Penelope, shall I?'

'No, no, Rodney. She's bringing someone, I'm sure.'

'No, no, Edvard. PH-D. Anna knows. We should talk about Nicholas.'

Thwistle hung up, leaving Tøssentern bewildered. He recounted the exchange to Anna.

'Oh, PH-D. Actually PH-D PhD. How nice.'

Tøssentern's bewilderment was undiminished.

'Penelope Hyffen-Dascher. I don't think you have met her, Edvard.'

'What is she, a dynastic punctuator? A printer's devil's daughter's compositor? Should I type her en or em? How ... wide is she?' Tøssentern was enjoying the mischief, but Anna interrupted.

'Edvard, of all people, you are the one who says always be respectful of names, never to make fun of them.'

Tøssentern looked undecided between contrition and fully abandoning the principle.

Anna continued. 'It's aristocratic, from Saxe-Coburg or somewhere. Anyway, Penelope's an engineer. I know her from university. She's an editor. She'll be fun.' She reflected briefly on the match with Thwistle, and added, 'That Rodney, what an old charmer he's turning out to be.'

In the event, Thwistle arrived alone, by bicycle, and PH-D a few minutes later, having driven from London. Penelope Loom and her companion Vissy were delayed by a gas leak in her neighbour's house that caused an invasion of emergency vehicles blockading the street. As she described the scene, the unpleasant odour, and hysterical public announcements to evacuate and avoid ignition hazards, Vissy, with consummate theatricality, mimed striking a match and lighting an imaginary cigarette. As he drew upon it and exhaled through pursed lips, she admonished, 'Vissy, put that out at once, you know we could all blow up.' Feigning surprise, he stubbed it out on the sole of his shoe. It was a virtuoso performance. Anna liked him.

After introductions, they sat at the long dining table in the conservatory. Both Edvard and Anna brought dishes from the kitchen, from which the guests were served. It was quite informal.

The purpose of the evening being to welcome Penelope Loom, much of the early talk was on life in Cambridge, the perils of cycling, property prices, and harmless chatter about Nazarene and its present Master. Tøssentern entertained with stories that even Thwistle hadn't heard, about a Nazarene Fellows' revolt in the 1870s when five logicians, calling themselves the Quintics, seized power. The chaotic, insolubly divisive two-year College Interregnum that followed ended only when Martin Gales, a gambler mathematician expelled from Oxford, was elected Master, and managed to rein back insurrection while clandestinely doubling, then twice redoubling, the Nazarene treasury.

When Penelope was asked about her areas of research, the discussion ranged from emergent glyph chirality to the nature of the heroic temperament, hermeneutics and the painstaking dissection of history from fiction, allegory from hallucination, amnesia from deception. Anna felt some anxiety that these themes of interpretation touched upon Edvard's recent preoccupations in his own life, around his recollection of the crash, and the obituaries.

But if he were disturbed, it didn't show. At one point, when Penelope mentioned the symbology of Cycladic figurines, Edvard rushed enthusiastically to his library and returned with a treasured example. It was passed around the table, each present offering an account of its meaning and purpose followed by a slightly boisterous round of applause. Interestingly, Vissy was the only one to imbue it with voice, speaking solemnly in what might have been a scholarly proto-Greek, or might have been nonsense. For the benefit of the others, he offered to translate, appearing to falter occasionally with the difficulty of the task:

You hold a womb of barren clay.
Yet it was living for the day
a labour line though undefiled
carried the chosen woman child
was broken from her water there
into Aegean circling air.

Came the golden Delian year
her blooded sweet adulthood near
Lord Eros graced where only this
would glisten his betrothing kiss.

Then mother from her mother learned
and issue into issue turned.

He then briefly addressed the sculpture in its own language, respectfully bowed his head, and passed it on. It was difficult to discern the serious from the satirical in Vissy.

And this being a dinner party in Cambridgeshire, it wasn't long before the conversation shifted to the vicar of Postlepilty. The subject was raised by PH-D, who reported that the gossip in London's editorial circles was that Simon Vestry had not been seen since that first letter from Barnabas Bending inciting riotous correspondence in the *Tribune*. For the second time, Tøssentern left the table, returning with a file of papers and clippings. He selected the letter in question, musing aloud as he scanned it.

'The Postlepilty symposium. Recognizing cant. I wonder how that will go. Anna and I couldn't even find the place.'

He passed the folder to Penelope Loom, who was the least informed of the party. The others were aware that no more theatrical reviews had appeared from Simon Vestry, but news of his disappearance was received with a good-mannered delectation for scandal. Tøssentern, always analytical, asked whether it was definitely known that Simon Vestry was a real person. Had PH-D ever met him? Might it be that he was an invention? Indeed, might he be an alter ego of the Reverend Barnabas Bending, himself the putative invention of Simon Vestry? Could it be that what they were witnessing was a mortal battle of two figments, a battle for endorsement, to be elected real? Or was there a third party, a master who falsified both? And why stop there: why not a concatenation of masqueraders having its origin who knows where? These ideas were so antithetical to the presumed order of things that PH-D confessed an impatience to return to London, and (in a phrase offered by Tøssentern) inseminate the city rumour mill.

Anna had known PH-D since student days. Though reading different disciplines, they shared a love of flying, and met through their university aero club. Together, they founded *Altimeter* magazine, which was noticed, acquired, and closed, by UITA Press. Anna, very occasionally, would still write a less formal invitation piece for the aviation literature, but for PH-D, the joint passions for aerospace science and writing had scripted her life. After postdoctoral work on propulsion management about collinear Lagrange points, she had advanced more rapidly in the publishing than the engineering worlds, and was now the London-based executive editor of the prestigious *Aviation Reviews*.

When the subject touched upon how she and Rodney had met, the less forthcoming Thwistle diverted the conversation.

'What is it you do, Vissy?'

'Well, I began as a classicist—not Hellenic, more declining Rome. Then declining fortunes, as a poet.'

'What sort of poetry do you write?' It was PH-D who asked.

'About incidents, characters. Not in the laureate tradition; nothing narrative, nothing pastoral.' He sounded reticent.

'Not in the style of Modern Tedium, the elegiac parochial,' murmured PH-D.

'Vissy, you should tell them about the rapper lyrics.' Penelope addressed the table generally. 'He's been sensational; it pays more than poetry magazines, or academia for that matter.'

Her manner now, suddenly enthusiastic and slightly disinhibited, contrasted oddly with the serious, scholarly woman of minutes earlier. It was a display of admiration, and quite endearing.

'You're a rap lyricist!' The voice and shift in posture betrayed PH-D as vastly impressed.

Vissy smiled politely, still reticent, evidently embarrassed. He, too, seemed a different person from the one who had clowned about cigarette smoking during a gas leak.

'Tell us about your characters,' asked Anna quietly. It changed the tone completely.

'Those I inhabit or those I write about?'

'I expect they're the same,' said Anna.

Vissy looked at her appreciatively. 'Yes, they're essentially one. A visitor, uncertain with words.' He hesitated. 'Often haunted, like all who have loved, by the past erotic.'

His voice and his look, still directed at Anna, were intense. She nodded slowly, returning his gaze.

'The past erotic. It sounds like a tense, if I might say so. Is that the new grammar?' It was Thwistle. Anna suspected he was dealing with discomfort. She had a little herself. Vissy looked at Thwistle.

'You are right. In poetry, it is the only tense.' From that point he was silent for a long time.

It was PH-D who returned to the subject of Simon Vestry, which had clearly continued to absorb her. She raised the matter as if there had been no intervening conversation.

'We should be able to figure out who invented whom; after all, who came before the other?'

Tøssentern was the first to respond. 'Well, that might not be sufficient. I think we should be mindful of the Halfpenny Set.'

'That's not a coin collection, I take it,' offered Penelope. She had been shuffling through the Bending file, and seemed unaffected by Vissy's seriousness.

'It could be—' began Tøssentern.

'The cash reserves of a modern superpower?' The interjection was PH-D's.

'But it's also about the limits of inference, named, as it happens, for Daniel Halfpenny.' Now the only response was inquisitive stares from around the table, and Tøssentern added, 'Let me illustrate with an experiment.'

He picked up a pepper grinder, and handed it to Penelope Loom, on his left. 'Pass this on to the person on your left, please.'

Penelope complied, and it continued around the table.

'Now someone observing any one of you in isolation, keen to invoke causation, and cognizant that cause must precede effect, might conclude that receiving the pepper grinder from the right determines in some way that you dispatch it to the left.

'Suppose now that he sees this same act by all five of you, still in isolation one from the other. If his ability to discern detail is limited, he may view it as repetitive behaviour executed five times by one undifferentiated individual, and propose an explanation accordingly. But if his inspection identifies that you are separate persons, he will theorize differently. Equally, if he can identify the object to be a peppermill, as distinct from, say, this figurine,' Tøssentern gestured toward it, 'he is likely to attribute different meanings in the two cases. The problem arises if he were to observe me.' Tøssentern took the pepper grinder from PH-D on his right.

'What he would see is that I gave it away on the left *before* I received it on the right. In my case, receiving it can hardly be in any way causal to dispatching it. If his inspection were further rescaled to include the connectivity of events, his explanation would again differ, and might account for the facts as we created them, though hardly our reason for doing so.

'What we must conclude is that there is no observable totality of events, and therefore no completeness of inspection. This was Halfpenny's insight: that observations commonly labelled evidential are not, in this example, scale invariant. That single fact can invalidate apparently sound hypothesis testing.'

'I'm not sure I follow.' Vissy had been virtually silent since the poetry discussion. Anna had a sense that he spoke for the others as well.

'Let me give another example.' Tøssentern addressed Vissy. 'Imagine you were not a classicist and opened a Latin dictionary, say, at the last page. You might conclude that all Latin words begin with z. Indeed, you would have no reason to suppose otherwise. But if you examine the fine structure of those z-words, the second, the third letters, and so on, you could conclude by an exhaustion argument that this could not be the case almost certainly, knowing the existence of more dictionary and the conventions of alphabetization.'

'But he could just look at the rest of the dictionary, surely,' suggested PH-D.

'Of course, if it is available to him. But that constitutes another inspection, in a scaling sense opposite to the fine structure inspection I've outlined. You see, it's perfectly possible that he can know there is more dictionary but cannot inspect it. For example, I might only provide him with a torn-out z-page. So,' continued Tøssentern, now looking at PH-D, 'you have said that Simon Vestry has not been seen since the vicar's letter. But was he seen *before* the vicar's letter? Our inspection of events, in Halfpenny terms, needs rescaling at least to include that. Looking at the rest of the Latin dictionary, as it were. For all we know, his theatre reviews were submitted by email and his remuneration banked electronically. What evidence does that afford for a real Simon Vestry? And, if he is not real, in what sense can he be said to have disappeared?'

To his friends, this was classic Tøssentern, and the critique seemed compelling. The discussion briefly moved to the general problem of identifying causal pairings in a noisy sequence. This eventually devolved to a quiet exchange between Thwistle and PH-D on Markov chains, followed by what seemed to be a mild disagreement about commutative groups. A moment later, indistinctly, inexplicably, their subject had shifted to harmonic analysis of an ancient Tibetan singing bowl reputed to sound the Tristan chord.

Those two made a compatible pair, thought Anna. She looked at Edvard, sitting at the other end of the table in earnest conversation with Penelope Loom about the quality of software for Greek typography. Vicar and Vestry, it seemed, were become ephemera of departed conversation.

Beyond Edvard, she had a view of the garden, and in the distance could see the greenhouse lit up; evidently, Thornton was working late into the evening. Anna thought about him, about being Thornton. If he looked back through the garden, his would be a reciprocal view of the brightly lit conservatory, looking very much like a greenhouse for these exotic people around her.

Thornton. There was a resilient man, who seemed to have

recovered fully from that strange swint business by simply handing over his distress. That was the therapeutic transaction: she accepted his anxiety, and issued reassurance in exchange.

So now the anxiety was hers, and in consequence the greenhouse had changed in meaning. It always brought to mind her visit to Walter Reckles in New Mexico, that odd discomfort about the separation of realities by some improbably fine artifice. Here, it was glass, beguilingly transparent but no less deceiving. Even closer, even more beguiling, within this room, in her company, it was the human face, a veneer of openness that masked the silent from the speaking self.

What had Walter talked about? Eigenvalues in the complex plane determining stability of flight. Maybe eigenvalues on some abstract surface determined stability of everything—relationships, identity, sanity. (One could certainly argue that complexity of the mind, like that of number, had real and imaginary parts.) A psychiatric diagnosis, then, might be no more than a column of numbers. *I'm sorry, your child has an eigenvalue problem*. And where would Thornton be located? Surely he was stable. Or Barnabas Bending? Or these people, the two Penelopes, say? The difficulty was, in their silent selves, everyone could be insane.

Vissy had fallen quiet once more. Somehow, in speaking least, he remained the most eloquent. Anna glanced at him and thought about his word, *visitor*. She found herself drawn to its poetry, into its alienation, and powerless to resist as its contour of meaning expanded to enclose her, then Edvard, in their own place, the conservatory.

Thwistle and PH-D had returned to the z-page problem and the matter of self-similarity in alphabetical orderings when, quite abruptly, Thwistle turned to Tøssentern and repeated the words he had used on the telephone: 'We should talk about Nicholas.'

Given the note of urgency, it seemed rather late in proceedings to raise the subject. Tøssentern, politely, interrupted to explain briefly to Vissy and the two Penelopes who Nicholas was.

Thwistle's news was that he had received a call from Nicholas's sister Millie (like Nicholas, a former student) concerned that his normally reliable communication with the family had completely stopped. In fact, they were unable to contact him in any way. Some weeks previously, Thwistle had emailed two other acquaintances whom he knew to be in Perth suggesting that Nicholas might be in touch, but he had now learned that neither had met with him. One, who was called Worse, had asked for more information and promised to make whatever enquiries he could.

There it was, thought Anna. Another disappearance. Barnabas Bending, Simon Vestry, Nicholas and, before it all, Edvard. Again, she disconnected from the moment, imbuing events with an uncharacteristic superstition and Gothic exaggeration; here was the ghost of *Abel*, here was a curse of the weaver fish. Perhaps disappearance was to be the signature of a new order, where the normal cycles of going and returning break badly and promised certainties regress to the tracery of missing pieces. Fracture, confusion, loss: the imagery was depressing, and thrust her back to where she was, seated in the conservatory. Even there, for all she knew, the house behind her might have vanished, as from a conversation.

The others were canvassing possibilities. Anna thought about Nicholas; she knew he was clever and resourceful, and was confident that an innocent explanation would emerge. She shared this optimism. Tøssentern was also reassuring, asking for little detail except wanting to know more about Worse. The others, respectful of Thwistle's concern, were quiet or positive. By the end, Thwistle himself seemed happier, resolving only to maintain contact with Millie, and with Worse in Perth.

Daniel Halfpenny was reportedly shot dead in an abortive Chicago jewellery heist before he had finalized his magnum opus *Probabilistic Reasoning*. The manuscript was completed and published with annotations and an introduction by Edvard Tøssentern (Lindenblüten, 2005). Every well-formed observation has an associated Halfpenny Set, being the set of all propositions refutable by the given observation. The set expands or contracts dynamically according as a fidelity function relating the observation to its object phenomenon. Fidelity takes account of empirical properties of the observation, such as resolution, scaling, boundedness, error and noise. It is increasingly the case that funding proposals in experimental research must define and argue the merits of a relevant Halfpenny Set, as competing applications can sometimes be decided on this measure alone. The interested reader is referred to Halfpenny's *A Fidelity Function*

Approach to Sampling Theory, and *Finite Halfpenny Sets* by T Thurdleigh. Less technical sources are *The Interpretation of Error* and *Partial Evidence,* op. cit. (It might be supposed that Tøssentern, in explaining to his audience the matter of evidential fallacy and observational scaling, would use as a prime example the Asiatic condor. However, of those present at the table, only Anna would be sufficiently informed to understand the allusion.)

[The following **Editor's Statement** is provided in the interests of transparency: After his death, it was revealed that Halfpenny led a second life in a totally different literature. Writing as **Timothy Bystander**, he was the author of the hugely influential *The Craven Soul,* and *Studies in Cowardice I: The Suicide Murderer,* as well as collections of poetry, *Moral Hazard,* and essays, *The Prophet of the One False God.* Moreover, based on concordance analysis, Bystander almost certainly authored **A B C Darian**'s *A Prayer Prepostery.* In turn, the admiring preface to that dark work, headed 'Imitation Believers' and attributed to the defrocked Abbess **Magdalena Letterby**, has long been suspected to be Darian's own. These findings have raised the question of whether other (perhaps inflammatory) materials were composed under pseudonyms of even higher order, a possibility that is currently the subject of intensive research. Unfortunately, this endeavour is itself complicated by spurious contributions from persons of unproven identity (for example, Darian claims to be real, living in Perth, and the true author of *The Figment Tree,* a work never before connected to that name). There are respectable conspiracists who believe such a trail will, at its end, force the conclusion that Halfpenny's death was not truly accidental. **Alison Pilcrow**, UITA Press]

Vissy Mofo (Captain Hate)'s latest release *Exegesis Christ* is available on the Acridaria label. Once asked how he acquired his name, the reply was: 'On account of causin' vicissitude to moh foes.'

16. Z-WORDS IN LATIN

Dear Edvard and Anna

Thank you so much for inviting me to your home yesterday. You provided a wonderful meal and delightful company. I will remember forever the transcendent flavour of seki fruit.

I feel that I should apologize if I seemed impolitely quiet for some time. On occasions I am withdrawn into other worlds, and the residuum left at table is a very dull guest indeed. It was certainly not for lack of enjoyment or appreciation of the conversation. On the contrary, that conversation transported me happily into my retired *dictionarium*, from which I send you a question. It is long, in a tradition dating from the Syllabine Campaign, and yet to have music arranged. But I think we share an interest in *zothecula*, for which in modern times a conservatory serves well, and in notions of conflation, for which zothecula serves well.

Sincerely
Vissy

> Could Zaleucus, lawgiver of the Locrians
> not in Zama, the town in Numidia
> where Scipio defeated Hannibal
> suffering zamia, damage, injury, loss
> nor in Zancle, now Messina in Sicily
> be zelotypus, jealous
> of three philosophers
> Zeno of Citium, founder of the Stoic school
> Zeno of the Eleatic school, teacher of Pericles, and

Zeno of the Epicurean school, teacher of Cicero
together comforted by
zephyrus, the warm west wind;
or of Zeuxis, painting in Heraclea
Helen, beauty and illusion of
possibly zmaragdus, emerald, beryl, jasper
or light and line of zodiacus, constellation;
surely not of critic Zoilus, scourge of Homer
undeserving of his subject's story's hero's
purple zona, belt or girdle;
nor even Zoroastres, lawgiver of the Medes
retiring to his zotheca
a private room in which to rest
reflecting on his place perhaps
and minor paradox
say, the longer but diminutive
zothecula?

17. RECOGNIZING CANT

Wagon des Philosophes
Paris Métro

Cher Reverend Bending

I am most honoured to be made a corresponding member of the Postlepilty Symposium on the varied meanings and fascinations of your excellent word. I fear that our French philosophers are ageing and tired and quarrelsome, and much in need of the Anglican vigour that you bring to their depleted discourse. Only one, my fellow citizen of the Métro, M Henri Fumblément, is capable of extended wakefulness. You are surely familiar with his textual analysis of the lyrics of Vissy Mofo (Captain Hate), where it is argued that to every line can be appended your very same term (such is its versatility), all without compromise to the artist's meaning or inspired rhyming!

But first I disclose a technical plagiarism. I confess that I draw upon my recent Induction Lecture to the *Academie*, dedicated, as is customary, to the First Lady of France. By tradition, that most venerable person becomes the owner of its content, and all my thoughts and expositions on the subject now vest in her.

And I apologize the more for I speak with an accent of the shamed. I refer to what our liberated women call *la maladie sans serif*, the tribal ignorance of the average Frenchman, who is famously inattentive to the subtleties and fine graces of what we discuss. I ask only that you imagine fattened, Gauloise-stained fingers, the smell of Citroën upholstery, and the breakdown lane of a national highway.

I confess also to some anxiety that you may view me more credentialled than I truly am. For we French share no ownership of your greatest ardour word, and despite a lifetime of earnest researches, my knowledge of Old Norse is limited. In this regard, I commend to you M Fumblément, a man of ravenous curiosity whose authority is, by reputation, Casanovan. (Whether he is practised in recognition, however, I cannot say.)

But some things I have learned. That here is a word infinite in form yet singular in virtue. That no other in man's lexicon is so repressed and more imagined. Its meaning, uniquely, is more displayed than conveyed. (Indeed, the common blush, becoming to the face, is sent from here.) Were English gendered, this would be feminine, and lightly scented. Its pronunciation is properly soft and slow and moistened on the tongue. It should never appear in a question, in the imperative, in the plural, or in the company of a moustache. It remains the foremost English cry of intimacy, of exploration and discovery, of invitation and acceptance; and it best belongs in a conversation for two.

A conversation for two that is forever experimental. A conversation between apprehension and desire, between suggestion and willingness, between consummation and a slow realization of the holy benediction in the word. That its meaning is a type of *kindness*, the embodiment and sublimation of *forgiving*, repeated and renewed with every utterance. (M Bending, as a priest, you will know this.)

Its finest expression is both music of the being and a symphony of the tongue; *largo* and *allegro*, *pianissimo* and *vibrato*—all composed in the moment, and conducted in the tempo of audience approval. Here is a performance where the lips are open but the voice is silent, or at least restrained, for the singing is the listener's and the aria is the word.

I assert that no other word in any other language contains such nuance and contradiction: of attraction and foreboding, transcendence and turmoil, promise and denial, paradise and enslavement. It is secretive, and clever in concealment; reserved, but expansive in good company; strong-willed, but open to persuasion; tight-lipped, but loquacious in private. Flirtatious with strangers and often generous to the needy, it befriends most the selfless, and wholly welcomes only the loving.

And should some cataclysm extinguish all of language save this one sweet syllable, the conversation of the world would continue undiminished, the eloquence of poets would not be undone, and the natural commerce of men and women would be no less subtle.

Alas, in our bleak times there are too few euros for our schools of Applied Philology and for now, regrettably, these meagre observations exhaust my scholarship. It remains only for me to recognize the tireless contribution of my research assistant, Mlle Marguerite Sallumer, to these absorbing studies.

Finally, I propose that my good friend, M Simon Vestry, attend in person to deliver my paper. I hope this meets with your approval.

Cordialement à vous

Napoléon Lecémot
Professeur

Regarding the 'cataclysm' assertion, Professor Lecémot seems unaware that such a circumstance has been tested historically. In *Cisalpinus* (circa 290 BC), there is described a race of **Syllabine Women** whose single utterance, *Can't*, served their every need in discourse. They were nonplussed into submission (and eventual annexation as the Roman province of Parsa) by tricky Latin speakers exploiting nothing more than two novel and devious linguistic constructions — the iterated negative and the very, very long question. Though not in themselves formally lethal, these were tactically upgradable, should hostilities require, to the dreaded *Z-Invectivus*, a barrage instrument of unsurpassed efficiency. Within a generation, the language of the Syllabines was lost, unrecognizable even to those who had been its native speakers. And with it perished that people's source repository of oral history, epic, poetry and drama. This is the earliest documented instance of language serving as a first-line weapon of imperialist conquest.

In the case of double, triple (and so on) negatives, the encounter also marks the invention of the modern parity check, foreshadowing the supremacy of number over word in the digital age. The Romans realized that there was no need to assimilate the cognitive reversal at each negation, but simply count their number. Lacking the binary vocabulary necessary to distinguish odd from even, it is unsurprising that the Syllabines succumbed to these aggressive confounding tactics. In our own times of inflationary coinage and the fatuous neologism, it is hard to conceive that for want of a word's invention an entire culture could disappear. (In turn, victorious Latin would similarly die of inertia, proving insufficiently profane to serve advancing civilization.

Its end was foretold by the Princess Periphereia (*Can't Can't*), known also as *Can't Can't Can't*, or the Prophetess of Parsa.)

Nevertheless, in the matter of parity, the Roman conquest was not without its difficulties. Division by II is not straightforward. (Who would suppose that $X/II = V$, or $C/II = L$, or $MI/II = DS$? Indeed, were it not for modern methods supervening, many a calculation begun in those times would still be unfinished. It is left as an exercise for the reader to evaluate S/II, and verify that $II/S = II\hat{}II$.) In the event, however, the Syllabines were vastly more confused than their invaders, and that is how conflict is decided. There does remain, it should be said, one consoling legacy for that defeated race: the Syllabine influence filtered through the entire Indo-European linguistic diaspora, and accounts for the silence content of conversations had in every descendent language. In consequence, we owe more to Parsan in our daily speech than we do to Latin. (See E Tøssentern, *Spoken Silence: Etymologies and Guide to Diction*; and N Misgivingston, *Stochastic Signatures of the Parsan Gap*.)

The expression 'suffer in silence' has its origin in the Syllabine experience.

More generally, and more insidiously, **Milton Noyes** in *Latin Aleatorics: Translations with Commentary* points out that Roman numerals introduced inherent bias into games of chance, and almost certainly subverted Imperial history. For example, the numbered die, as cast before the Rubicon, was unbalanced, with only IV and VI having equal turning moment. Extraordinarily though, in this particular instance, the outcome may not have been corrupted by that fact. Noyes explains the relevant sample space (that is: to cross, and not to cross), and strongly affirms a remark of Martin Gales (made in a Lindenblüten lecture on gambler's ruin, in 1879, and scandalizing historians at the time) declaring it unthinkable that Caesar would not choose instead to toss a *denarius*. We now believe that he did, but reported the other as more literary. This appalling licence has left Noyes sceptical that the Rubicon was even crossed at all, arguing in any case that Caesar's military genius would compel the more strategic, more tactically surprising (but less eloquent) advance on Rome by anabasis into Parsa Syllabina, then striking quickly south. Rather sadly, Noyes' ambivalence about his own discoveries is evident in a footnote to that chapter, where he meditates on how these archetypal scenes, woven into our language and our art as metaphors of destiny and decidedness, are proving to be crassly falsified.

The reader should be made aware of this: In all of history, every setting out, and every tread and turn that follows, has probability underfoot. That said, only one other example from Noyes, a Biblical chance event, will be mentioned here—at Calvary, the soldiers' die, being evidently tetrahedral ({I, II, III, IV}), could not possibly have been fair. The Seamless Robe would have been more equitably quartered after all.

Further notes added in proof It has been brought to the author's attention that the argument linking parity with the 'want of a word's invention' warrants elaboration. We formalize matters as follows. Let $S(w, n)$ be a sentence having word count w and containing n negations in series. Then S is affirmative (negative) according as n is congruent to 0 (1), modulo 2. Whilst it is not necessary to employ n distinct counting terms for this determination (because sequential negations can be assigned alternately to each of two registers signifying progressive n odd or even, disregarding cardinality of n), it is clear that a binary vocabulary (and, *a fortiori*, a monologic language) is not sufficient to define and justify the operation. Exactly what might be sufficient is still unknown, and is part of a more general unsolved problem, the so-called Syllabine Task, which continues to torment modern symbolic language researchers.

The terminology introduced here provides for a technical specification of the aforementioned *Z-Invectivus*. For this we have (1) *S* is interrogative; (2) Excepting negation forms, *S* is composed of z-words exclusively; (3) *w* is free to increase without limit; (4) *n* is free to increase without limit; (5) Negations may be concatenated, as in *non non non ...*, or *aaa ...* in prefix, to any order; (6) Style variants are permitted. (One of these, the *Expectoratus*, can still be found in certain languages.) The power and tone and speed of abusive delivery from specially trained and fearsome centurions can only be imagined.

Finally, there have been numerous requests to expand on the life of the Prophetess. Despite the depredations of the Roman invaders, we can be grateful that among their number were historians and poets who rendered into Latin something of the Syllabine heritage, including many of the prophecies of Periphereia. These have in common a unique triadic structure that has often been compared with sonata form (it has also been suggested that they are syllogistic, but the case is considered weak; they certainly lack any Aristotelian formalism), and are thought likely to have had a musical cadence in the Syllabine that is not preserved in translation. They are also unusual in antiquity, being almost devoid of the oracular, instead having a disturbing profundity of insight into the human condition. Her most famous, and most enigmatic, pronouncement is incomplete, appearing to be missing its recapitulation. Normally, the latter would offer a degree of internal correlation, and its absence makes interpretation more problematic. It begins:

The flight of silver half-brightens the earth.

Almost all scholarly attention has focused on this line, and the catalogue of proposed meanings, including the night lunar transit and an oblique forward reference to Judas Iscariot, is too extensive to discuss. However, the ideas of Milton Noyes, who is the acclaimed modern authority on the writings of the Prophetess, should be recorded. Noyes is a probabilist by training and instinct, and is naturally drawn to the image of a tossed silver coin, perhaps catching the sunlight as it spins in the air. The inclusion of *half* is wholly corroborative, this being the defining probability in such a Bernoulli trial. Of course he is led, irresistibly, to a mention of Caesar's lie, but his programme is vastly more ambitious — nothing less than a grand exposition of a Syllabine preoccupation with balanced dichotomies, such as light and shadow, good and evil, free-will and fate. In a radical 're-reading' ('reading' because its script has never been confidently decrypted) of an occult Parsan Greek text which includes an array of signifiers previously assumed to represent some important genealogy, Noyes believes he has uncovered a nascent Pascal's triangle. From that, in what must be acknowledged as a triumph of mathematical–historical synthetic research, he develops the coin toss theme into an all-pervading cultural philosophy founded on a sacred arithmetic of chance, specifically a rudimentary version of binomial statistics; for this, he summons extensive supporting evidence — most notably the characteristic quincunx design and a possible forked-path motif found on late Syllabine pottery.

(For all this manifest complexity and sophistication in Syllabine abstract thought, we are still left with the fact that, for want of explicit words to denote odd and even, their civilization perished. The lesson we must draw is that language evolves not for civil communication, not for the expression of ideals, not even for its measured containment of silences, but for the rebuttal of insults. In this, of course, the Romans excelled, and still do.)

Frustratingly, however, none of this brilliant exegesis contributes to our understanding of the second line:

> The flight of gold half-darkens the sun.

Here, Noyes is silent, joining a cavalcade of scholars who have offered no enlightenment on the intention of the Prophetess. Obviously, many have been tempted to invoke an astronomical, perhaps ecliptic or zodiacal, explanation for these words, but the reader will easily conclude that the moonlight metaphor of the earlier line is disqualified analogically. In short, no hypothesis has been found remotely convincing, and the hermeneutic challenge remains wide open.

But there is much more to this extraordinary figure than the prophecies. For this author, she is best celebrated as the first to draw freehand a faultless circle, using sable brush and oil of lampblack. Not content with the one beauty, she destroyed it in the quest for another. Employing methods that anticipate modern techniques of titration and colorimetry, she compared the quantities of ink in its circumference and diameter. The perfection of her hand can be judged from the result transcribed in *Cisalpinus*:

$$\text{III . I IV I V IX II VI V ...}$$

(The expansion here becomes indecipherable.) We name this ratio pi (the initial letter of her name in Greek) in her honour.

18. WORSE

The physics of falling bodies is well understood, but not the metaphysics.

So mused Worse as he stepped safely back from the gaping elevator shaft. There seemed an urgent need of redress, and the makings of a disquisition came untidily to mind. A tribute to the author of the *Principia*. Arcane theorems of existence and uniqueness, addressing first *Am I?* followed by *Am I alone?* A homily on fallen man. Last lessons in futility and abandonment. The fall into love, and love's disrepair. The fall as narrative, spoken one level at a time. Argument and irrevocability begin at 33; 33 is the cause of 32, and 32 of 31, and so number of annihilation. And the fall as enlightenment, which is to find one's place in parable.

Here was the meditation of a falling man, admittedly compressed into five and a half seconds. Its conclusion might conduct to attentive listeners in the basement car park, but only silence returned to level 33. Metaphysics, Worse could safely surmise, had not interceded, and wholly temporal last words might have been more fitting. Perhaps, *I don't think you appreciate the gravity of your situation.* Or, *Here's something for nothing, fucker. That's why we call it a free fall.* Worse instantly felt ashamed. Somewhere in the mass of any man there were surely atoms of goodness, deserving of (one could say) gravitas.

In any case, there was much to be said for a falling death. At least the physics was straightforward; the kinematic equations were easily solved and, as any thoughtful student would enjoy, linked immediately to observation. There was also kindness in the constants, a humane good fortune about the speed of things.

Death came not so suddenly to be unforeseen, but without prolonged uncertainty either. There was none of the confusion and ambiguity and unpunctuality of a decline into terminal illness. There was no attendant metabolic or pharmacologic delirium. In the state of falling, certainty and lucidity made terror sensible, and a man could properly summon his readiness to die. In short, the speed of reason was in perfect harmony with the fall, knowing and comprehending into the final centimetres of awareness.

And falling was a true leveller. Feather and stone, man, woman—none slower nor less graceful than the other, all made equal by a universal law. Of course, for those inclined to human exceptionalism, that ideal was incidental to a humbling indifference of the natural world. For them, the romance of the dangerous height, the flirtation and fear and vanity of the climb, even the science of flight, were inventions of defiance. Nevertheless, if some commoner should excel, and overreach, there remained one uniform justice: that he who had risen further, fell further.

Worse stared at the void. It had proved ideal for bulky and awkward items. In seven years at the Grosvenor apartment, he had now disposed of two armed intruders along that same slight parabolic arc to their final resting place: an unlit, unvisited, concrete winch-pit. One day, he would remember to throw in a sack of builder's lime as well, for antisepsis.

Bending down, he removed a screwdriver wedging the track, allowing the outer doors to slide faultlessly to a close. He examined the paintwork and door seals for traces of interference. Noting that the lift car was at the forty-first floor, he re-entered his apartment and secured the door behind him. In the bathroom he washed his hands and face, studying himself in the mirror. Before drying he washed again, more attentive to its sensations.

He collected together his assailant's loose possessions and carried them to an office desk, where he switched on a bright reading light and began a careful study of each object. A slim wallet contained Australian and Hong Kong banknotes, a driver's licence, credit cards, a hotel key card, and some club passes — not all bearing the same name. Separately were a rental car contract, car keys, some meal receipts, an airline boarding pass, a watch, and a mobile phone. The licence and the contract were both in the name of Zheng.

Worse examined each article before photographing it and setting it aside. Then, taking the mobile phone and camera he walked across a hallway into a long narrow, windowless room set up as a galley office. Along the right-hand wall was a bench bearing several computer terminals and assorted peripherals. Two of the CPUs were uncased. At the far end, looking more like a workshop than an office, was another bench covered by a sheet of thick black rubber. On this was a steel instrument rack containing oscilloscopes and other electronic test gear, along with a soldering-iron, a vice, assorted loose tools, and small tray sets of meticulously labelled circuit components. Most of the other long wall was furnished with shelving containing a technical library, manuals and reports. Just inside the entrance, on the left, a small table held a microscope and a fibre-optic light source.

Worse went to one computer and downloaded the photographs, encrypting them. Then he rolled his chair down to the workshop end and, removing the casing of the mobile phone and extracting the SIM card, applied fine probes to the circuitry as he watched first an oscilloscope and then a computer screen. Satisfied that he had accessed the phone ID data and downloaded its entire call register, he encrypted the files and reassembled the phone. Then he moved to another terminal.

Within the building security profession, problems at the Grosvenor were well known. Over its seven-year life there had occurred, apparently at random, puzzling failures in the building's communication and surveillance systems. At first, these were investigated thoroughly, and more than once declared eradicated, yet they still returned. Over time, because no catastrophic incidents had ever implicated security failures, and because on every occasion the faults seemed benign and self-limiting, the concern of the early years was replaced by bemused acceptance. For those in a position to know, these inexplicable 'transients' were part of the building folklore, and no longer elicited security alerts. Only to Worse, who had occupied his suite at the Grosvenor for the whole seven years, did their origin hold no mystery at all.

Entering a code, Worse called up a program labelled Peepshow; displayed before him was the complete building security status along with a fault listing. Cameras on odd numbered floors from 19 to 39 were still out. He now shut down surveillance in the basement car park, as well as interrupting central monitoring of elevator locations.

Collecting Zheng's car key, he assembled a small toolkit together with a torch and a fresh set of gloves, and left the apartment. He rode the lift down to level 29, opened the door, and checked that the corridor was empty. Then taking the screwdriver from his coat pocket he created, within a few seconds, subtle but forensically incontrovertible evidence of interference with the outer door seal.

Back in the lift, he felt both good and bad. But calling to mind the unpleasantness of Bishop Mesmerides on 29, he was quickly relieved of ambivalence, and pushed express to the basement.

The descent was rapid and he imagined being in free fall, summoning a magical force to save himself. He relished the physical sense of deceleration and return of weight, enjoying the audacious power as his tiny frame of reference slowed to a precision stop. *You should have thought of magic, fucker.* But Worse was ever careful not to displease his single deity, the author of irony; simultaneously, he offered silent penitence to determinism and the natural world. As if his apology had been accepted, the doors opened and he stepped safely into the car park.

Worse knew exactly what to look for: the vehicle description and registration were on the rental contract. He also guessed accurately where he would find it. Zheng had parked right beside the elevators in a bay reserved for commercial vehicles, oblivious to clearly displayed regulations about visitor parking. Worse had sometimes entertained capital punishment for people who did that, and felt a perverse gratification. At the same time, he was pleased that the car was in range of a surveillance camera directed at the lift station.

He walked past the car, studying it casually. For several

minutes he stood half concealed behind a concrete column some metres away, watching. Still watching intently, he activated the remote unlock. Now confident that an accomplice had not drifted to sleep inside the car, he walked over and entered by the front passenger door, closing it behind him.

On first impression, the interior was bare. The only personal items were a refolded city map above the instrument panel and a screwed-up food wrapper on the passenger floor, which imparted a nauseating odour to the enclosed air. A portable GPS device was wired to the lighter plug. Using his torch, Worse examined every recess and storage site, but his only discoveries were a car manual and roadside assistance information in the glove compartment. He placed the map and GPS in his bag, mentally noted fuel gauge and odometer readings, and set about his next task.

Using a fine screwdriver, he levered off a loudspeaker grille in the fascia. On its underside he carefully positioned and secured with glue a barely visible pin-like object, then replaced the grille. The microphone had a short transmission range, and he next concealed within the upholstery under the driver's seat a more powerful repeater incorporating a GPS beacon. Finally, he reached underneath the fascia and, by feel alone, disconnected audio output to the speakers. Now any conversation in the car would not be made inaudible by the sound system. Of course, Worse reasoned idly, the conversation might be nothing more than some blaspheming exchange over the lack of entertainment. To test the microphone he opened and closed the car door, then said quietly, 'Why the Christ doesn't this work?' Followed more angrily by, 'Did you switch it on, dickhead?'

Ensuring that he had left no visible traces of his visit, he stepped out of the car and checked inside the boot; it was empty. Then leaving the car unlocked with its key in the ignition, he returned to his apartment.

There was still work to do. First, using Peepshow, he searched for the closed circuit vision of Zheng arriving in the building and exiting the elevator on level 33. After making copies, he excised these segments and replaced them seamlessly with repetitions of featureless frames. Then he restored building security to fully operational status.

Next, he moved to a computer that was partly disassembled, with circuit boards on view. Wires connected exposed CPU components to other devices on the adjacent bench, and to a large flexible aerial attached to the wall. Here was the receiver for microphone transmissions, which were recorded for offline reprocessing and signal enhancement. From the other machine, Peepshow streamed video from the basement camera, so that audio and visual data would be synchronized. Finally, Worse programmed the computer to direct-dial his own mobile phone the moment the listening device was sound activated. In that way, wherever he happened to be, he could overhear events within Zheng's car.

Satisfied, Worse collected his mobile and walked through the apartment to a balcony. It was now nine in the evening, and he looked downward, marvelling how a thousand tiny fairy lights in an avenue tree could coalesce into an impression of one. He imagined individual bulbs as information bits such that the illuminated tree displayed some complex message, the output of a computation, a solution. Yet by simple negation that meaning could be wholly reversed if one particular bulb, unresolvable to him, were to be extinguished.

His attention then passed to the traffic, and the anonymous, untidy, intriguing business of the city. His eye followed approaching cars, imbuing them with occupants and purpose, wondering who might be another Zheng, and which would turn into the Grosvenor, and for what reason.

He had almost forgotten his intention. Raising the mobile to his ear he pressed a button. Immediately he heard a familiar thump, then: *Why the Christ doesn't this work? Did you switch it on, dickhead?*

He went inside to begin filling a spa bath, poured a glass of wine, and made some phone calls. Returning to the bathroom, he placed his own and Zheng's mobiles within reach of the spa and dimmed the light. Undressing, he threw his clothes more with rejection than direction into a laundry basket, then stepped into the bath, progressively sinking into hot, slightly soapy water. He sat motionless for several minutes, before sinking further until his feet were in contact with the far end, and he began to float. Then he closed his eyes and for the second time that day imagined falling. He submerged his head, and after a full minute began to push his feet against the spa wall. As the force increased he experienced again the reassimilation of his inertial self that had occurred in the lift.

But something was different. Within the darkness, into his weightlessness, came a new, unwanted companion sense. Ill-defined yet insistent, it grew stronger and more urgent until it enveloped and compressed him, entering his body and bursting into meaning as profound asphyxiation. He sat up violently, his face in air instantly cold, eyes open, lungs filling with new breath. Zheng's phone was ringing.

19. ZHENG

Worse stared at the phone, both attentive and incurious. He had expected a call, and his preparation was thorough. A computer had opened a dummy connection and initiated a trace; already, in the workshop, there would be valuable caller identification and location data.

The ringing stopped as, by design, a messaging service switched in; Worse was not inclined to advertise the state of affairs. This was also a signal to close out the day's business, attend briefly to ordinary chores, and get some sleep.

His mind had been playing with the notion of representing a person as a set of attributes, analogous to characterizing a material object by its physical and chemical properties. Then at any point in time that person would be fully described for the purpose of, say, argument. From this point of view, he already knew a great deal about Zheng, and he was confident of discovering more.

But the idea had limited usefulness. His thoughts advanced to a different metonymy, one better subserving explanation and prediction with respect to events and behaviour. This was the idea of a person as the centre of a defining complex of implications changing over time. Beginning before birth and ending after death, this existed in parallel to ordinary biography and objectified everything causal connecting the person to the world. The implicative signature that he might label *Zheng* would persevere, though radically changed, after the man's death. The ringing phone was an illustration of this, and he felt the same distaste and trespass on his private space as he had with Zheng in person.

But for now, those emotions could be put aside. The importance of the model was that Worse should consider himself a variable in *Zheng* with essentially unknown logical connections. Further analysis could wait until morning; without checking the results in the workshop, he retired for the night.

By midmorning, Worse had a comprehensive picture of Zheng the man. Five days earlier he had flown to Perth from Hong Kong, rented a car at the airport, and immediately driven south. There were no credit card or other data to indicate exactly where he went, except for the purchase of petrol about two hundred kilometres down the coast. On the basis of the odometer reading, petrol usage and some telephone evidence, he probably drove quite some distance further. These facts were consistent with a stored GPS entry for a point west of Margaret River. He had returned to Perth two days previously and checked into The Excelsior, and his return flight was booked for twenty-four hours hence.

For the time being, Worse planned to conclude his research by hacking into Hong Kong bank accounts associated with Zheng. One alias account showed a number of deposits ranging from twenty to fifty thousand US dollars, going back about three years. Some looked reasonably traceable, given a little effort. But Worse's attention was fixed on the most recent, credited ten days before, and this one was entirely different. Worse knew a lot about electronic money transfer, how to conceal it and how to uncover it. Much of his consulting work over the last few years was concerned with exactly that. And within a few seconds of trying to identify the origin of this payment it was clear that here was very sophisticated concealment indeed. He played with it for about an hour, peeking, pushing, unwrapping, poking, tricking, cajoling. He learnt a little, but not enough, and certainly not what he wanted. He decided that he would resume the task later with special software.

Meanwhile, there was something comparatively easy that he could do. Returning to the accounts page, he withdrew the fifty thousand dollars last credited, dragged it through some muddied cyberspace, and rinsed it squeaky-clean on the other side. Mr Zheng had generously donated to a police charity.

During all these investigations, Worse was continually evaluating his own security. It was clear that Zheng knew where to find him, but careful reconstruction of the previous day's events, along with no evidence to the contrary in the man's effects or electronic communications, strongly suggested to Worse that his personal appearance remained secure. Not only would this simplify management of his safety, it constrained the possibilities regarding the identity of Zheng's paymaster; Worse was also canvassing hypotheses of motive.

The conclusion regarding his own identity, though provisional, afforded some confidence for his next project. He hacked into the security system of The Excelsior and planted appropriate camera faults. Then he changed into a business suit, pocketed Zheng's room key, gathered the remainder of the man's belongings in a briefcase, and set off for the hotel. It was five blocks distant, and Worse chose to walk. He entered via the lobby, took an elevator to the ninth floor, and found Zheng's room. Checking that the corridor was empty, he inserted the key card and stepped inside.

The room had been serviced, but the usual paraphernalia of the business traveller was lying about, intermixed with the glossy debris furnished by management. Wearing gloves, Worse set about a systematic search. The bedside telephone flashed messages, and his first act was to pick them up using the television screen. There were two, both requesting that Zheng return the calls urgently, but offering no identification. Worse noted the relevant times. He then scrolled through the menu to examine Zheng's progressive account. Everything was consistent with what Worse already knew, though it served to fill in some details about where the man had eaten, his diet, his appetite for beer, and his predilections for fantasy in pay movies. There were no telephone charges.

As the search progressed, a picture emerged of someone depressingly plain. Worse humoured himself with indignation that he might have met his end at the hands of this amalgam of the unsavoury and the very dull. Clearly, the previous day's thoughts on falling, offered as a sort of prayer, would have been completely wasted on this man.

Having examined every item of paper, clothing and luggage, Worse turned to potentially his most challenging task. Although he was confident of opening the safe, he knew that it could be time-consuming. He had brought some electronic aids, but was hopeful that they would be unnecessary. And so it proved. On his first guess, using six digits from Zheng's mobile phone number, he heard the pins retract and the display rather fatuously flashed Open. Whenever he did this, he was reminded of Feynman's wonderful memoir piece on safecracking, and resolved to re-read it.

Worse swung open the door and reached inside. There was a box of ammunition, a passport in Zheng's name, a card recording account numbers and obvious passwords (most of which Worse recognized), and a roadmap of the state. This had been refolded to display the South-West tourist sector centred on the famous wine region. Slipped into the pages of the map was a sheet from a hotel notepad. On it was written 'Grosvenor poss 33 male'. Worse was quietly delighted, and put the map and note in his pocket. He then took from his briefcase Zheng's wallet and watch, placed them in the safe, and closed the door. Other possessions, apart from the mobile, he distributed naturally around the room. Finally, leaving the key card on top of the television, he opened the door, glanced down the corridor, and stepped out.

Just as he rounded a corner leading to the elevators he saw two men approaching. They walked side by side making no concession to others, and Worse found himself waiting behind a room-maid's cart to let them pass. They were scanning room numbers, and both glanced at Worse without special interest. The indifference was not reciprocated: something triggered Worse's attention, and by stopping to wait he gained extra seconds to study their appearance. One was mid-thirties in age, the other mid-twenties. Both wore dark clothing, the older a fairly modish suit with grey shirt and light tie, the younger a waist-length leather jacket with blue shirt and buttoned collar. Neither carried anything in his hands. They looked out of place, not businessmen, not tourists.

After they passed, Worse hesitated, listening carefully. Out of sight behind him he heard them knocking on a door. Rather than risk spying around the corner he walked confidently back, approached another room as if it were his own, and placed one hand on the door lever and another in his inside jacket pocket. Then as if he had discovered on his person whatever he had returned to collect, he walked briskly back towards the elevator. This charade legitimized his glance at the other men. They were knocking impatiently on Zheng's door.

Worse sat in the main lobby with his back to the elevators, looking at a newspaper. After a few minutes, the two men appeared, looking around as they walked to the entrance. Worse casually put down the paper, picked up his briefcase, and followed. They had parked on the street in a loading zone. From a discreet distance, he watched them enter an empty car and drive away. He memorized its registration, then set off to enjoy the walk home.

20. NEWTON'S BY-LAWS

Back in his apartment, Worse's mobile alerted him that something of interest was happening in the basement car park. He listened as he walked through to the workshop and stationed himself before Peepshow, where he was unsurprised to recognize the two men whom he had seen at The Excelsior. One was seating himself behind the driver's wheel of Zheng's car.

'The key's in it!'

The second man opened the passenger door and sat with one foot outside the car. 'That's fuckin' weird. Has he just come or something?'

'It was supposed to be yesterday. Christ, the doctor will be pissed if there's been a screw-up.'

'C'mon man! A pro against a nerd—how could he screw up?'

'Yeah.'

There followed a few seconds' silence, then a soft clicking noise. Worse's surmise was immediately confirmed.

'Stone fucking cold.'

'Jeez,' His companion said, 'so he just left it here.'

'Yeah. We'd better check it out.'

'Shouldn't we call in? He said just look, don't go up. The place'll be crawling with pigs gawking at the stiff.'

'Jesus, Kev, does it look like the place is crawling with pigs?'

Kev considered this. 'Do you really think Zheng could've screwed up?'

'Well, something's wrong and we should check it out. Maybe we'll get to do the job properly.'

'Yeah. Look good, wouldn't it, pro flown in, big bucks, screw up, and we fix it.' Kev relished his fantasy to the point of first practicality. 'We dunno what he looks like.'

'Yeah, well, that's easy. We just go to the thirty-third floor and blow the brains out of every weedy little nerd in sight.'

'Fuckin' great. Let's do it!' said Kev.

Two thumps signalled the end of this unedifying screenplay. They walked confidently to the lift station and waited. Worse watched them enter an empty elevator, saw the one not called Kev (characteristically, Worse corrected himself: the one not known to be called Kev, though Kev and Kev would seem farfetched) turn to press a button, and the doors close.

From that moment, definitely Kev and possibly Kev were prisoners of Peepshow's repertoire of faults. Worse isolated the elevator from official monitors, and listened via the emergency intercom. At 33, the doors wouldn't open. He heard Kev, with inimitable redundancy: 'The fuckin' doors aren't opening.'

His companion wasn't perturbed. 'Press the open thing.'

Peepshow registered repetitive requests for *Door Open*. Worse held them there about a minute, until Kev's mentor instructed impatiently, 'Press another level, fuck.'

Kev, either for want of imagination or from misgivings about the whole proceedings, pressed for the car park. Simultaneously, the lights went out and they accelerated, not down, but upwards.

'Fuck, fuck, what did you fucking do?'

'Nothin', fuck. I just pressed down. Like you said,' Kev added inspirationally, rebalancing the implicit blame. The elevator hurtled to 74 and stopped.

'Open the door for Christ's sake.'

'I can't see a fuckin' thing.'

Worse had removed power from the panel.

'There must be an alarm or intercom or something.'

'Yeah, but I can't see a fuckin' thing.'

'Use your fucking phone for some light. Jesus.'

Worse sent them downwards, pausing at the basement, and returned them to the top. He repeated this, then parked them at 13, a plant room where their protestations would go unheard. They had no idea where they were. Holding his mobile obviously gave Kev the idea of using it as a phone.

'Let's ring someone.'

'Oh yeah.' The sarcasm indicated prior consideration. 'Like the Doctor?' Kev's companion fell silent, probably reflecting that the contravention of orders was his responsibility. 'Fuck.'

'What about Smudge? He might keep it quiet,' suggested Kev.

'Yeah, maybe. He's gone to Sydney doing drive-bys but he could find out who to ring, the management and all.'

'Do you think they know there's a problem?'

'Christ knows. Jesus.'

'I reckon they'll be onto it.' Kev didn't project conviction.

'Get Smudge anyway, fuck.'

As Kev presumably fumbled with his phone, Worse spoke into the intercom. 'Is there anyone in there?'

'Yeah, yeah,' shouted Kev eagerly, possibly answering for both.

'Oh good. I'm the service manager. We know we have a malfunction. We'll get you out of there.'

Kev's mentor had recovered full bravado. 'Jesus, fucker, do it now.'

'Yes, as soon as possible. We're working on it. Meanwhile, there's no cause for alarm. Now, how many of you are in there?'

'Two, two of us,' replied Kev.

'Good. Now it's important to stay calm. How fortunate there are two of you. Imagine what it would be like on your own!' He added innocently, 'Try to keep each other company, we're doing everything we can.'

'Get us out, fucker,' said Kev's companion.

'Now gentlemen, do you know each other?'

'Yeah,' answered Kev, 'we're together.'

'Good. My name is Mr Newton. You may have heard of me. And you are?'

'Kev.'

'Definitely Kev? Kev definitely?'

'Yeah. What do you mean? I'm Kev.'

'And your friend's name?'

'Ritchie,' said Kev.

'Get us out, fucker,' Ritchie introduced himself.

'Stay calm, Ritchie. You're not in any danger.'

'You're the one in danger, fucker.'

'Ritchie, and you too, Kev. I know it's disconcerting, being trapped in an elevator, but everything really is okay. The shift engineer is on her way. She's called Jill. And we have procedures in place. Everything's fine. Were you having a nice day? Are you visiting friends in our great building? Can I contact anyone for you? Any messages for those on the outside?' Almost imperceptibly, Worse hesitated and dropped his voice a semitone to pronounce the final word.

'Shut up, fucker.'

'Ritchie, I do need to inform you that our building has special by-laws against using foul language, that sort of thing. We have little fines; they go to charity.'

'You haven't heard foul yet, fucker,' growled Ritchie.

'Ritchie, he's trying to help.'

'That's right, Kev. Definitely, Kev. Now Kev, look after Ritchie. He's feeling the pressure. I think we should make you the spokesperson. You can choose the charity for Ritchie. But you'll both be out of there really soon. Kev?'

'Yes, Mr Newton?'

'Would you like to listen to some music? Would you like to play word games?'

'Shut up, fucker,' responded Ritchie.

'Kev, are you there?' Worse knew that Kev would be comforted by the redundant.

'Yes, Mr Newton.'

'I need your help, Kev. Kev, I want you to look up at the ceiling and there's a kind of fresh air grille there. Can you tell me if it looks open?' Again Worse modulated the last word, not quite subliminally.

'Fuck, fuck, it's dark in here. We can't see Jesus Christ!'

'Is ... is He there, Kev?'

'What do you mean? Ritchie's here.'

Worse incompletely covered the microphone and spoke to his empty workshop. He ensured that the two in the elevator would hear. 'Jesus, the lights are out! I think they're saying Jesus Christ is with them but they just can't see Him—they're losing it for sure. Fuck. No power means they can't do procedures. It's looking like the big one. We do have braking, don't we? Tell me we've got braking!' He mumbled an inaudible reply, waited a few seconds, and uncovered the microphone.

'Kev?'

But Kev was already talking. 'What about the brakes, what was that about the fuckin' brakes?'

'Nothing, Kev. That's a little fine for you, Kev. I'm noting them all down for you. Kev, how is Ritchie doing?'

'Shut up, fucker.'

Again, Worse spoke aside. 'They know about the brakes. Where's Jill? Oh for Christ's sake. Get her at the hairdresser's then. Foils? Fuck. Myrtle, what's the cable test showing? What's the cable over-strain, for Christ's sake?' He paused. 'Jesus, it's not that difficult. Figure it out, Flossie. It's only calculus, for Christ's sake.'

'Jesus Mr Newton, is everything okay?'

'Of course everything's okay, Kev. Just hang in there. Kev?'

'Yeah?'

'Kev, it might be a good idea not to talk too much now. Just to conserve your energy.' Worse pronounced it air-nergy. 'Are you recumbent?'

'I dunno.'

'Well, why don't you both lie down, for any jolts, you know. Only little jolts, of course. I'm afraid you'll need to be patient. We'll have you out of there in no time at all, celebrating with nice sparkling sweet wine and fresh windfalls, and you'll think it's the funniest thing that's happened in your whole day. Kev, look after Ritchie, he's feeling the pressure.'

'Shut up, fucker.'

Aside again: 'Has Jill answered? Is her hair done? Henna? Really? I would never have imagined. Lucille, stop the giggles; this is serious. Freckles, are we go for brakes? Where's the power overload at, Jezebel? Are we still dead-zoning on the main linkage, Gertie?' He paused. 'Fuck it all, Ginger. I already know the free fall numbers. Don't give me worst case. Jesus, give me a survival scenario at least, can you?' Immediately, he sent the elevator to the basement, up to the top, and back to 13.

'Jesus. What's happening?'

'Why, Kev?'

'We just went up and down and shit.'

Actually, thought Worse, it was down and up and down.

'Hold on, Kev. The s-word, that carries a little fine. And the blasphemes, they're a double, I'm afraid. So the double blasphemes, like, you know,' Worse hesitated and intoned solemnly, '*Iesus Christos*, they're double double. For example, s, f, J-C all said together would cost you six fines. I'll add it all up for you both at the end. In fact, why don't I set up a little spreadsheet to make it easier? Anyway, while I'm doing that, I'll try to find out what happened to the lift.' Worse paused. 'Let's see ... the manual calls that a gravity fault. Mm. That could be a problem with the universal law. Might take some time. Do you know about the law, Kev? But we won't worry about that just now. It says stay calm. That's how Bishop Mesmerides managed. Have you heard of the Bishop, Kev? He's our most famous resident. Once he got caught in an elevator for forty hours. Had to relieve himself and all. May have been the same elevator. Anyway, he prayed and prayed. He prayed so much he collapsed. Not from starvation. Not terminal thirst. Not even from abject terror. Collapsed from pure faith. Collapsed from praising the Lord. Seeing Jesus and all, Kev, like you didn't. When he got out he said the forty was special, like in the wilderness. He made a famous sermon on it, called *A Guide for the Cataplexed*, about salvation I suppose. Kev?'

'Yeah?'

'I am required to inform you that we do have a by-law against fouling the elevators, all the same. Kev?'

'Yeah?'

'Do you pray?'

Before Kev could respond, Worse spoke aside. 'Jesus Christ, if you can't get Jill, get Samantha. Or Mary-Lou. Or Desdemona from Ramona. I want someone who knows what they're fucking doing! What? Me? Oh, fuck the fines.' After a few seconds, he added soberly, 'Maybe we should get the Bishop's help, then.'

Worse then returned to the intercom. 'Kev, Ritchie, we're doing everything possible. We've got fire brigade, police, ambulance, Jill's crew, counsellors. We think it might just be a computer crash.' He slightly stressed the last word, drawing further attention to it by virtue of substitution. 'A computer glitch. We're about to raise our weedy little nerd-in-residence to help.'

Worse allowed the potential implications of that statement to sink in. After several seconds he spoke again. 'Kev? Good news!'

'Yes, Mr Newton?'

'All the other elevators are working just fine. Wasn't it funny you chose this one!'

'But we didn't know this would happen, Mr Newton.'

Worse almost felt sorry for him.

'Kev, I need to leave the mike for a while—there's a tow truck driver going berserk in the basement. Naturally, we have by-laws about parking, you know. I trust you left your vehicle in an approved visitors bay. Meanwhile, just stay calm. Remember not to talk unless it's important. Kev? Is Ritchie breathing okay?'

'Yeah. I think so.' Kev's reply somehow conveyed wide eyes. Ritchie was less in doubt.

'Shut up, fucker.'

21. FIENDISCH

Worse reviewed the basement security to identify Kev and Ritchie's car. Then he shut down car park surveillance and put together another toolkit, along with something known in the profession as a bitter almond. From a locked safe within a refrigerated fume hood in the laboratory next to his workshop he took a canister the size of a small torch. He unscrewed the casing at one end and inserted batteries from a supply in a lab drawer. Using fine forceps as a pointer, he entered data into a miniature keypad, then carefully replaced the screw cap and transferred the device to his bag.

The laboratory had a large window, offering natural light and a view of distant hills. Worse walked right up to the glass and looked out. There were occasions when he felt as if he lived in a fortress, and then he used these views, of the hills, of the Indian Ocean on the other side, and from the balconies down, to recivilize his world with perspective. He disliked his interaction with the two in the elevator, but his motive was to prevail; powerlessness, humiliation and discouragement were his psychological weapons. Most people who knew Worse would agree that he lacked genuine malice entirely. What he did not lack was objectivity, and he used these quiet moments to strengthen his trust in the factual, and his resolve in dealing with threat.

Placing a laptop computer and an assortment of cables in the bag, Worse left his apartment. In the car park, he went straight to their vehicle and opened the driver's door using a wire hook. There was a phone attached to the car charger. It was probably Ritchie's, thought Worse, and partly explained why Kev was instructed to make the calls in the elevator. The discovery slightly altered Worse's plan. Instead of wiring the car for voice he took the phone apart and inserted a miniature relay switched to a dummy open line. Not only would calls via the mobile be transmitted to his computer, the phone would also eavesdrop on any conversation within range. Before reassembling it, he downloaded the call register and contacts file. Then he searched the car, confiscating a few items. Finally, he took the canister from his bag and carefully concealed it underneath the driver's seat.

Collecting his computer and toolkit, he left the car locked and walked through the car park to his own vehicle. There he linked both phone and computer to the car power supply, established the connection to Ritchie's phone, and opened Peepshow. Satisfied with these preparations, he moved his car to a bay from where he could see the lift station and switched off the engine. Without any further communication, he brought the elevator containing the two men to the basement and opened the doors.

They were lying down and spent several seconds apprehending light and freedom before springing to their feet and leaping out. Ritchie turned and kicked the doors as Worse closed them, then strode angrily to his car. Kev briefly leaned against a concrete column, but his returning composure was destroyed by having to run to the car before Ritchie drove off without him.

Worse followed. His driving manner was relaxed as he didn't need to keep them in sight; incorporated within the canister was a GPS beacon which identified their movement on his satnav screen. They headed west out of the business district and across to the coast, then followed the urban beaches south. The two were largely silent, except for Ritchie instructing Kev to inform someone named Karl that they were running late. Karl replied that he also would be late.

Their destination was Vlamingho's, a restaurant off the coast road with panoramic views of the ocean. As Worse pulled into the car park, he saw Ritchie and Kev disappearing through the main restaurant door. Close by was their car, parked in a bay reserved for disabled drivers.

Worse positioned himself overlooking the beach at a point from which, through the passenger window, he could see the restaurant entrance. Ritchie had placed his mobile on the table, little realizing that it served as a perfect microphone. Worse listened to them order coffees, and some desultory interactions signalling that each was preoccupied. This allowed him to divide his attention between events inside and the more alluring, rolling waves in the same ocean that had borne Willem de Vlamingh's ship, in 1697, just out there. Worse imagined himself returning a curious stare.

He also watched the restaurant clientele coming and going. After about ten minutes a flamboyantly polished black BMW pulled into a reserved bay next to Ritchie's car. From it emerged a tall man wearing a dark business suit. Through half reflecting glass walls Worse could see the figure walk directly to a table. At the same time, he heard some cursory greetings. Kev, rather nervously, seemed to address the newcomer as Doctor Fiendish. That would be Fiendisch surely, thought Worse, Karl Fiendisch.

'What do you have?' Fiendisch said.

Kev replied eagerly, 'Coffee' and was ignored, while Ritchie began a surprisingly honest account of events at the Grosvenor. He finished on a slightly apologetic note, saying he thought it better to report in before doing more. His final remark revealed exasperation.

'Yes, yes. You did well.' The accent was German. Worse sensed relief in the other two.

'Interesting. Do you think your experience was entirely by chance?'

Ritchie didn't answer immediately and Fiendisch himself filled the silence.

'It doesn't matter. Just be very careful. Even more careful. Don't return to that building until I say. I need to understand more.'

In the background, Worse discerned a regular ticking sound, as if from cutlery tapping china. This would be Fiendisch, he thought, and the metronomic accompaniment imbued his speech, already musically flat, with a slow tempo of threat. On aural grounds alone, Worse disliked him.

'We have to ask, what has happened to Zheng?' Fiendisch continued, 'And, what has happened to our enemy?' He was silent for several seconds. 'But we should probably assume that Zheng has failed.'

'What'll we do?' asked Ritchie.

Again there was silence but for the tapping sound.

'Nothing for now. I need to consult. I will be in touch.'

No more was said. Fiendisch appeared at the entrance and walked to his vehicle. Leaving the car park, he drove south. Worse allowed two vehicles to pass before entering the coast road in relaxed pursuit. He wasn't concerned about Ritchie and Kev; their movements and conversations would be recorded for later study. But Fiendisch was a valuable find, and he might be about to confer with others.

The BMW headed through the industrial periphery of Fremantle, crossed the river, and was soon negotiating the narrow, heritage streets of the old port city. Briefly, Worse wished that he had placed a tracking device on the car when it was unattended, but reminded himself that this would have been too risky. As it happened, the task of following at a distance proved undemanding, and when Fiendisch turned into a private off-street parking area Worse was able to pull over and park with unexpected ease. There were several paid minutes remaining on the kerbside meter, and he stayed in his car watching the street ahead. There was no further sign of Fiendisch.

Worse got out of his car, walked around to the meter, and forced some change into the coin slot. With each insertion the remaining-time indicator advanced minutely with a squeak of machine ill will. Then he set off along the footpath. About fifty metres ahead he passed the driveway on his left where Fiendisch had turned in. The BMW was parked, with three other cars, in a neat, gravelled yard surrounded by high walls. On the right was a side entrance to the adjoining building, the street frontage of which Worse now passed. It was two-storied colonial, with a grand entrance and wrought iron window grilles at street level. Once a port authority chambers or prosperous mercantile office, it had been superbly restored, and a polished brass plate in period lettering identified its present incarnation: HUMBOLDT BANK. Opening Hours 9.30 am – 4.00 pm.

Worse continued on, not wanting to appear too curious. He

crossed the street and sat at a café, looking back. No arrivals or departures enlivened the bank's entrance, nor its car park. After about thirty minutes, he paid for his coffee and walked back towards his car. From across the street he now registered detailed information about the bank building, access, roof design, windows, main door and security. His gaze rested for a few seconds on the brass plate. At that distance, the smaller print was indistinct, but he remembered: Closed 4.00 pm – 9.30 am.

22. THE HUMBOLDT BANK

Close to the wall, where Worse preferred to walk, the gravel was uncompacted by car tyres, and his black sneakers elicited a soft crunching sound with each step. The stone was blue metal, and from the safety of deep shadow Worse admired the surface of glints where moonlight was reflected in thousands of quartz facets.

It reminded him of the boulevard fairy lights seen from his balcony, and as with those, brought to mind ideas of information and inference. If he walked over there a trace would remain, memorialized in light, and to a knowing observer it would betray his passing. As likewise things hidden were betrayed to him: a glint was evidence of moonlight, and moonlight evidence of sunlight. And if a stone in the yard of the Humboldt Bank informed him of the sun and the moon, how much could he learn from all the records concealed in the building itself?

He sidled along the wall to the doorway leading from the yard to the bank. There was a latticed-iron outer gate with concealed hinges. The lock looked manageable, but he couldn't appraise the recessed door until he reached it. Also, the entrance was probably alarmed, and if he were the owner, there would be motion-sensor lighting in the alcove. On balance, he felt further exploration would be more efficient.

He continued past the gate, still in shadow, to the back wall. This was about three metres high, but its rough stone composition afforded manageable toeholds. Within a few seconds, Worse was sitting astride its capping, surveying the property on the other side. It was also a parking area, and several business vans were left sleeping for the night. The adjoining buildings were in darkness, except for a yellow glow from lighting in the next street over. Beside him, the wall of the bank stretched upwards, and his gaze focused appreciatively on a feature that he had noted the previous afternoon. A metre above him was a decorative brick course that projected several centimetres from the stone face. He adjusted his small backpack and continued the climb. Once above the brick ledge it provided a valuable purchase for his toes as he edged sideways to the first of two second-storey windows that overlooked the yard. Reaching it, he grasped the mullion tightly and felt safe for the first time in several minutes. He looked down. From this angle the surface of the yard was pitch-black: no glint, no moon, no sun.

No depth. He might have been clinging to the face of a bottomless mineshaft. Only by memory, and faith in object persistence, could he know that down there was a blue-metal surface, that if he slipped it would be five metres, not a thousand, and to a familiar crunching sound. But even his own body was invisible, and for a moment conviction loosened inside him. Then his fingers tightened their grip and, by the hardness of masonry, his corporeal world was affirmed.

But the effect of that was to feel suddenly exposed and vulnerable. The discomfort drove him on; within a minute, the window was open and he had lifted his body onto the sill. Slipping his feet to the floor he closed the window behind him, then stood listening for a full minute. A vehicle passed along the street and he watched its tail-lights disappear at the first corner. Otherwise, the building was completely silent, and he began to explore, using his torch sparingly. He had entered what appeared to be a storeroom. High shelves were stacked with archive boxes of files, and along one wall a table served as mortuary for lifeless computers. He tested the thickness of dust; this was a room infrequently aired.

Opening the door carefully, Worse found himself on the upstairs landing. There were several other rooms, all but one with closed doors. That revealed a kitchen cabinet, sink, table and chairs—evidently the staff tearoom. Next to this were two doors with bathroom semiotics. At the front of the building, extending its full width, was an elegantly furnished boardroom.

Before exploring further, Worse knew he must deal with

the security system and set up a strategy for exit. He made his way downstairs, avoiding a carpet runner that might conceal pressure sensors. On the bottom step, he hesitated, in order to study the layout. Slung from the ceiling of the central hallway was a binnacle with three cameras trained on the front entrance, the side hall leading to the car park, and opposite to this, a door which Worse guessed might conceal a vault room. He pulled a balaclava over his face and proceeded towards the front entrance, walking near to the wall on his left. Along both sides were hung paintings of modern Australian Masters. Worse cast his torch on each admiringly; anyone watching would suppose him an art thief agonizing over choice.

A few metres past the presumed vault there was a closed door bearing the name DR KARL FIENDISCH in gothic script. Worse tried the handle; it was locked. He continued to the front door. The security panel was on the wall opposite. It was a system with which he was familiar and even from where he stood, Worse became aware of something unexpected: the building was not alarmed. He crossed the hallway in front of the main door and confirmed his impression. Some careless employee, the last to leave, had exited without card-swiping the panel. An implication was immediately evident to Worse; the electronically armed main door would not be deadlocked. He stepped back and verified this by opening it enough to reveal a vertical slice of the outside world. Then he closed it quietly; he now had at least one escape route.

The Fiendisch office would take some effort to unlock, and he decided first to search the rest of the floor systematically from front to rear. On the south side of the building, opposite the security controller, the front office was a reception area with comfortable seating, a coffee table piled with financial newspapers and company reports, and a high counter behind which were two distinct secretarial workstations. Two windows were furnished with closed wooden venetians, and no light penetrated from the street.

He quickly located his first objective, ineffectually concealed in a false drawer. It was the videodisk recorder for the security cameras in the hall. He opened the drive to remove the current disk and for the second time was surprised. The device was empty. For a bank, the security standards seemed appalling, and Worse's confidence was briefly strained. Perhaps the Humboldt Bank had nothing to hide, no secrets. But he instantly reviewed the implicative thread, Zheng to Ritchie to Fiendisch to this building, and continued the task.

Apart from some unwrapped stock, there seemed to be no other videodisks around. He sat in a secretary's chair and redirected his attention to the nearest computer. The live screen provided enough light to dispense with his torch, which he pocketed. Within a few minutes he had mapped out the bank's IT platform, and was scanning files on Fiendisch's computer via the company intranet. Much of the mail was encrypted, and Worse spent a few minutes in cursory analysis. The challenge of breaking the code was enticing but he put it aside. That was an exercise to be continued in safety.

Removing his backpack, he took from it a flash memory stick and attached it to a computer USB port. But this was not for the purpose of making dumb copies. Deep inside the operating system, hidden within the arcane text of machine code, he inserted a discreetly camouflaged subroutine that would periodically transfer the hard disk's contents to an untraceable email address. Satisfied with the installation, he returned the terminal to its original state, replaced the memory device in his backpack, and walked to the door.

The computer screen cast an eerie glow into the main hall. Worse paused to look at a large Whiteley nude on the opposite wall, and wondered if ever before it had been observed under such strange lighting. Unusually, it was elegantly mounted, giving the effect of a luminous canvas framed by thin shadow, floating weightless off the wall. Combined with the subject's beauty and the style of mixed naturalism and abstraction, it was mesmerizing.

He decided to tackle the locked door. Against the wall between him and Fiendisch's office was a pedestal with spindly carved legs, supporting a preposterously large flower arrangement. It looked unstable, and he gave it wide berth. He was still distracted by the painting and absently feeling for his torch as he stopped before Fiendisch's door. When his eyes moved up to examine the lock, he froze. The door was ajar.

In an instant, a whole new construct of events was revealed to Worse. As he re-rationalized his discovery of the disabled alarm and the missing disk, he admonished himself. But there was little time for analysis. The door was opening, the same eerie screen glow spilled into the hall, and a dark figure backed out of the room.

Instinctively Worse turned in the direction of the front entrance. The only cover was the pedestal and in the single second needed to reach it he realized that, while he was closer to a means of escape, he was moving further into the same light that only moments before had held him entranced by art. He crouched down and watched. And again he rebuked himself, re-examining his assumptions: there may be more than one. If this one came in his direction, Worse could not possibly remain undetected. He saw the figure bend to lock the door, then turn and, possibly curious about the source of light from the front office, walk towards him.

Worse believed that he still enjoyed the advantage of surprise. Since leaving the secretary's station he had been holding his backpack. Now, covertly, he adjusted his grip. As the figure loomed beside the pedestal, two things happened. Worse sprang like a cat, and the other's head, oblivious to this, turned away in the direction of the Whiteley. And so the strap of Worse's pack passed easily over beret, over face, and tightened on the throat.

For a moment, Worse was in control. When strangled from behind, most people react instinctively by bringing their hands up to their throat in a vain attempt to loosen the band, their efforts quickly weakened by asphyxiation. But a defensive tactic of experienced fighters is to twist to face their aggressor so that the band is no longer strangulating, then counterattack. This one twisted.

Jesus. Worse seemed to find himself constantly recalculating. Reflexly, he turned slightly sideways and raised one knee in front of his groin, just in time to block a savage knee-kick. Simultaneously, he brought both arms across his front, protecting himself from the knee to the face. This deflected a sharp elbow punch to his chest.

Worse's left hand still held the pack, with the strap around the other's neck. He pulled it sharply forward and down, stepping aside and behind while re-slinging the strap so that once again it was across the throat. In the same action he pressed a foot into the back of his opponent's knee, while twisting the backpack into a tightening noose. The other's frame collapsed to the floor, and Worse secured its full submission with his weight.

The speed and emotion and automaticity of his actions left Worse somehow retarded in time, his consciousness tripping to catch up with events. Only now did he remember, and by remembering regain the present. In the midst of the struggle, his silent, powerful adversary dimly backlit by the Whiteley, he had felt something incomprehensible. In that same instant the screensaver had switched and his eye was drawn from the twisting silhouette to the painting behind, to the floating nude that seemingly shone brighter in the moment of darkness.

That image, eidetic and remote, and other contradictions, now demanded his attention: enchantment and fear, softness and firmness, contour and shadow, impossibility and touch. And suddenly he understood. What he had felt was a woman's breast.

Jesus. He found his torch and shone it obliquely on her face. She looked completely calm. Worse felt ashamed.

'Listen to me,' he said quietly. 'I am not going to hurt you.'

Her expression didn't change.

'I'm going to let you go. Please think about this, though. We are two intruders. Perhaps we're looking for the same thing. Perhaps I've already found what you want. We should talk. We could help each other.'

As he spoke he loosened the strap and raised it over her head, at the same time removing his balaclava. She slowly sat up, one hand tenderly stroking the front of her neck. Worse was sitting against the wall beneath the painting, his torch lying on the polished jarrah floor, his gaze fixed on the triangle of yellow light. He continued speaking, partly to her and partly to himself, in a voice woven with reflection, explanation and contrition.

'I thought I was alone. I thought you were a man. I thought there could be more than one of you. I thought you might be armed. You were leaving the office of a man who wants me killed. I had nowhere to hide. There was no time to think. I'm sorry.'

She reached for the torch and studied his face. 'What are you going to do?'

Worse wondered if her question carried the coda 'with me', and felt more shame. 'I was thinking of going upstairs and making a pot of tea,' he said.

23. EMILY MISGIVINGSTON

A motley assortment of staff tea mugs, some name-tagged, was scattered on the draining board. Above the sink a glazed cupboard contained fine china presumably reserved for the boardroom. Worse took down two cups and studied their interiors.

'Have you read my friend's *A Scrutable History of China*?' he asked absently.

'Has anyone?'

Worse ignored her. 'Frances Shin Wah. She could hold these like shells to her ear and recite the secrets of the boardroom.' Worse placed them delicately on saucers and poured from a matching teapot. His actions seemed ceremonious.

'What is your name?'

'Millie. Millie Misgivingston,' she replied.

Worse was instantly attentive for two reasons. Misgivingston was the name sent in an email introduction from Cambridge. He hadn't yet had the opportunity to follow that matter up. It was also, in an odd sense, a family name. His expression changed with the satisfaction of discovering a connection. Millie misread him.

'It's not amusing. It's a fine old English name.'

'I know, I know. The Magnacarts and the Misgivingstons, when they stopped feuding, founded parliamentary democracy.' Worse pronounced it Marnacourts.

Before she could question him on this he added, 'Millie for Millicent? Mildred? Mildew?'

'Millie for Emily.'

He pushed one cup across the table, then sat down opposite her. The kitchen was windowless, and he had closed the door and turned on the light. As they tasted the tea, Worse reached for a discarded newspaper which had been folded to expose a half solved crossword. Taking a pen from his pocket, he wrote in an answer. It amused him to think of his intrusion both adding and subtracting a clue.

Millie had been watching inquisitively. Worse realized that he had hardly looked at her. When he did, her eyes held his for several seconds. She seemed about thirty. He was privately bemused that he had mistaken her for a man.

'Did you find what you were looking for?' he asked casually.

'No.'

'What was it?'

'Who is it,' she corrected emphatically.

Worse's eyes signalled his interest. He was judging when to indicate that he was more informed than she could have expected.

'My brother worked here for about three months and then six weeks ago seems to have disappeared without trace.'

'What does the company say about it?'

'They claim to know nothing. That Fiendisch character says that Nicholas was a lazy employee and just didn't show for work. He basically said good riddance. And yet they had headhunted him specifically, tracked him down to a research station in Asia where he was a volunteer. He has a superb CV and works like a maniac.'

'Have you come from the UK looking for him?' asked Worse.

'Yes. We couldn't get any sense out of Humboldt or the police from over there; just hours of telephone and email frustration. My parents wanted me to come to see what was going on. So far I've achieved nothing. The police don't want to know me. Fiendisch—can you believe that name?—effectively showed me the door.' She hesitated, as if re-experiencing the events, then continued more reflectively.

'I must say, I had started to wonder if Nicholas was becoming unhappy about his work, but he always kept in touch. We're a close family.'

She had been holding her cup with two hands, elbows resting on the table. Now she lifted it to her lips and sipped distantly.

'What was your brother's role in the bank?' Worse was not insensitive to his choice of tense.

'He's a mathematician,' she answered, 'we both are.'

'What's his area?' asked Worse immediately.

'Well, he has several interests, financial modelling—quantitative analytics—being one. That's why he was here.'

'Go on.'

Millie fixed him briefly with an evaluating stare, and continued. 'Derivatives pricing, bundle design, adaptive risk management, reinsurance strategies, quite a lot on neural net methods. Very innovative, actually. Then he moved into language studies; did a lot of work on statistical properties of Parsan gaps—it was Nicholas who discovered that you can infer with reasonable accuracy what language people are speaking by analysing their silences. After that, he did another amazing thing, obtaining redundancy bounds for something known as the Syllabine Task, the outstanding problem in computational linguistics, apparently.'

She hesitated. Worse remained attentive, and it seemed that sisterly pride led her to fill the silence with further detail. 'Once, he found some rate he needed by linking seventeen derivatives, then managed the integration. That's not lazy. They awarded him the highest accolade in mathematics.'

'A Fields Medal?'

'A department afternoon tea party. The FM is way second.'

'Who was that with, the linguistics work?'

'Rodney Thwistle's group in Cambridge, and Edvard Tøss—'

Worse nodded slightly. Almost suddenly, she wondered what all this might mean to the man across the table. 'Have you heard of him?'

'Thwistle? Yes. What's your area?'

'Stochastic processes. That's amazing, you knowing RT. Are you a mathematician?'

'No.' He offered no elaboration, but continued looking at her. A black denim jacket was buttoned to the neck, and the beret, skewed forward, shaded her eyes from the ceiling light. She was beautiful.

'When you say Nicholas kept in touch, was that by email generally?'

Millie nodded.

'Can you still access them?'

'I can. Are you offering to help?' She was still holding her cup, amphora-like. Above it, from shadow, her eyes stayed upon him, analytic. He finished his tea.

'Of course. Actually, extraordinary as it may seem, I've already been asked to help. I'm hardly ever in contact with Thwistle these days but I did get an email recently asking me to look out for Nicholas. What with a paid killer shooting at me, I hadn't given it any attention. My name is Worse, by the way.' He held out his hand across the table.

'You're Worse! I was told to contact you.' She shook his hand, smiling.

'Well, you certainly did that, downstairs. Did Nicholas ever mention the name Charles Finistere?'

'No. I made note of everyone he mentioned in order to contact them for information. Why do you ask?'

'Oh, last night I researched this company a bit. That was the name of a director.' Worse appeared to lose interest in the subject. He glanced at his watch. 'How did you get into the building?'

She unbuttoned the top of her jacket, and from an inside pocket removed a credit card. 'Nicholas is obsessive about back-up. He copied his staff swipe card onto this.' She placed it on the table. Nicholas had reprogrammed the chip in an expired Visa card. Worse was impressed. 'I found it amongst his things, what was left of them. He's done it before so I guessed what it might be.'

'What do you mean, what was left of them?'

'His flat had been ransacked when I arrived.'

'What's happened to the place?'

'I'm staying there, I've taken over the rental.'

Worse suppressed his immediate concern. He sat back in his chair, one arm stretched out, fingers rotating the empty teacup back and forth on its saucer. She found him looking at her with a new intensity.

'I have offered to help. Do you want that?' His manner was matter-of-fact. Millie also sat back, meeting Worse's gaze for several seconds.

'Yes.' It was a measured syllable, and elliptic. 'But I would like to know more about you.'

Worse acknowledged this with a nod but was otherwise not forthcoming. 'Then I advise you to move out of Nicholas's flat. Tonight.'

'Do you really think I'm in danger?' From the tone of disbelief she clearly expected reassurance to the contrary.

'I do.' He stood up, collected both cups, and washed and dried them thoroughly before replacing them in the cupboard.

'Apart from that one irresistible vanity,' Worse nodded toward the crossword, 'my plan was to leave my visit undetectable. Was that yours?' He pushed the Visa card towards her.

'It was. That is, until a man saw me in the main hall.'

Worse ignored the sarcasm. 'So you left Fiendisch's office as you found it?'

'I did.'

'I need a quick look in there. Since you've done the lock already, you might open it for me. Did you take the videodisks?'

Millie nodded and Worse continued. 'I think we should leave them and take copies. We'll keep tonight's and put another used one in the drive. Corrupt it. If they don't suspect a break-in, they'll probably just archive or overwrite without ever viewing it. Do you mind doing that?'

They were standing by the door. Worse had his left hand on the door handle, and his right, which now held the torch, was reaching for the light switch on the adjacent architrave.

'I don't mind, if you don't mind something else.' It was a new voice, lighter than before. Worse turned questioningly, looking at her directly.

'Do you mind if I carry your backpack in the dark?'

As the light switched, he glimpsed her smiling. There was irony and trust, and playfulness. And like the Whiteley nude, her image persisted into blackness. To Worse, there was little in the moment itself. Its meaning was convolved with everything that had gone before. He had attacked this woman, and beneath the surface of their conversation had found himself distracted by remorse. This voice and smile he took to be the beginning of forgiveness.

Leaving the kitchen door open, and using torches, they quickly checked each upstairs room. Worse wondered when Millie would be curious about how he had gained entry. They were in the storeroom, Worse waiting by the door, when she said, 'Is this where you came in?'

'How did you know?'

'There's a window, its full of business records but you've shown less interest than in the bathrooms. I wondered if you had already been through it.'

If Worse had a weakness, it was clever women. 'Time to open the vault,' he said casually, with no hint of a slight nervousness he felt.

Worse searched in Fiendisch's office, then spent about twenty minutes examining the vault security. He estimated it would take about an hour to open, and he couldn't guarantee that the intrusion would go unnoticed. Not wanting to arouse suspicion that might endanger his embedded code, he abandoned the task and sought out Millie.

He found her in an accountant's office off the north side of the hall. Deciding that their search was otherwise complete, they left by the front door, their furtive movements unrecorded on a damaged videodisk.

Richard Magnacart and **Richard Misgivingston**, both knights of the Crusade, resolved to settle ancient wrongs by way of single combat. Their chosen weapon was the battleaxe. As recorded by **Grant Pontage**, a King's tax collector present on the day, the affair was organized with great pageantry, there being festive tents and ale stands and roasting spits set up across a neutral ground thereafter to be known as Mingle Common. The standards and ancestral colours of both families were on display, and each had a crested dais, musicians, games and falconry, a team of seconds and servants-at-arms, and supporters all shouting 'Sir Richard!'.

The battle raged for five hours, the two brave knights exactly matched in strength, agility and stamina. As evening came, great torches were fired, their light glinting red on arcs of sharpened blade and the plate and mail of heaving armour.

The people there gathered grew restless and dispersed about their business of the night, children were taken to their beds, and ladies of both houses retired to the tents. The musicians fell silent, and the cheers were few. Still the knights fought.

Then, at the fateful moment, one saw advantage, and the other also. Each swung his axe with such symmetry of speed and force that both were cleanly struck, enough that in the instant of his soul's departing each glimpsed victory in the other's full beheading.

And where their blood mixed on the stirred earth, there was seen a crimson vapour rising, and it shone with such a brilliance that the brightest torch was darkened, and it swirled and ran and billowed now into the face of Christ, now the ramparts of Jerusalem, now the swints of Calvary—whilst to every watcher's thoughts at once there came a prayer for absolution.

According to the Pontage chronicle, such was the power of this vision that all inheritance of hate was drawn within, consumed as in a fire, and the lamentation left beside was turned to celebration. He describes Magnacarts and Misgivingstons of all ages dancing freely on that field, two families joined in blood and faith, in miracle and worldly fortune, and by oath of mutual caring from that night on.

The modern location of **Mingle** (or **Mingler** or **Mingleton**) **Common** beneath urban London has so far proved untraceable, largely because of unfortunate lacunae in historical Registers of Deed, a dearth of evidence in the cartographic record, and negligible clues in nomenclatural or lexicologic threads. We do know that over the centuries the area variously accommodated the first Mercifuls' Chapel (in which would convene the Brimstone Assizes), a monastery school 'w swinthrie lofte', a knight's house having a *quadratum cavaedium*, the Priory hospital of St Clement (with 'an hospis fr thos infirme of bottomical paine w blockige') and, curiously, an 'Embalmes palas fr Yeomen of't Hoom Cantys', owned by one John Chalmers Esq. This history of built settlement gives reason to hope that excavations might one day uncover crypts or other structures housing reliquaries and similar artifacts dating to events recorded by Pontage. Rather charmingly, there is identified one minor residential square, nowadays very plain, that has attracted some eccentric interest. Amateur historians linked to a London chapter of swint fanciers propose it as the site of Mingle Common, solely on the grounds that swints appear to favour resting in its gardens before their further pilgrimage across the British Isles. Needless to say, this argument has attracted no scholarly attention, and has insufficient substance in itself to justify the granting of an archaeological licence.

24. THE NIGHT WATCHMEN

Millie, who had walked from Nicholas's flat, accompanied Worse to his car. He had parked in the same place as on the previous afternoon, and acknowledged the expired meter with a good-natured tap on the face.

As they got in, Millie asked what his earlier enquiries had revealed about the Humboldt Bank. Worse explained that it was an unlisted investment bank and, not being a public company, there was little compulsory disclosure to the Securities Commission. The building was occupied in the 1980s by the Port Building Society, which in a phase of poorly managed expansion had transformed itself into a bank. That business almost collapsed in 1987, and was taken over by VolksBank-AA. They never really prospered; the retail business declined and was subsumed by the majors. The nascent merchant banking section was bought out by venture capitalists and reinvented as the Humboldt Bank in 1999. Humboldt had a very low public profile. It served an exclusive private client group, and mostly dealt in currency trades, foreign exchange derivatives, and venture capital placements. Its ownership structure was not transparent, and only two directors were identified, Fiendisch and Finistere.

At that point, Worse excused himself, reached for his phone and pressed a single character. His call was answered immediately. There were no salutations.

'I'm out and safe ... Interesting ... Is your spare room free? ... Yes ... In the bank ... Thanks.'

'Who was that?'

'A friend, Sigrid. She was to come by with liniments if I fell off the roof.'

'Is she putting me up for the night?'

Worse glanced at the time. 'Is that all right?'

'Sure. I don't understand why I'm suddenly in mortal danger, though.'

'The fact isn't sudden. Your being apprised of the fact is sudden. Where is your place?'

Millie named a street nearby, familiar to Worse. He started the engine and pulled out from the kerb. As they passed the Humboldt, both glanced at the dark facade. It seemed an unlikely home to the surreal drama of only minutes before. He wondered if Millie was thinking the same.

'What do I need to pack?'

'Everything. I'll help if you want.'

She became quiet. Worse wondered if behind the silence she were examining her trust in him. Certainly he thought about his own risk. Thwistle had not mentioned a sister, but Worse was comforted by the knowledge that he could check the veracity of what she had told him. Clearly, they both had an interest in the Humboldt, or at least Fiendisch, and it might be that Nicholas, through email traffic, was the explanation for Fiendisch's interest in him.

'Who is Sigrid, apart from being your friend with a spare room?'

'Sigrid? Psychiatrist, logician. Worked on probabilistic reasoning and psychosis. Markov madness, you could say. Might afflict you one day. Early doctoral work on Kant's legacy in the modern world. Thesis published as *Recognizing Kant,* apparently a runaway bestseller, if in a vanishingly small market. Now writes books on things called credules. You'll like her.'

Again, Millie fell silent. Worse turned into her street and asked where her place was. He pulled over in a spare bay about fifty metres further on, and was intending to go in with her. Something made him hesitate. Excusing himself, he reached for the laptop that was on the floor by Millie's feet and cabled to the dash. He made a short keyboard entry, watching the satnav screen, then looked in his mirror.

'Fiendisch has people watching your place.'

'How do you know?' She sounded just a little incredulous.

Worse had turned his head away, looking back along the street.

'They're in a white Commodore on the other side twenty-five metres back.'

He thought about the fact that he had driven right past them, and was thankful for some subconscious vigilance.

'How do you know?' The inflexion had changed while somehow preserving the incredulity.

'Listen.' Worse entered another command. It was as if he had tuned the car radio to one of those depressing early-hours talkback quiz shows. Millie glanced at him with a theatrically pained expression. Worse raised a finger to his lips. Suddenly, with much clearer reception, a man's voice was broadcast into the car.

'It was DiMaggio, fuck. They're losers. Jesus. I'm gonna ring, I'm gonna ring.' It was Kev's voice.

'Just cool it, will you? You ring and that makes you a loser. Fucking shut up about it. Watch the road. No more stuff-ups.' Ritchie was an eloquent mentor. After a few seconds, he added, 'That Benz a minute ago. Pulled over and no one's got out.' He had apparently been observing in his mirrors. 'Did you make out who was in it?'

'Nah. Light's too bright.' After some delay, Kev added, 'D'you think it could be our bitch?'

Worse glanced at Millie. She was staring fixedly at the stereo controls.

'Why would she park up there? You got more of those?' There was a sound of crinkling wrapper.

'Maybe she's pissed off. Fuck. The loser. DiMaggio, ya prick. Ring 'em Ritchie.'

'She hasn't pissed off. All her stuff's still there for Christ's sake.'

Millie drew breath audibly.

Ritchie continued. 'She's just on a fucking night out, where else would she be? She'll be back.'

Worse reached to mute the transmission, but Millie stopped him.

'She could be screwing some fucker all night.' An idea of Kev's mythic woman was conveyed by the lust in his voice.

'Yeah, well, she's got to stop sometime. Then she comes home. Then bang. No more all-night bitch. No more big-sister fucking trouble.'

'What's the bitch like, Ritchie? You gonna do anything first?'

'Jesus, Kev, keep your fucking mind—'

Worse switched off the sound. Millie made no objection. He settled back in his seat, staring through the windscreen, the computer half on his lap, half against the steering wheel. He wanted to reach for Millie's hand, to acknowledge her vulnerability, and reassure her, but at the same time he was inhibited to test her trust. The sordidness of what they heard somehow weakened the human being in him. His generosity was deadened; he felt ashamed to be a man.

'How do you know they're waiting for me?' Her voice was quiet and reedy, as if she were about to cry. Worse continued looking forward. Unexpectedly, as he spoke, his concern took the form of irritation.

'Their names are Ritchie and Kev. They're killers. They take instructions from Fiendisch. I've seen them all together. Therefore they're connected to Nicholas. They're in your street. They mentioned big sister. Tell me the likelihood.'

He immediately regretted the harshness of his inference, and its cruel appeal to the probabilist in her. 'I'm sorry. I'm really sorry.'

She was silent for several seconds, then asked, 'How is it that you can listen in on them?'

'Yesterday they came to my place to kill me. I'll tell you about it later. Anyway, I managed to distract them and hide a microphone in their car.'

He had been thinking about the bitter almond in the Commodore. He could press a few keys and end their lives. He could listen to them die. He could walk back along the pavement and watch. He could even ring Ritchie and say: 'You're about to die, fucker.'

'Emily, hypothetically, if you had means to end the lives of those two here and now, sitting in their car, would you do it? Guaranteed result. No incrimination.'

She considered the question. 'If I could remain safe from them in the meantime, I would rather wait till I'd found Nicholas.' Her voice was becoming defiant.

'That's what I was thinking,' said Worse. 'Can I pass this to you?' He closed the computer and handed it to her. She rested it on her lap. For the first time since parking, he looked directly at her.

'I'm really sorry you heard all that.' It was spoken without obviousness, and brought to the space between them his concern, and kindness. For Worse, it was also an apology for the awfulness in men.

As he rested his hand on the gear selector, Millie turned to him, acknowledging his words with a tilt of her face. She reached out and placed her hand lightly on his. 'I'm so worried about Nicholas.' She was almost tearful.

'I know.' At last, Worse's humanity found expression in his eyes. 'We should leave.' He pulled into the street, half watching the Commodore and its ugly conversation recede into rear vision.

For readers unfamiliar with **credule theory**, the following brief introduction may be of interest. Any given belief can be partitioned into irreducible, monadic elements (of belief) known as *credules*. Credules can be identified under special tests of atomicity, details of which are given in S Blitt's *Elements of Belief*. Every credule is epistemically independent of every other credule, except in the case of negating pairs (see below) where clearly they have correlation negative one. A (non-null) belief, then, can be defined as a set containing at least one credule, disregarding negating pairs (this condition is implicit in several definitions that follow). The number of independent credules contained in a given belief is referred to as the *order* of the belief. Any complex belief can be discretized into *unit-beliefs*. A unit-belief is one having least order capable of motivating an act. (A sentential definition is used in some formalisms.) The algebra of sets provides a methodology for analysis; for example, intersection defines belief in common, or agreement. Two beliefs (sets), A and B, are *identical* if and only if every credule in A is contained in B, and vice versa. Otherwise, A and B are different beliefs. If A and B are different but have one or more independent credules in common, they are said to have semi-agreement (denoted *congenial* beliefs by some authors). If no credule in A is contained in B, A and B are called absolutely different or, equivalently, *disjoint* beliefs. Note that two disjoint beliefs cannot be the joint premises of a valid syllogism. The precise correspondence between set membership and order is subtle, and treatments differ according to author. For Blitt, a belief A is called *null* if, for any disjoint belief B, the union $A \cup B$ has the order of B. Every null belief is defined to have zero order, and to be identical to every other null belief. A credule a is said to *negate* the credule b (and vice versa) if the belief $\{a, b\}$ is null. In general, a belief containing mutually negating credules is not rational.

There have been many attempts to develop clinical models from this theory, particularly applied to delusional ideation. (Strictly, a belief is *false* if it contains at least one credule that is false. A credule is false if it belongs to the Halfpenny Set of any made observation.) Much of the modern psychiatric endeavour here can be viewed as identifying and repairing pathological credules. Typically, psychotic beliefs tend to be of very high order. Interestingly, religious beliefs are also of high order, unless agnostic, when they are null. Recent research has focused on the distribution of the unit-belief order statistic, which differs between sexes, appears to vary diurnally, and is altered by antipsychotic drugs (A Camenes, personal communication).

Evidence is also emerging of a totally novel psychotherapeutic modality premised on credule count censoring; a recently discovered ligand, auric sekitriptyline, specifically reduces the order of certain religious beliefs (toward the null state) with apparent conservation of conscience and no other discernible central nervous effects. The theological promise (not welcomed by all clerics) is that residual faith studies will identify the one true god.

The strong analogical connection between false credules and ordinary pathogens (including infectivity, resistance, and a form of antigenicity) has stimulated new avenues of research with profound implications for public health. It is reasonable to expect that effective surveillance and prompt detection of particularly virulent credule isolates, allied with conventional epidemic control measures, will assist in arresting the spread of popular delusions and mass hysterias, and even eliminate endemic variants. New credule conversion techniques, and targeted drug therapies using sekitriptyline-like agents, are expected to revolutionize these efforts and, longer term, immunization programmes may be possible.

In another fascinating development, some authors, particularly in the sociological literature, have advanced the hypothesis that credules are heritable. This is partly to account for the common observation that traits such as criminality and religiosity are familial but not always attributable to nurture. At least two plausible mechanisms have been advanced: (1) Credule determinants with intensionality are encoded in parts of the genotype subserving language (it is very rare to find criminality expressed before language develops); and (2) Credules are embedded in dreams, and inherited *pari passu* (the favoured hypothesis). The suggestion of heritability, which would seem incompatible with Sidney Spoker's idea of generational renewal of conscience, is distasteful to many ethicists, and this might explain why funding for the required multicentre longitudinal studies has not been forthcoming. If proven, the concern is that affected persons and progeny will be subjected to open-ended state-sponsored credule rehabilitation therapies. But such programmes are not new; the very same, using spiritual and corporeal methods, has long been the prerogative of world religions.

Finally, in respect of translation science, a theorem states that two beliefs are *Thortelmann equivalent* if and only if they contain at least one credule in common. It follows that a true belief and a false belief can be Thortelmann equivalent.

25. THE STRAND RECKONERS

It was almost 4.00 am as Worse chose the coast road to return to Perth.

'I think it might be safer if you stay with me for the time being, rather than Sigrid.' His place was far more secure, and he was thinking 'safer' for both Millie and Sigrid.

Millie didn't reply. After a full minute of silence, she asked, 'Why did those men come to kill you?'

Worse gave a summary of events beginning with Zheng's visit, and finishing, 'So, at the moment, it comes back to Fiendisch, though he apparently confers with someone else. I don't know why they would want me dead.'

He had been glancing periodically at the satnav screen. Ritchie's car had not moved.

'Are you scared?' Millie looked at him.

'Scared? Appropriately, I would hope.' Worse was thinking of the recent struggle in his apartment, and Zheng's fatal miscalculation. He turned his head, looking past Millie to the white water glints on the black sea. They reminded him of the quartz scintillation earlier. He appeared to change the subject. 'Have you heard of Leonardo di Boccardo?'

'No.'

'No. Few have. A Florentine political philosopher and earliest known victim of aggravated identity erasure. He was the luckless progenitor of all those airbrushed out of history in fascist times. Despite that, he projects an appealing sort of mentorship across the centuries, I find.'

'Airbrushed at least hints of a certain artistry; now we would be digitally remastered from the record,' said Millie, rather technically. 'Anyway, what about him?'

'He advised that, in conflict, one need only be as fearful as one's adversary is clever. From what I have seen of the two outside your place, that would be not very. In the case of Fiendisch, more. Definitely more. A small advantage is that I suspect they're not completely sure of my identity.'

'As I am not,' Millie responded drily. She also looked briefly at the ocean, then ahead. 'Do you think their interest in you is connected somehow to Nicholas disappearing?'

'Increasingly.'

Worse called Sigrid to say that her house guest would not be arriving. He gave no explanation.

When he had rung off, Millie continued her enquiries. 'Why would they conceivably want you dead? I mean, what is it you do? Ordinary people don't get killed off by gangsters for no reason.'

'It is troubling, isn't it?' Worse said. 'Generally, I just quietly mind my own business. Occasionally I might meddle in someone else's—only bad people, though.'

'Did you go to the police?'

'No. I was wanting to figure out more for myself first.'

When they were nearly at the Grosvenor, Worse pulled over and asked for the computer. He instructed Peepshow to blind the security system to their arrival. As he drove into the basement car park he noted Zheng's car, but made no comment. In the elevator, all he said was, 'Thirty-three,' as he pressed for the floor, for Millie's benefit.

Worse actually had two adjoining apartments, occupying the whole north side of his floor. When he referred to his spare room, it was more like a spare apartment. Millie was not aware of this, and when he showed her to what was clearly a main bedroom, she asked rather pointedly where he would be sleeping.

'Through here,' he said, ignoring the imputation. They walked into the side that was primarily his home.

'I'll be here if you need me. The security's good. I'll show you around in the morning.' He glanced at his watch. 'Well, later today.'

He had carried the computer and backpack up from his car, and now put them down on a hall table.

'How can you afford all this?'

Her curiosity exceeded good manners, and within the lifetime of the question Worse detected an apologetic inflexion. But he did answer politely.

'Indebtedness. Mine and others'. Consulting fees. Some modest royalties.' He was tired. 'We'll make a plan tomorrow. There's a lot of research we can do from here. We need to unravel the strands of our respective mysteries. I'm sure we will find them joined somewhere, which can only be helpful, actually.'

They were standing in the hall outside his computer room and he gestured inside. 'We can find you some clothes and whatever as well. Go shopping, I mean. We may also be able to get back into your place soon. First we should make a judgement about your level of continuing risk. Let's plan to start at ten.'

He walked through to his kitchen and assembled some fresh items on a tray, then led her back to the other apartment. He put them in her refrigerator, and pointed to other supplies in cupboards.

'Towels and so on are in the bathroom. Washing machine and dryer in there. You could do your things overnight. If there's anything else you need, just come over and call out. You should feel completely at home.'

'Thanks. It's great. A definite improvement on where I've been recently.' The thought of Nicholas interrupted the pleasure in her face, and she looked down.

'I was meaning to ask,' said Worse, 'do you have your credit cards and so on with you or are they at the flat?' Millie patted her denim jacket.

'Good. I mention it because if they were back there, you might have considered cancelling them.'

'And my travel documents are in safekeeping at a bank.'

'Not the Humboldt, I trust. Goodnight.' As he left, he added, 'By the way, I have a regular commitment on Thursday evenings. I'll be out tonight.'

He closed the link door behind him.

Worse was up and working by 8.00 am. The first thing he did was check the location of Ritchie's car. It was still in Millie's street. He scanned the voice recording from Ritchie's phone, making some notes as he did. There had been little conversation over the past four hours as the two took turns at watching the house, and sleeping. Worse also prepared another computer, specifically for Millie's use, with safeguards for both her and himself.

Millie appeared at exactly 10.00 am, opening the link door and calling out. Worse answered, and she followed his voice to the workshop. She looked surprisingly refreshed, and seemed pleased to see him. He marvelled at the art of dressing differently using the same clothes.

'By the way, I don't know your first name,' she said brightly.

Worse hesitated. 'Richard. Have you eaten?'

'Yes, thank you.'

Worse stood up and moved to the computer he had dedicated to her.

'This is for your exclusive use. You can do everything on it. It's important you don't touch any of the others, please. Printer's online. Here's your email address.' He pointed to a sheet of paper on the bench. 'Username. You need a ten-character password, case sensitive, the usual string caveats. You can set up access to your UK address using these instructions,' he gestured again toward the sheet. 'It calls an encryption routine. Obviously, don't mention where you are, or me, in your messages.'

'Where am I, anyway?'

'Level thirty-three, the Grosvenor. Did you sleep well?'

'Yes. I took a while getting off, but then I was fully out to it till the alarm.'

'Do you have everything you need for the moment?'

'Yes, thank you.'

'I'll make coffee while you set up your mail.'

'You said that you'd sensed that Nicholas was becoming unhappy in his work. Why did you think that?' They were sitting on the main balcony, where Worse had served coffee.

'Well, he had been hired to develop a suite of specialized instruments for the wine industry—futures, options, hedge products, insurance tools and so on. It was exciting stuff. They seemed like a very sophisticated business, they wanted the best, and they were prepared to pay for expertise. They treated him very well at first, professionally and socially. He was loving it here.'

She fell silent, and Worse waited. 'Then his last few messages seemed different. Early on, they'd left him to get on with it, and it was going really well. He was at the stage of testing prototypes—basically running lots of simulations—when I think Fiendisch started interfering.'

'Do you know what that was about?'

'I gathered that they disagreed about parametrization. I don't know any details. Nicholas wondered if the bank was under financial strain. That was in his last message. I've printed them off for you.'

'What did the parametrization issue mean to you?'

'I don't know. I haven't thought that through. Margins, maybe. Acceptable risk, profit projection.'

Worse was silent for several seconds. They sat in canvas chairs, both facing out, with a small table between them. The project seemed sound in principle. The Australian wine industry had made enormous advances in recent years, and had become a billion-dollar export earner. Conventional economics would prescribe profitable management for each stage of harvesting, production, packaging, marketing, shipping, retail, associated tourism, and so on. As far as Worse was aware, the industry was successful in those respects. But bankers and brokers would inevitably want more. A specialist derivatives market would assist in capital raising, risk management, portfolio gearing and, above all, provide another layer of opportunity for profit. It wasn't surprising that a boutique investment bank like Humboldt had seen the potential for niche financial products and set about developing them.

But something else made a connection for Worse. His reconstruction of Zheng's final days placed the killer in the heart of the South-West premium wine district. For a man with a mini-bar tab listing beer only, the visit was surely not for pleasure.

'Coffee okay?'

'Great.' She hadn't yet tasted it, and was prompted to reach for her mug. As she did, and unpredicated by anything spoken, they exchanged glances with such exact coincidence that Worse felt slightly unnerved, as if embarrassed by trespass and discovery. It was one of those events that, however trivial, draws attention to itself by virtue of improbability. But for Worse it was more than that; he knew from experience that it signalled in him a particular curiosity and self-consciousness around another person. Even looking away, he sensed her smiling as she raised the coffee to her lips.

'Tell me what you think has happened to your brother.' The shift was sudden, and she seemed to startle slightly.

'Well, even before meeting you I was worried about something awful. I told you that it's completely out of character for Nicholas not to keep in touch. And I found his flat burgled. All that might have had nothing to do with the Humboldt, except that the mood of the emails did change, and Fiendisch behaved so oddly, nothing like you'd expect of a business principal with even ordinary concern for a staff member.'

Worse was always entertained by disjunctive pairs such as odd and even in the same sentence, and turned to look at her. His momentary distraction went unnoticed.

'Anyway, I thought the bank aspect of it looked sufficiently strange to sneak in for a look around. I mean, Nicholas would have had an office there. No signs of that last night.' She gestured negation with one hand while resting her coffee on the table with the other. In doing that, she looked at Worse.

'Now, of course, from everything you've told me, I'm really worried. For Nicholas. And for myself, I suppose.'

Worse stared at the balcony railing, and took the conversation back a step.

'Is that something you do regularly, breaking into banks?'

'I didn't really break in,' she said defensively, 'I had an entry card. No, of course I don't. Do you?'

'Denial, fallacy, protest, deflection. Very infrequently. Weren't you scared?'

'Absolutely. Especially when—'

'The flower arrangement sprang into life. I'm sorry.' Worse was looking into his coffee, but was aware of her grinning.

'You're forgiven.'

He looked at her as he rose from his chair, collecting her mug. 'Well, you scared me too, and you're forgiven.'

Worse had been thinking about the best course of action. There were two mysteries. The first, Zheng's attack, was his. The second was Millie's—what had happened to Nicholas, and why she herself had been targeted. The relational complex *Zheng* implicated Ritchie implicated Fiendisch, though not necessarily the Humboldt. *Nicholas* implicated the Humboldt and Fiendisch, and as well, *Nicholas* implicated Millie implicated Ritchie, though not necessarily Fiendisch or the bank. It seemed inconceivable that the two sets of events were not related, at least through Fiendisch, and if that were the case, Worse believed that finding Nicholas should take priority. He shared these thoughts as they walked through the kitchen to the computer room.

On the way, Worse briefly showed her the other lab, explaining that should the need arise, they could do basic forensic work in-house.

'Why do you have all that stuff at home?' she asked.

'I used to be interested in it.'

'I hope you're not some kind of arch-criminal and I've been completely hoodwinked.' She was being humorous, but Worse was blunt.

'I'm not.' A moment later, before she could formulate something apologetic, he added, 'Hoodwinked is a nice word. We should use it more.'

Millie stayed quiet.

'I don't think I told you about our spyware in the bank's IT system,' Worse said as they entered the computer room. 'We have a copy of everything there is.'

'Wow,' Millie almost whistled appreciatively.

'First, I think we should independently record everything we can remember about all the rooms in the bank. Then combine notes. Then we'll start mining the computer records: keywords Nicholas, Zheng, Grosvenor, for example. I'm also going to find out more about Fiendisch. Interrupt me at any time. Otherwise we'll discuss progress over lunch.'

Millie assented briskly by sitting at her desk, turning to give Worse a stack of printed emails. Worse had already thought about the fact that these represented her last contact with Nicholas, and he accepted them with slight formality.

Before beginning his own tasks, Worse checked on Ritchie and Kev. The car was no longer at Millie's address. He streamed through the record and found what he expected, a phone call from Ritchie to Fiendisch reporting a lack of sighting of their target. The latter had instructed them to leave the scene and get some sleep. Worse called out to Millie.

'Another link established. Those two watching your place are taking orders about you from Fiendisch. Not surprising, but now confirmed.'

Millie looked up. 'Are they still there?'

'No.' He was pleased to report that.

Worse was keen to find out more about Fiendisch, and follow his movements. He began with the banker's mobile phone, accessing the account file and copying the numbers dialled. He recognized those of Ritchie and Zheng, but it was another that caught his attention. This was a frequently called fixed line number in Margaret River. Worse pursued this, to find it was registered to Verita's Wines, a fully controlled entity of the unlisted Providence Portfolio, having directors Karl Fiendisch and Charles Finistere. Providence itself was a subsidiary of Humboldt. As he discovered these connections, Worse copied relevant material into a research folder, as well as writing some notes on a pad. After several minutes, he sat back, staring at the screen. Strand within strand; every thread of enquiry seemed to unravel another.

For the moment, he decided to return to Fiendisch. The mobile account led him to a home number. Worse noted the address. After this, he wanted a break, and collecting the sheaf of emails from Nicholas he walked through to his bedroom and lay down, his head supported on three pillows. He first confirmed they were in chronological order, then read the last first.

Hi M. Sorry to hear about Pico. Has he got alternatives worked out? Good luck with the marking and remember to be kind. If it gets too awful you could run away like me. Actually, things aren't so great here at the moment. I thought my stuff was going brilliantly. Retrodiction tests for Autonomous Trader have been unbelievable, 32pm12% virtually guaranteed. For some reason Dr F doesn't seem pleased. He wants big changes with parametrization that look dangerous to me. They're way off for the market behaviour. I don't think he understands all that much, though his doctorate (he says) was in economic modelling. He does seem OK with programming though. Anyway, his mood has changed the last few days. He really was quite kind to me before but I'm feeling fairly uncomfortable now. I suppose the bank may have hit some difficulties. I'm not party to the general business. Two of the front office staff seem to have quit last week. I'm not sure I'll want to stay much longer myself if the unfriendliness continues. Do you think I should be upfront about it?

Do you remember Hiro Wasabi? He was the one who found the problem in RT's draft proof of Fitzsimmons III. Pointed it out with infinite politeness of course. I don't think you ever met him. Anyway, I discovered that he has a visiting professorship over here. We've talked on the phone and plan a Japanese meal out next week. I think I'll try to get to their weekly research seminars too, to keep in touch. It's a bit isolating professionally here, which is saying something, after where I was before.
Hope all's well. Love N.

Worse stared at the page for several seconds. He then went back to read the earliest, working forward chronologically. There was a definite change in sentiment in the penultimate message, where Nicholas mentioned some unexpected, and evidently unreasonable, pressure to get the project completed. It was a comment that might have passed unnoticed, its significance only illuminated by the subsequent message, and events. Worse noted the dates. The last fully optimistic, unreservedly positive email was on August 12; two days later the mood was changing.

'Did Nicholas write letters by post, or only email?' Worse had left the printouts on his bed and walked through to Millie's desk.

'A couple of postcards early on, that's all.'

'Did you chase up the Hiro Wasabi contact?'

'I did. Actually, I ended up having that meal out with him myself last week. Nicholas was to phone Hiro to confirm the arrangement, but never did. Hiro tried email and phoning the bank, only to be told that Nicholas had left the company.'

'Were there emails, Nicholas to Hiro?'

Millie hesitated, possibly thinking she should know. 'I don't know.'

Worse glanced at Millie's screen, but didn't ask about her progress. 'When you have time, it might pay to search for Nicholas's email files. There may be versions of things written but not sent, internal memos, correspondence with other colleagues. Whatever.'

Millie nodded agreement but already Worse was moving to another terminal.

He had been unable to trace the origin of payments to Zheng's account. However, the problem could be greatly reduced with a little more information, essentially by searching for a link from both ends. Over the next few minutes, Worse remodelled the task by incorporating accounts associated with Humboldt Bank, Fiendisch or Finistere. It remained computationally demanding, and he fully expected the analysis to take days. But now he was confident of success; in the end there would be a result, some pathway of maximum likelihood connecting Zheng to an account number, a password, and the name of a person of interest.

26. SIGRID BLITT

'Why do I think there's trouble afoot?'

Knowing his friend's capacity for play, Worse examined each word for obliquity, especially 'afoot'.

'Afoot? A foot,' he pronounced carefully. Sigrid eyed him patiently. He continued. 'It's funny you should say that. A foot has been the sort of gestalt of my day. I've seen an amputee on crutches, a young man in a wheelchair with a leg in fixators, a shop window full of right-hand shoes, and kids playing hopping games in a car park. Now you say afoot. Why is it a one-legged day?'

He seemed genuinely intrigued, and Sigrid, not quite sure of the comic temperature, said seriously, 'It's Scalene Thursday; you should know that. In many cultures it's an important festival. You're meant to cross your legs for luck.'

Worse looked at her suspiciously, but with no shift in tone began to describe in detail the events of the previous few days, keeping his account factual and largely free of opinion or inference.

Sigrid listened without interruption, showing concern, surprise and amusement as the story unfolded. From time to time he stopped talking, as other diners or café staff moved close to their table. He concluded with a précis of his conversation with Millie just prior to leaving the apartment that evening. It was about taking a look at the Fiendisch house later in the night. When he finished, Sigrid stared at her water glass, eventually looking up.

'Have you talked to the police?'

'Not at this stage.'

'Could the Zheng attack be to do with SpeakEasy?'

It was a natural question. SpeakEasy was an internet site managed exclusively by Sigrid and himself, dedicated to commentary that would normally invoke the hopelessly archaic and repressive Australian defamation and contempt laws. Sigrid and he as editors, and any contributors, were protected by Worse's own DPA encryption code and a distributed virtual server system using cuckoo programs that switched rapidly and randomly across almost a million public access servers.

For over three years now they had offered a forum for essays and critiques on subjects such as censorship, judicial impropriety and incompetence, law of contempt abuses, parliamentary privilege, political nepotism, conflict of interest, and corporate bullying. It was the modern incarnation of a dissident printing press, and their regular pamphleteers' dinner on Thursday evenings dealt with editorial matters for the following week. Obviously, the site had many enemies, and it could easily be that Fiendisch had reasons to attack SpeakEasy unrelated to the Nicholas business.

Their meals had arrived, and Worse was carefully dissecting bones from his grilled fish.

'I'm investigating that, but it's looking very unlikely—no irregularities, no security flags, nothing direct and nothing statistical.' He was referring to automated self-checks embedded in the operating system. After a few seconds, he added, 'I need to understand exactly what purpose Fiendisch had in hiring Nicholas, and if it changed. Anyway, has anything unusual been happening in your world?'

'My patients. They're all unusual.'

'I thought you made them normal.'

It was Sigrid's turn to scrutinize her meal. 'Well and normal are different things. What would you like me to do?'

'I was hoping you might look after SpeakEasy this week. Maybe a BenchPress edition; you could use the judicial activism material we worked on.'

'Yes. I could do that.'

'I'd also like you to apply your mind to what I've told you. Give me any ideas.'

Sigrid looked serious. 'I think you should talk to Spoiling.'

'I thought you would say that. How much should I tell him?'

'Everything. Except whatever could incriminate you. Leave out your little contingency gift in Ritchie's car, for example. And where Zheng rests.'

Worse accepted the advice with a slight tilt of the head.

'Call him now.' She reached for the water bottle and refilled their glasses.

Worse removed a mobile from his jacket pocket and dialled a stored number. Almost immediately, Sigrid could hear, 'Worse, how are you?'

'Hello Victor. I have a perplexity for you.' Worse and Spoiling shared a private vernacular.

'I feel a headache coming on.'

'Victor! You enjoy perplexities.' There was mock hurt. 'It's about the Humboldt Bank in Fremantle, a director called Fiendisch, and a missing person, Nicholas Misgivingston. Can we meet tomorrow?'

'Of course, for coffee.'

'Thank you, Victor. I will call you. By the way, I have a name and number for your Sydney colleagues looking into their shootings.' He gave Smudge's contact details taken from Ritchie's mobile. As he pocketed his own phone he reached thoughtfully for his water glass.

'Any concerns?' Sigrid eyed him searchingly.

'About Victor? No, I don't think so.' Worse was ruminative, using an unopened sugar sachet to corral scattered breadcrumbs into a neat square. After several seconds, Sigrid re-enquired.

'I mean, do you feel better or worse, less or more disturbed, after speaking to him?'

'Better, less,' he answered. He pushed his chair back from the table and crossed his legs, one knee over the other.

'That good luck thing, does it last through midnight?'

The theoretical basis of a **defective pixelation algorithm** (DPA) had been advanced by Worse in 1995. The essential idea was that data were intentionally encrypted with embedded random errors. This rendered conventional code breaking approaches almost useless, but the trick was to modulate the error statistics such that security was maximized while decryption remained possible. If it were slightly wrong, either everyone could read it, or no one.

It could be shown that, in principle, error frequency should vary with the Shannon information content in the message, but no one had determined the critical relation. The proposal attracted brief interest in the literature including discussion of suitable error processes, and a short paper by a student of Thwistle's applying classical signal-noise theory. Most came to view the problem as intractable. Worse used a different approach, viewing it as a sort of inverted sampling problem, and the essence of his solution was the crucial discovery of an equilibrium structure exhibiting nested orthogonalities. From this followed a family of elegant symmetry results, which in turn led to very surprising computational efficiencies.

As it happened, when this work was completed, he was planning the SpeakEasy project, for which a unique encryption algorithm would be very advantageous. He therefore decided not to publish the algorithm, and shared the result only with Sigrid. At the time of writing, this and the underlying general optimization theorem remain unpublished.

27. BITTER ALMOND

Millie was driving, and as she pulled over to the kerb Worse glanced at the dash clock and thought of Sigrid's reply. 'For a year,' she had prescribed authoritatively.

Half past midnight; enough time then. Millie switched off the engine and turned to Worse, who was unbuckling his seatbelt. He pointed through the windscreen.

'It's the third one along, with the limestone wall. Built 1930s and restored with the good features preserved, typically renovated for comfort and security. These properties go down to private beaches on the river. Very nice.'

Millie sat back comfortably, but her glance settled on the Fiendisch residence.

'I know what you'll say,' she began quietly, 'but do you think Nicholas could be in there?' Her eyes stayed focused on the house.

'What will I say?'

'Exactly.'

They fell silent. The degree of danger to which Nicholas had been exposed was obvious to both of them, but his possible fate had never been explicitly raised. In reference to Nicholas, Worse had been careful, in the tense and mood of his language, and in its context, to convey a presumption that his disappearance would be explained and he would be found alive. He was waiting for Millie to broach the worst of possibilities. She seemed to be thinking about it now, and he decided to speak.

'I think Nicholas became extremely valuable to them. He was made party to, or discovered for himself, some criminal activity in the bank, probably related to his software project there. Either he escaped into hiding or they have him working for them under some kind of duress, even confinement in some form. I think the second is more likely, bizarre as it seems. I don't think he's otherwise been harmed. I think he's alive. If Fiendisch wanted to hurt him, he would use Ritchie and Kev, and they're stupid enough to talk about it. There's nothing on the voice recordings.'

Worse was vaguely relieved that he had managed to convey these ideas without using 'dead' or 'killed'. But he was a little troubled by his own last point, by the possibility that Zheng had been instrumental in Nicholas's fate. He was still looking along the road when he added, 'But I'd be very surprised if he's in that house.'

Millie turned to face him with a look of intense seriousness.

'Thank you.' Just two syllables, very quietly, were enough to expose a voice slightly broken with emotion. Worse met her gaze; even in the near darkness, he could see distress, resolve, and trust. He suddenly had a sense of enormous responsibility, and it mixed uncomfortably with the compassion he already felt around her missing brother. He turned to look forward, and remained silent.

After several seconds, he reached for his mobile, adjusted it to silent mode, and opened up a line to the car phone, which Millie answered. Then he fitted a miniature wireless speaker to his left ear, tested communication both ways, and placed the mobile in a jacket pocket. Millie would speak to him if anything untoward happened in the street. His plan was simple: to place a tracking device on Fiendisch's car, and to take whatever opportunities presented to explore the premises generally.

Worse turned to grasp his small backpack from the rear seat, and in the single move of swinging forward and opening his door they exchanged glances. A moment later the door closed, and he was almost lost in the shadows of the treed verge. Millie sat forward, staring intently into the gloom. She could just make out his dark figure climb to the crest of the boundary wall, hesitate, and disappear over the top. In that moment she felt acutely alone, and a mild but unfamiliar anxiety entered her thoughts. She reached out to the dash and central-locked the car.

From the top of the wall, Worse surveyed the front of the property. Between him and the house was a dense native garden, through which he could see some dim lighting in the ground floor. Across to his left was the driveway, protected from the street by large iron gates. He twisted his body and, grasping the capping as best he could, lowered himself to the ground, the last few centimetres being in free fall. Immediately, he ran his hands over the inner surface of the wall, feeling the roughness for points of purchase, for toeholds. Satisfied that he would have little difficulty in scaling its height even in haste, he crouched down and observed the house for a few minutes. The lighting remained subdued and there were no sounds. The second level window curtains were drawn closed. He noted a security alarm under the eaves.

His plan was to edge along the internal face of the wall to the driveway, but once there he sighted a motion-sensor spotlight directed toward the gates. Any further progress would be easily detected. He therefore retraced his steps about five metres, headed across the garden directly to the front of the house, and emerged on a path connecting the driveway to the front entrance. From there he moved leftwards and, keeping low, passed to the rear of the sensor range. At that moment he heard Millie's voice in his earpiece.

'Car coming from my direction.'

Worse moved into the garden, and watched how the vehicle's peripheral headlight briefly illuminated the point in the driveway where he had just crossed.

'It's a taxi. Driver, one passenger, I think; turned left at the end.' He nodded slightly, as if Millie could see.

The driveway widened to lead to a single lock-up garage, as well as an uncovered bay to its left, where the BMW was parked in the open. From his temporary refuge in the garden, Worse studied the roller door of the garage. There was an exterior handle and lock, but it was clear that opening it would be a noisy affair.

He moved forward between the BMW and the left wall of the garage, finding a path leading toward the rear. At the end of the wall, he stopped and peered around the corner. In front of him was a large paved outdoor living area, partly roofed by a vine-covered timber pergola. This connected to the house proper via French doors, through which could be seen a dimly lit kitchen. Beyond the patio was a swimming pool, and adjacent to this a small building that Worse supposed housed the filtration machinery. Arrayed about were seating areas, one protected by a sturdy canvas market umbrella. Past that, the property sloped away into darkness.

Of immediate interest, though, was the rear wall of the garage, in which was a door affording access from the terrace, and a window. Worse slipped around the corner and looked in the window, one hand simultaneously reaching for the brass door handle and gently turning it. The window was obscure, but the door opened easily and he stepped through, closing it behind him.

He stood motionless in the gloom for several seconds. The window transmitted minimal light, yet he was gradually able to make out the general disposition of things around him. To his right, beneath the window, was a workbench with a vice and assorted tools. On his left were garden implements, lawnmowers, and various edging and pruning tools. In front of him was a passage between two tall storage cupboards, along which he could see the metallic gleam of a vehicle.

In his research on Fiendisch's finances, Worse had not discovered ownership records for a second vehicle. He moved between the cupboards, and recognized a late model Range Rover. Shining a subdued torchlight on its registration plate, he memorized the number; he also noted reddish mud on the tyres and wheel arches.

It was parked close to the garage wall on the passenger side, and was unlocked. Worse made his way to the driver's door, using his torch judiciously to examine the interior. There was nothing of interest on the front seats, and he moved to the rear door. The back seat was folded down to enlarge the luggage tray and he could see what looked like a large pile of crumpled blankets.

Worse had put much thought into what he might find and what it would imply about Nicholas's fate. Conversely, the fact of Nicholas's disappearance implied certain possible findings, and he was not surprised at what he now saw. If Nicholas had been restrained and transported hidden under those blankets, Worse might find some indication as to whether he had been physically harmed first.

As quietly as he could, he opened the rear passenger door,

switching on the dull interior ceiling light. Holding his penlight in his mouth, he began to fossick amongst the blankets, progressively adjusting his weight further into the car in order to complete the task systematically.

He was searching the armrest pocket of the opposite door when the briefest flash of light, hardly perceptible, alerted him to danger. It was the starting flicker of a fluorescent tube. Within a second, the garage was flooded in blue-white light, and Worse heard the workshop door close, rattling its adjacent window. At the same time, the ageing roller door to the front drive began to grind open.

There was no opportunity to escape either way undetected, and Worse had to act instantly. He launched himself fully into the vehicle and pulled the rear door shut, its sound subsumed in the noise of the garage door, and covered himself with blankets. He heard the driver's door open and felt the suspension react to the weight of a new occupant. The door slammed shut and the engine started. As they reversed out, Worse found his mobile. Awkwardly, with one finger, he sent a message to Millie: *In range rover. Follow.*

Millie replied through Worse's earpiece. She could see the front garden now floodlit, and the remote-controlled gates opening. Worse heard her start his car. He felt the Range Rover reverse over the road verge, then set off down the street. Although he had the tracking device in his pocket, he had not instructed Millie how to access its signal through his laptop or the Mercedes Comand system. He switched his phone to GPS; at least he could keep informed of their movements. At the same time, Millie had position indication on the car GPS, and mentioned whenever the street name changed. Once, when he thought she was too close, he messaged her: *Hold back a little.*

Curled up tightly on the hard luggage tray, and fully covered by blankets, Worse was desperately uncomfortable; he felt his joints stiffen and from time to time was forced to suppress a threatened cough or sneeze excited by dust or fibres in the blankets.

It was half an hour before he was certain who was driving, when the silence was broken by Fiendisch speaking on the phone. 'Where are you? ... I'm being followed ... I don't know ... I can't see ... On the freeway ... Verita's ... Because the Admiral wants matters finalized ... I will stop at the roadhouse, let me know when you are a few minutes away ... No, bring Kev ... Forget the girl for now.'

Nothing that Worse heard was unexpected. It would be virtually impossible at night to trail a car from Fiendisch's house to the freeway without being noticed. And their destination, Margaret River, was no surprise. He messaged Millie: *F has spotted you. Keep up now.*

Over the next hour, Worse was constantly updated by Millie about progress. Fiendisch had put on music; surprisingly, it was loud rap with, even more bizarrely, Latin lyrics, and not at all to Worse's taste. Eventually, Millie told him that they were approaching a roadhouse on the left, and he heard the clicking of the car's turning signal. As a sound, it was welcome relief from the music.

'If he goes inside, you may get a chance to get out,' said Millie. 'I'll let you know when it's safe.'

Under the blankets, by feel alone, Worse found the tracking device in his pocket. He had intended to secure it to the BMW before leaving the Fiendisch property, and was pleased not to have done so already.

The vehicle slowed to a stop; Worse heard the driver's door open and the seat springs ease.

'He's buying petrol,' reported Millie.

Worse was acutely aware of the sounds involved, including that of gushing fuel entering the tank only centimetres from his ear. He heard the cap replaced, the flap closed and latched, and the fuel nozzle reseated in the pump.

'He's walking in to pay. Get out the driver's side ... now.'

Worse had already slipped the tracker under the driver's seat, locking it magnetically below one of the steel rails. He opened the door and stepped out, rebunching the blankets into a heap, then closed the door and looked around. Millie had pulled up in a parking bay serving the restaurant, which was closed. Worse ran to his car, glancing at the office as he went. Fiendisch was just entering, still with his back to events.

Worse eased himself into the passenger seat, smiling warmly

at Millie, and immediately reclined the seat fully. Millie had left the engine running.

'I need to stretch. I think my joints are welded into foetal flexion. I'm going to lay low. There's no reason why we should tell Fiendisch that there are two of us. Did he look at you from the pump?'

'He tried to. I watched him through the wing mirror.'

'Would he have recognized you?'

'If he did, he's pretty smart.'

'There's no doubt he's smart,' replied Worse. 'What's happening?'

'He's returning to his car ... getting in ... driving off.'

'Follow. We're post-subtle now; he knows our business. I heard him call those two crooks from outside your place to chase us.'

Millie reversed from their parking bay, swinging the car around. Worse was still lying down.

'Post-subtle. How well that describes our world,' Millie said as she rejoined the highway.

'Oh yes. Post-subtlety. It's a stunning new movement in the humanities. Invented by those philosophers who live on the Paris Métro. Solves for the great unknowns by progressive elimination of substance. Quite Gaussian in its genius. Ideally suited to frugality of expression and perfunctory dialectic. Permits insults, for example. Silences discouraged, unless they're antisocial. I expect its defining contribution in mathematics will be blank pages of proof. Surely it has reached Cambridge? Anyway, we must now view ourselves as participants at risk in its chase variant.'

'Don't annoy me with that stuff; it may have reached Cambridge, but not mathematics, thank God.' Millie was surprisingly short. Worse managed to lace the apologetic with more irritant.

'By follow, I was respectfully suggesting that you don't overtake and then propose that we are in pursuit from ahead. And as a probabilist, you must surely agree we are in a very interesting queue. Perhaps you could model it.'

But Millie's immediate attention on the mathematics seemed to insulate her from further provocation. 'Actually, queues are one of my special interests. Queues and entropy.'

'Fascinating. Claude Shannon, wait in line.'

Millie fell silent. Worse had reached for his laptop and now pulled up the map signal from the Range Rover. Next he did the same for the tracker in Ritchie's car, discovering that it was only ten kilometres behind them, and travelling fast. Finally, he opened the monitor line to Ritchie's phone. He then told Millie what he had done.

After a short silence, he spoke again. 'Have I upset you?'

'No, no. I'm thinking about Nicholas, that's all.'

'Yes.'

The next voice was Ritchie's. He had phoned Fiendisch to report that they were passing the roadhouse. They heard the reply.

'Good. Catch up. It's a light-coloured Mercedes staying quite close. I think there is only the driver. I will put my hazard lights on so you will know it's me. Phone again when you see us.'

A few minutes later, Worse tracked Ritchie's car closing in. He returned his seat to upright and looked behind. Headlights were coming up fast. Ritchie called Fiendisch.

'We see you, and the Benz. What do you want us to do?' he asked.

'Use your special expertise. Stop him following me. I'm going to pull away from your line of sight. When that's done, meet me at the winery.'

They heard Ritchie instruct Kev to pull alongside for an easy shot at the driver.

'When Fiendisch speeds up, follow as closely as you can,' Worse said to Millie, reopening the laptop. After a few keystrokes, he folded it closed.

'Excuse me.' He reached across to flick the headlights on to high beam. 'Let's make it difficult for Fiendisch to see what's happening.'

'What is happening?'

'We're using our special expertise.'

They were now doing one hundred and fifty, one hundred and sixty kilometres per hour, keeping up with the Range Rover, but the high-powered Commodore was still closing in behind them. Worse was turned in his seat, looking backwards. He used his mobile to contact Ritchie, and spoke without introduction.

'Might I remind you both that you are yet to pay Mr Newton's swearing fines? There is, of course, a growing interest component, as well as fees, levies, incidentals, penalties, surcharge, tax withheld and petties.' He hardened his voice to add, 'And fucking stay in line. Don't fucking mess with Millie's entropy.'

Worse rang off. The Commodore was starting to fall back. They heard Ritchie speaking to Kev.

'That was fucking weird. You know that fucker in the fucking building with the fucked-up lift—Jesus, Kev, what's that fuck-awful stink? That is fucking foul. What have you been fucking eating?'

'It wasn't me, fuck.' From early childhood, Kev had perfected a succinct blend of profanity and denial. It worked best when coupled with a corollary of shifted blame: 'It must have been you.'

'Fuck it wasn't me.' Ritchie found his originality in small permutations, and was not to be outclassed in gracing evasion with expletive. Evidently, he was still puzzled by Worse's call. 'It's the middle of the fucking night and that Newton fucker wants his fucking fines paid, Jesus. Had the fucking balls to warn us off. Said we're messing with some bad sister called Millicent Ropey.'

'Who the fuck is Millicent Ropey?'

'I dunno. The way he said her name, though, she must be some kind of major league fucking attack bitch, like we're in serious shit. Fuck, what have we done to her? Fuck, we're just minding our own business. Fuck, how could he have my number, anyway?'

'Forget it, fuck. That fucker Newton's just a building clerk, some fuckin' fall guy for the super bitch. Anyway,' Kev counselled consolingly, 'you'll feel better when you've magged out on the fucker in front. Remember, it'll be your twenty-first. The boys are going to throw a celebration.' He paused, apparently forming a plan, and added confidently, 'Then we can sort out this Ropey bitch, and drop the clerk fucker too, if you want.' His words were beginning to slur.

Worse shared a small amusement with Millie. 'There's an attribution for the hip historian. Newton: the fall guy ...'

'Watch out, Kev!' shouted Ritchie.

The Commodore had slowed and was wandering on to the gravel edge.

'Slow down, let Fiendisch get away,' Worse instructed Millie.

They heard some indistinct words in the other vehicle. Worse watched as Kev lost control and the car left the road, became airborne on a small embankment, and lodged about a hundred metres through the scrub, upright and still quite close to the road.

'Stop.'

Millie pulled over to the side, and they both looked back at the wreckage of the Commodore. Its headlights were still on, casting an eerie swathe of light that seemed to dim and swirl as they watched. Millie took a moment to realize it was an effect of smoke. Almost immediately, they saw flames; there was an explosion, and within seconds the whole car was ablaze.

Worse turned to look ahead. Fiendisch's tail-lights were out of sight.

'Let's get going,' he said, 'someone else can call the fire service. No need to hurry. Let Fiendisch think we're finished.'

As Millie pulled away from the edge he addressed an unspoken question.

'They were dead before the fire, quite humanely.'

'What killed them?'

'Millicent Ropey, then chemistry.'

Millie didn't respond. Worse looked down to the laptop and began to track the Range Rover.

Worse's signal actuated a miniature solenoid, enabling stoichiometric admixture of potassium cyanide and sulphuric acid, and releasing pressurized **hydrogen cyanide** through a sintered glass membrane. The reaction is exothermic, intense heat (in combination with an integrated jacket containing a gelled accelerant) eventually destroying all trace of the device and igniting plastics and upholstery locally, as well as detonating leaking fuel. There is no reactant residue and, following incineration, no post-mortem evidence of the metabolic cause of death. Bitter almonds are not available to the general public.

Worse's last comment refers to the fact that a contributory cause of death, in a setting of lethal threat, was the confusion, distraction and irrationality occasioned by unchecked *figmentation*, here instantiated by 'Millicent Ropey' and taking the form of an acute *folie à deux*. Of course, such psychological instruments are not discoverable at autopsy, but are conservatively estimated to be causative in approximately fifty per cent of unexplained deaths.

Indeed, most people, most of the time, negotiate the world disadvantaged by impaired or illusory mental constructs. (The experience of surprise is virtually pathognomonic. Their contrived fabrication and collapse is a basic mode of humour, and of cruelty.) These might introduce inefficiencies, puzzlement, disappointment, or embarrassment, but they are not ordinarily life-threatening. The role of 'imagination' in their genesis is easily overstated, as they form quite naturally around errors of perception and errors of logic, which are both common. The figment 'Millicent Ropey' originated in a false perception where a suite of possibilities as to what Worse might have said was restricted by Ritchie's ignorance of entropy; that accepted, and within the mental universe of Kev and Ritchie's car, the progression of thoughts would not seem fanciful. Far more fundamental though, and more problematic, is that given correctly perceived facts, figmentation arises from erroneous hypothesis-forming about reality—a limitation of inductive reasoning.

Aspects of this subject are explored in the context of religious delusion in Timothy Bystander's *Studies in Cowardice I: The Suicide Murderer* (previously cited). There it is asserted that corrupted figmentation is routinely exploited by cynical elders in the tuition of perpetrators. The author shows that widened culpability (and, importantly, cowardice), if not moral revulsion, extends categorically from any such atrocity. (Note that the charge of cowardice is proven when conscience, in respect of an act's consequences, is intentionally excised in the act itself. Bystander conjectures that some human conduct is so evil that such an excision is its necessary condition. The alternative, which supposes impossible moral accommodation, would declare protagonists formally non-human; this is disallowed by political nicety, though the weaker 'inhuman' is commonly applied—albeit wrongly to the act rather than the individual.)

28. PRUSSIAN BLUE

An hour later, they were driving through the town of Margaret River, centre of the South-West wine industry. The main street was deserted, with little public lighting. As Worse expected, Fiendisch was heading for the same map reference that he had found in Zheng's GPS. He had turned toward the coast, then north on Caves Road. Worse estimated that they were ten minutes behind, and was happy with the gap. Millie was still driving, following instructions from their own satnav, which Worse had programmed.

'Are you hungry? Restaurants look closed,' he added, 'but I have some take-away.' Worse had reached for a shopping bag on the rear seat. He tore a piece of olive bread from a small loaf and passed it to Millie, then took some for himself.

Worse was constantly checking Fiendisch's movement on the laptop. He wondered if Millie shared his own sense that they were getting closer to finding Nicholas, or at least, an explanation for his disappearance.

'He's stopped. We turn right in a kilometre. He's about a kilometre inland from there. It'll be a minor road. Start slowing down. As we turn in, switch off the lights.'

The turn-off wasn't difficult to see; it was signposted 'Verita's Winery. Wine Tasting. Cellar Door Sales.'

'Who's Verita, do you think?' said Millie.

Worse replied as if changing the subject. 'Did you know that there are now more apostrophes in the world than locusts?'

The side road was narrow but sealed, winding slightly through stands of karri forest. From time to time there were unsealed tracks disappearing off on either side. After about six hundred metres, Worse told Millie to slow to a crawl, and turn into one of these. It was rough, and hard to read the surface without lights, but they found that it led to a clearing and what looked, in the moonlight, to be a gravel pit. At Worse's request, Millie turned the car to face back toward the road, and switched off the engine. Worse opened the sunroof and they sat quietly, listening to the sound of the forest, breathing in the scent of eucalypt.

'What's the plan?' Millie said.

'The plan? Search, rescue, destroy, punish, celebrate. Easy.'

Worse reached forward to the Comand panel and pressed for telephone. He dialled Spoiling. The call was answered promptly but wearily.

'Worse? When I said meet for coffee, I was thinking, like most sane people, about ten o'clock. I forgot you were not in that company.'

'Sorry, Victor. So much perplexity, couldn't wait. Take this down before anything else.' Worse gave their GPS position.

'I'm just out of Margaret River with Nicholas's sister. We've followed Fiendisch down.' The call was on speakerphone, and Millie heard Spoiling sigh. 'He told his employees to kill us earlier. And just so you're not taken by surprise, you'll hear news of a brushfire off the Old Coast Road. In the fire is a car. In the car are two bodies. With the bodies I expect there are two handguns. Possibly more. That's why you'll be brought in.'

'And what part did you play in their unhappy fate?'

'Nothing. They were driving too fast, overconfident, lost control. Hit a kangaroo, maybe. Fortuitous, for us.'

'Mm. Worse, I've been making some enquiries about Fiendisch since our last conversation. He's no ordinary banker. Fiendisch is an alias; his real name is von Fierssenbad—'

'Fiendisch was an inspired substitution,' said Worse.

'I have to tell you he is dangerous. He has a bulky Interpol dossier. I'm very distressed that my suburban colleagues didn't take the sister's complaints seriously enough.'

'Millie,' said Worse.

'What?'

'The sister is named Millie.'

'Oh yes. My apologies. Worse.'

'Yes?'

'Try not to cause too much havoc.'

'Havoc? Havoc?' Worse sounded incredulous. 'Oh, you mean pandemonium. Of course not, Victor.'

Again there was a deep, audible sigh. 'At least keep Millie safe, even if you've no sense of what that means for yourself.'

'We've pulled off the road about four hundred metres short of the winery. It's called Verita's. We'll go ahead on foot and see what we can find. You should come on down. Margaret River's the ideal destination for an action-packed, and yet, intriguingly relaxed, getaway. Why, there are forests, caves, wineries, beaches—'

'Worse. No. No. No havoc. Enough perplexity. I feel a head-ache ...'

'Nice to talk, Victor.' Worse ended the call. He glanced at Millie. She was smiling.

'He's a very good man, very smart and very good. A philosopher detective.'

'I think I can hear that.' Millie hesitated. 'What was all that about a kangaroo? That was for my benefit, right? That's a local joke; you're having me on?'

'Unfortunately, no. It's a real hazard at night. Many a car has been written off and many a life lost. Kangaroos largely, of course.'

Millie was eyeing him suspiciously, her fixed smile suggesting she wasn't sure what expression to adopt. She found it hard to read Worse; the serious seemed enmeshed with obliquity and even the occasional fantastical. What about that post-subtle business? She had never heard of philosophers actually living on the Métro. For all she knew, all that was made up in the moment, just to needle her. She felt it was time to clarify something that had bothered her for days.

'What was that you were saying the other night about a feud in my family? Who was it with?'

'Oh, the Magnacarts,' said Worse. Again he pronounced it Marnacourts. 'Why do you bring that up, after kangaroos?'

'Because I've never heard of it, and it's my family.'

'The spelling is Magnacart, by the way.' Worse sequenced the letters. 'And I'm not surprised you've never heard of it. The feud was settled in the thirteenth century, and the story is passed only down the male lines of the two families. You'll need to ask Nicholas about it. Of course, he may feel he shouldn't tell you; that's been the tradition for seven centuries.'

Millie was indignant. 'Nicholas knows? Nicholas knows and hasn't told me?'

'Well, you'll have to ask him.' For Worse, this was a strategic assertion that Nicholas would be found alive. 'Just don't be surprised if he says he knows nothing about it.'

Now she was outraged. 'How do you know about it, anyway?'

'Someone once told me.' Worse drew the exchange to a close by opening his door and going to the boot, returning with a bag.

'Take this.' He handed her a small torch. 'Silence your phone. Leave the keys under the seat.'

He transferred a few items to his backpack, closed the roof, and without looking at her said, 'Ready?' In response, Millie opened her door, and they made their way to the sealed road, turning left toward the winery.

After about three hundred metres, the forest thinned, and they could make out the cultivated rows of a vineyard, just perceptible in the cloud-diffused moonlight. The road widened and split. On the left, a sign indicated parking for tourist coaches. On the right, there was a car park. Ahead was a grand turning circle in front of a large building. There were no lights showing. A large sign read Cellar Door, with an arrow pointing to the left. To the right was a more industrial frontage, probably the production area of the winery, thought Worse.

He whispered to Millie, 'The Range Rover must be parked at the rear. There's probably a private residence. Follow me.'

Worse ran to the right-hand side of the building, edged forward, and looked around the corner. He fell back, and told Millie what he had seen.

'There is another building, with lights. And his car. I want to have a look here first.' He gestured back toward the cellar door, and they moved in that direction.

When they reached the large corrugated iron sliding door on the winery side, Worse tried to open it. There was no give at all, and no visible lock. To one side, there was a smaller access door, and Worse pushed on it pessimistically. To his surprise it opened, and he turned to convey his satisfaction to Millie. They both stepped through, and he closed it behind them.

They stood still to listen, and accommodate to the gloom. The space was suffused with a dim fluorescent light from safety and exit signs. They were in a truck loading-bay, and above their heads were two heavy-duty chain blocks suspended from a steel girder. To one side was parked a forklift tractor. There were several pallets loaded with cartons of bottles. To the rear of the building there was a soft glisten from gigantic stainless steel vats and crushing beds, and to their right they could make out a floor-to-roof rack system. Worse briefly shone his torch on some of the stacked plastic drums. Preservatives, precipitators, flocculants, and pure ethyl alcohol.

On the left were steel stairs leading to a mezzanine floor. Worse took Millie's hand briefly so she would follow. On the upper level were offices and an assay lab, and they worked their way along to find another staircase at the rear. They descended to floor level, moved between the vats and some enormous oak barrels, and found themselves in a bottling area. This led around on the left toward the public cellar door entrance. Here, the concrete floor was polished, there were free-standing racks of bottles and comfortable seating, and the walls were decorated with vineyard scenes and posters portraying historical winemaking. A large timber counter faced the entrance, and Worse slipped behind it, noting wine-racks, sinks and a dishwasher, and a cash drawer with electronic payment facilities. For the whole exploration, he had paid particular attention to the floor, but had nowhere found it breached with a trapdoor. Without mentioning his purpose to Millie, he had wanted to assure himself that Nicholas was not secreted in this building.

Worse motioned for Millie to follow, and led her back to where they had entered. From the storage racks, he lifted down three drums of ethyl alcohol.

'They supplement fermentation with this,' he whispered, 'Fortifying. Perfectly legal. Hold your breath.'

He broke the seals with a pocketknife, unscrewed their caps, and poured the contents onto the floor. When the last one was empty enough to manoeuvre easily he lifted it to pour alcohol over other containers in the lower racks, and then laid a liquid fuse to the door. Putting it down, he bundled Millie to the access door, and out into the fresh air. Only then did she become aware of how polluted was the atmosphere inside. Worse reached into his backpack and handed her a box of matches.

'Stay hidden here. Don't go back in under any circumstances. I'll text you if we need a diversionary fire.' As he spoke, Worse entered the message into his phone in preparation.

'It will just say "Now". Be careful. Most of the ethanol will have vaporized and it could go off like a bomb. After lighting it, run to the vines and hide. I'll find you.'

He pointed to the neat rows of wired vines in the semidarkness, and touching her hand gently, addressed the subject that he knew to be the most important in her world.

'If Nicholas is here, I will find him.'

Worse slipped away without looking at her response. He was still holding the backpack and, out of Millie's view, he removed Zheng's pistol and put it inside his jacket, then reshouldered the pack.

From the corner of the winery he now surveyed the other building more carefully. It was about thirty metres distant, singlestoreyed, and he could make out a large satellite dish, along with a few smaller ones, on the iron roof. There were more interior lights on than he had noted before. Fiendisch's vehicle obscured the main entrance, and Worse used it as cover to cross the open space. When he reached it, he could see that the rear tailgate had been left open. He glanced inside; the rugs that had concealed him earlier were undisturbed. Through its windows, he could now examine the main entrance to the building. It was recessed within a trellised portico area accommodating a garden and some ornamental trees.

The front door was open—Fiendisch was expecting Ritchie and Kev, reasoned Worse—and he could now hear voices. He made a dash to the garden on the right side of the entrance, almost colliding with a wheelbarrow in the dark. Moving under the cover of the trees, he was able to reach the wall only two metres from the door, through which some weak yellow light was falling on the paved entrance. Worse was straining to interpret what he could hear when suddenly the glow he had been staring at shifted and darkened as somebody inside moved close to the front door. One voice was now clear.

'Where are you taking me?'

Two men emerged from the door, one in front stumbling and obstructing, his wrists evidently bound behind, followed by a large bald man pushing him roughly toward the Range Rover. Next appeared Fiendisch. In one hand he carried a pistol, from the other swung an elastic luggage tie.

'Somewhere scenic. Very nice. Be quiet.'

Worse, well aware of Fiendisch's ruthlessness, was still shocked by the ice in his voice. Their prisoner was resisting, making progress slow. He briefly broke free of his escort's grip and turned back toward Fiendisch and, in the light from the house, afforded Worse a clear view of his face. It was Nicholas, recognizable from a photograph that Millie carried.

'I have codes embedded. You need me. You will lose your accounts. You will lose defences.' Nicholas's voice was impressively matter-of-fact. If this had any effect on Fiendisch, it didn't show.

'Keep a grip on him, Stronk. We need to get to the cave and back before the staff arrive.'

Worse weighed up his options. Challenging them now while Fiendisch had his gun drawn could be very messy. And he didn't know who else might be in the house. On the other hand, once they got to the vehicle, giving chase would be difficult as the Mercedes was hidden nearly half a kilometre away. Moreover, Nicholas was clearly in imminent danger. It was time for a diversion, time for some big sister trouble, as Ritchie had put it. Worse shielded the glow from his mobile screen and pressed send.

Even to Worse, the result was spectacular. The others had still not reached the Range Rover when there was an enormous explosion, the whole winery end of the roof lifting off as if carried by a cushion of blinding yellow light. Worse had instinctively dropped down against the wall, but the other three, more exposed to the shock wave, were pushed back. Several windows of the Range Rover were blown out, and Worse was aware of falling glass from house windows just along from where he was hiding. Burning debris started raining down on the clearing, some coming close to the house.

Worse had immediate concern for Millie. He edged further back into the shadows, as the front of the house was now illuminated as if in daylight, and reached for his phone. Immediately, there was a message from Millie: *I'm ok. Was that big enough?*

There were further smaller explosions from the winery. Fiendisch was the first to speak. 'Get him back inside and locked up. Ring the fire service. Then come back and help me.'

Stronk said nothing, but began manhandling Nicholas back inside. Fiendisch ran a few metres toward the burning building and stopped. He had pocketed his gun but still held the luggage tie. Now he took out his mobile and made a call, half protecting himself from the heat behind the Range Rover. At one point, he turned to stare back at the house. His spectacles made two yellow discs as they picked up reflected firelight. Worse couldn't hear his words above the roar of the fire. He was now lying down against the wall, but still felt badly exposed. Burning cinders were filling the yard, getting very close to him. If he were Fiendisch, he would be thinking that the winery was beyond rescue, but the house might be saved.

Worse had calculated that if there were others in the house, they would have shown themselves. There was another enormous crash as more of the roof collapsed. Fiendisch, still on his mobile, instinctively turned away to look at the winery, and Worse took his chance. He sprang up, crossed to the entrance, and darted in through the open door.

For the next few seconds his actions were automatic. He drew his pistol. He kept to one side to be out of sight to Fiendisch. A bulky key ring had been left on a side table; he pocketed it. Before him was a wide hallway leading to glass doors at the rear. Through these he could see Stronk struggling with Nicholas. They seemed to have entered another wing of the building, not visible from the winery. Worse glanced around to the front door; Fiendisch was still on his phone, looking at the fire. That must be a very important conversation, thought Worse; I would be hosing the roof of the house to extinguish flying embers. That was the rule in this part of the world.

Worse ran to the glass doors. They were unlocked. He passed through quietly and found himself in a glass-roofed link area. Stronk and Nicholas were out of view in the next section, but he could hear Stronk trying to inform the emergency services of their location, while suppressing Nicholas from shouting into the open line. At the end of the link Worse entered a large, carpeted office. Stronk was pushing Nicholas across the space to a door at the other end. Neither saw him. He glanced back to check on Fiendisch; there was no sign of him. Worse then crossed to his left where he had a wall behind him and could see the entrance he had just used.

The others were still unaware of his presence when he called loudly, 'Stronk. Let him go.'

Nicholas had the sense to take advantage of Stronk's surprise, and break away. His hands were still secured behind him. Stronk turned to see Worse's pistol pointed steadily at his head. The range was three metres.

'Stronk, don't even begin to move. You, come here. Don't get between us.' Worse addressed Nicholas without taking his eyes off Stronk.

As Nicholas crossed the room with surprising composure, Worse was unable to suppress his delight. 'Dr Misgivingston, I presume?'

'I am. Who are you?'

'I'm Worse.'

'Worse!' repeated Nicholas, with a confused relief. 'Worse, he's got a gun.'

'I'm sure he has. Stand to my left with your back to me.'

Nicholas did as he was asked. Worse took out a pocketknife and placed it in Nicholas's hands.

'Open it by feel,' he instructed, still looking at Stronk.

Nicholas did so and Worse used it to cut the tie between his wrists. He closed the knife with one hand and repocketed it. Stronk seemed suddenly to work out who he was.

'Worse? But, but Zheng.'

'No longer with us.'

'You killed Zheng?' Stronk looked incredulous. 'You're in fucking big trouble. He was like a son to the Admiral.' Now he looked murderous.

Worse was acutely aware that Fiendisch was expecting Stronk outside to help with the fire, and wanted to close business off with him quickly. However, here was a promising line of enquiry; maybe the Admiral was the person to whom Fiendisch reported.

'Zheng was a cheap killer, and not very good at his job. He even gave me this.' Worse waved the pistol slightly.

'They'll fucking kill you badly. Fucking badly.' Stronk seemed almost sympathetic for Worse's fate. That ugly, shaved head was quite expressive, Worse decided. 'I've been told about them.' Now Stronk appeared to be relishing the thought.

'You weren't just being told. You were being warned, you fuckwit,' said Worse.

Stronk's face flashed through vacant to comprehending to murderous again.

'Lie on your stomach with your hands behind your back. Nicholas, tie him up, will you? Don't get between us.'

Nicholas retrieved the cut tie and refashioned it to a suitable length.

'So, Stronk,' Worse continued casually, 'where do I find the Admiral? I have, of course, condolences to offer.'

'They'll find you, fucker, and you won't like it.'

'Tell me, Nicholas, how well did this man treat you?'

'He's a cruel bastard, Worse. He's kept me locked up for weeks. Calls himself Bad Warden, always threatening me. He was just telling me there's a secret limestone cave somewhere on the property and they were going to dump me in it.'

'Admiral's orders,' inserted Stronk defensively. Now the expression was conciliatory.

Worse was surprised that Fiendisch hadn't come to investigate the delay; he moved back to the link for a quick glance toward the front of the house.

Stronk timed his move to perfection. He rolled onto his side, unbalancing Nicholas, and his right hand, lightning fast, reached into his coat.

Worse saw the movement and the glint of gunmetal, but his line of sight had Nicholas too close to Stronk. Instinctively, he improved the trig by launching himself sideways across the room. Halfway to the floor he had the shot and fired a single round. Stronk fell back, his face bearing a coin-sized token in the centre of the forehead and an indelible expression of surprise.

Nicholas jumped up, staring at Worse.

'Can't reason with them. Take his gun,' was all Worse had to say as he stood up, rubbing the shoulder that had taken the fall. He looked again along the link room to the front of the house. Then he pointed to the rear. 'Where does that lead?'

'It's all the operations centre,' said Nicholas. 'That's where I was imprisoned.' His voice was shaken.

'There's no one there?'

'No.'

'I'll look later. We'll go out the front. There's one Fiendisch and three of us.'

'Who else is here?'

'You'll see.'

Worse took Stronk's gun carefully from Nicholas and checked it. It was a revolver, with a round in the breach.

'Do you know how to use this?' asked Worse.

'I think I have the general idea.'

Worse applied the safety, making sure Nicholas understood its action, and handed it back.

'Don't use it unless I tell you to. Let's go.'

Worse led the way toward the front door, checking each side for Fiendisch. Once through the door, he pushed Nicholas into the shadows that had previously provided his own cover. The fire had now shifted its intensity to the sales end of the building, and there was an intermittent crashing of broken glass and small explosions. There was less light from the fire now, but dawn wasn't far off. Worse's plan was to deal with Fiendisch only if forced to; his priority was to regroup with Millie and get her and Nicholas to safety.

He led Nicholas further around the edge of the portico garden, intending to make a run for the vines and find Millie. Worse was concerned that a whole lot had happened since they had last communicated, and decided it was probably safe to call her quietly. He took his mobile from a jacket pocket and speed-dialled her number with his left hand, the other still holding his pistol. He wasn't expecting the reply.

'So you are Worse.' It was Fiendisch's voice. He had read the name on Millie's phone.

'Hello Fiendisch, I thought it was time we met,' said Worse.

'I have the girl.'

'That's very melodramatic for a banker, Fiendisch. Shouldn't you be saying "I have the mortgage documents ready to sign", something like that? Anyway, you haven't time for this; you must have interest to calculate, exorbitant fees to invent, that sort of thing.'

'You will not be so amusing dead, Worse.'

'Do you have the Admiral's permission to speak like that?' Worse was deliberately needling.

'Come into the clear with your hands in the air, or I kill the girl.'

Worse had a sense that Fiendisch was quite close, that what he was hearing was part telephone, part conducted voice. He covered the phone against his thigh and whispered to Nicholas.

'Whatever you see, whatever seems to be happening, don't do anything. Leave it all to me. Trust me.' Nicholas nodded. Worse raised the phone and addressed Fiendisch.

'How do I know you've got the girl?' It was the exchange's first reference to another person that Nicholas had heard. Fiendisch rang off.

'Stay hidden,' Worse whispered to Nicholas. 'He might think you are locked away inside.'

They saw Fiendisch edge out from behind the Range Rover. He was pulling Millie close to him, his gun pressed against her temple. Worse guessed that the luggage strap was around her neck. She was completely quiet, and in the gloom, Nicholas couldn't see who it was. Worse moved further around the garden, away from Nicholas and away from the light at the front door.

'Come out with your hands in the air, or I shoot the girl.' Fiendisch repeated.

Worse stood up, pointing his pistol at Fiendisch. The latter adjusted his posture rapidly, indicating that Worse's position had surprised him.

'Drop the gun.'

'Fiendisch, you're not a killer. You're a banker for God's sake.' Worse was delaying. Every minute toward sunrise gave him more light for a clear shot. 'How is the banking business, anyway?' Worse's pistol was still aimed at Fiendisch.

'Drop the gun.'

Worse was acutely attuned to the resonance in the voice, particularly its authority. He would test it once more, deliberately adopting the given name.

'That reminds me, Karl, we were just having an interesting talk about post-subtlety. Have you heard of the post-subtle, Karl? In the banking world, I believe, it would once have been called the unapologetic. In Europe, it's—'

'Drop the gun.'

Very slightly, the voice had changed again, shifting just a nuance from command toward request.

'Speaking of banks,' continued Worse, 'and tarnished wealth generally, I was thinking only yesterday about the oxidation states of gold. Did you know how—'

'What are you talking about, Worse? I said drop the gun immediately.'

'Karl, you're a numbers man. You must have studied some elementary game theory.'

'I don't play games. Drop the gun or I kill the girl.'

Worse judged it was time to add some mild insult into the confusion and draw hostility toward himself. His tone, which had been relaxed and conversational, and not at all consonant with the act of pointing a weapon, now hardened slightly.

'You really don't have a Prussian blue, do you? Have you not heard the expression "every tread and turn", Karl? Let me acquaint you with some priors. Zheng, gone. Ritchie, gone. Kev, gone.'

Worse waited. He saw Fiendisch look toward the front door, no doubt hoping to see reinforcement in the form of Stronk. Then he added pointedly, 'Stronk, gone. For a man who doesn't play games, you should at least take notice of the odds.'

In the improving light, Worse saw Fiendisch's gun waver slightly.

'You killed Zheng?' The emphasis on the name was mixed disbelief and reverence.

'He suffered, shall we say, a workplace accident. Perhaps I tipped him over the edge a little. But does he weigh heavily on my conscience, Karl? Precisely *mg*, as might a feather, Karl.'

'What are you talking about, Worse?'

'By the way, where should I repatriate his unpleasant mortal remains? To an Admiral somebody, I think?' Worse was hoping for information.

'He will kill you, Worse.'

'How is that possible, the very same being your intention? Are you thinking you might fail, Karl?'

The light was better, and Worse had a clearer target. He could almost recognize Millie, and hoped that Nicholas couldn't see her that well. His gun was still pointing at Fiendisch, and he began to walk toward him.

'Stop right there, Worse. Drop your gun.'

Here was the endgame, and Worse was sure that Fiendisch didn't understand. He continued walking, pistol held at eye level, gaze locked along the Prussica, aiming steadily. Worse said nothing; control and confidence were draining, one man to the other, with every step.

Seven metres, six metres, his advance unhurried, all the time both becoming more discrete targets. Worse remained silent: *My enemy's incomprehension is become my power.*

Then Fiendisch complied exactly as Worse anticipated. Judging Worse to be the greater threat and Millie a diminishing asset, he turned his gun from Millie to Worse. Before it lined up, Worse fired; another single shot to a centred roundel on the forehead. *And my enemy's power will obtain my preferment.*

Millie slipped her head out of the ligature, pulling away. Fiendisch's body toppled slightly, collapsed forward onto the tailgate, then to the ground. Worse hurried forward, pocketing his gun. Millie was shaking, eyeing him with caution. Then she put her arms around him.

'It's over, Millie. You're safe,' Worse said kindly. 'And Nicholas is safe. He's here.' Worse turned and called out, 'Nicholas.'

Nicholas leapt from the garden and hurried over, his recognition of Millie increasing as he ran.

'Millie? Millie! What are you doing here?'

They embraced, sobbing quietly.

Worse stepped back, removing his backpack. He collected Fiendisch's weapon, put the safety on and placed it inside. Then he held out his hand for Stronk's gun, also checking its safety and putting it away. He looked for Millie's mobile and found it beside Fiendisch's feet; he decided to return it at a later time.

It was almost sunrise, and in the distance they could hear sirens of the country fire service. The winery was burning quietly, beyond rescue, but the house looked undamaged apart from broken windows. The crew would soak the wreckage, put out the ember fires, and start an investigation.

'What do we do now?' asked Millie.

'You should know the routine by now,' said Worse, remembering a similar question at the Humboldt Bank. 'We go inside and make a pot of tea.'

Worse's description of **Victor Spoiling** as a philosopher detective was accurate. Apart from contributions to journals and conferences, he had written two monographs, *Unsteady State: Power, Protest and the Polis,* and *Moral Discriminators in a Policed Society.* The latter contains his widely quoted lemma (with proof, by *reductio*) that every volitional act has moral content. There is little doubt that had these works been read and understood within more senior ranks, their author would have found himself eased from the force as too thoughtful, or tactfully promoted into the company of the epauletted.

Worse's **locust inequality** is easily proven without recourse to laborious enumeration, using a mapping argument. For every single locust's sighting, an apostrophe is recorded, whereas for at least one occurrence of an apostrophe (Verita's) a locust is not.

29. *IN VINO* VERITA'S

Nicholas had never been allowed freedom of movement in the main house, so they explored together. They found the kitchen off to the right of the main hall at the rear, with a view of what Nicholas had called the operations centre wing on the left. To the right, into the distance, beautiful, rolling vineyards were taking form in the dawn light.

Millie and Nicholas sat at the table while Worse sorted out the facilities, getting the kettle started and putting out some mugs. As he searched for loose leaf tea, he phoned Spoiling. The line sounded odd and he guessed the reason.

'You're in flight, Victor?'

'Worse, what choice did I have? I keep getting reports of extraordinary things. You tell me about a burnt-out car that turns out to have assault weapons in the ashes. Then an explosion rocks half the South-West, then a giant inferno on your coordinates—'

'I saw that too, Victor,' interrupted Worse.

'And now some poor devil of a volunteer fire chief has just found a body in the car park.'

'How unfortunate. That would be Fiendisch. I'll keep the other body hidden in the house. What's your ETA?'

'Fifteen. What other body?'

'Seriously though, Victor, you might want to secure the Humboldt premises in Fremantle, and freeze all assets and transactions involving the bank, Verita's Wines, and Providence Portfolio. Also, there's a Charles Finistere in the picture. He needs to be interviewed, with respect.'

'Yes, yes. What do you mean, seriously? And what other body?'

'I'll have tea ready for you in the kitchen. Out.'

Worse had found only teabags, and was agitating them in a pot. Placing it on the table, he excused himself. He walked through to the front of the house and across to the Range Rover. Two fire volunteers stood nearby, staring at Fiendisch's body.

'Make sure no one interferes with this,' he said, gesturing as he approached.

Ignoring his own injunction, he bent down and secured a wallet and mobile from Fiendisch's clothes. Then he reached inside the back of the vehicle, and after removing his tracking device, pulled out one of the rugs, flicking it free of broken window glass. Before he covered Fiendisch, Worse spoke quietly, almost kindly, to his face. 'It was every tread and turn, Karl.' Without a glance at the others, he returned to the house.

In the hallway, he stopped to scan the call history of the mobile. The most recent contact, the call Fiendisch had made just after the explosion, was to a non-standard number. Worse recognized the ID prefix of a satellite phone. He returned to the kitchen and sat down opposite the others.

'What was going on here, Nicholas?'

'As far as I have managed to work out, they've set up a secret trading platform, a kind of stock exchange for criminal assets. People trade shares in illicit drug transfers, money laundering operations, internet scams, arms deals, banned exports, that sort of thing. I think they also buy and sell illicit software like skimming programs. The most frightening thing I saw was ignition code for a nuclear trigger. I recognized it because their clock subroutines have a super-criticality architecture with characteristic cross-links. They're known as loopstraps; the Soviets called them Manhattan Transfers and the Americans, Kremlin Ties. They're not mentioned in programming textbooks. A kid from Belarus told me about it years ago at a junior maths camp.'

Nicholas caught the instant concern on the others' faces, and hastened to add, 'Naturally, I corrupted it. It wouldn't switch on a light bulb now.'

'I miss the simple, gloomy humour of the Cold War,' said Worse, relieved. 'So, you are saying that an individual could have beneficial ownership without identifiable culpability?'

'And without getting their hands dirty, as it were. It took me a while to figure it out but I'm sure that was the idea. As well, of course, there's potential for an options market. On top of it all, the bank gets commissions and broking fees, loan interest, business introduction fees, currency trades and arbitrage margins.'

'Yes. I'm sure no avenue of usury was unexplored,' said Worse.

'I became too curious when they had me modelling insurance pricing for transactions that were non-existent in commodities that were undefined for risk scenarios that were more to do with discovery and interception and confiscation than acts of God. Naturally, they disguised the terminology, but it didn't take a lot to decipher the language. Given I had been told that I was developing financial instruments for the local wine industry, the whole enterprise started to look suspicious.'

'I'm not surprised,' observed Worse. 'Why did they isolate you? What happened that drove them to bring you here by force?'

'Well, I suppose I started to question some of the material I was asked to work with, model design, parameter settings, basic things. I've always seen discussion and debate to be part of the process of research and development and refinement.'

'Rightly so,' said Worse. Millie nodded in agreement. She had a hand on Nicholas's arm.

'Anyway, it wasn't well received by Fiendisch. He said things like: just write the software and make sure it works. It all soured quite quickly, actually.' Nicholas's words slowed, and he stared reflectively into his tea. Worse and Millie gave him time to continue.

'Naturally, I've spent a lot of time thinking about things. The day his thugs tied me up and bundled me into the back of an off-roader—that very day, I had received an email from Paulo in the Ferendes.'

'The Ferendes?' questioned Worse.

'That's where I had been working before coming to Perth. Paulo is in charge of the language research station there. It's run from Cambridge by Edvard Tøssentern. Ferent languages are very special historically.'

'Tøssentern of inductive graphs?' asked Worse.

'The same. He knows Rodney Thwistle, and it was RT who emailed you and me setting up an introduction. I regret I did not meet you earlier.'

'I suspect that email was what brought their villain Zheng in my direction,' said Worse.

'Anyway, I've figured out there's a special connection between the Humboldt and Banco Ferende. Paulo's message about the extent of Chinese logging in the north set off some kind of alarm.'

'Can you explain to us the Chinese connection?' said Worse.

'I wish I could. Fiendisch was definitely not the top person. He took orders from someone called Feng. I'm sure he's the one they also call the Admiral. I don't know where he's situated. They had me setting up Société Générale accounts and after a while I realized it was nothing to do with that reputable French bank, but a rather facile camouflage for the gang of generals who seem to be involved in international crime. Their financial centre seems to be the Banco Ferende in Madregalo. I think all the development was being done here, using Fiendisch's expertise, and mine for that matter, with a view to operating out of Madregalo, and probably the Humboldt as well. There's another thing: I need to let Paulo and Edvard know that there's more than rapacious logging happening on the northern plain. The commodity signatures point more to mining, and I suspect they're helping themselves to mineral sands and rare earths.'

Worse leaned back in his chair, looking at Nicholas. He was calculating the size of their problem.

'Do you think the criminal operations are sanctioned by the Chinese government?' he asked.

'I think that's very unlikely, as Beijing periodically orders exhibition trials and harsh punishments to discourage official corruption. But the People's Liberation Army is a law unto itself, and there were certainly PLA assets deployed in the Ferendes. There could well be a blind-eye factor in play, of course, but when I was there our belief was that the logging scam was run by a cadre of senior and probably retired officers abusing their privileges.'

'In which case, if the whole enterprise were exposed, Beijing is likely to prosecute on the side of good rather than be disgraced.

Excuse me.' Worse stood up. He had heard, before the others, an approaching helicopter.

The pilot chose to put down behind the house, and Nicholas and Millie had a view through the kitchen window of a short, middle-aged man wearing a green anorak step to the ground and walk across to Worse. They shook hands, embraced briefly, and spoke for a minute, before Worse led the way around into the house. As they entered the kitchen, Worse made introductions.

'This is our missing person, Nicholas Misgivingston, and Nicholas's sister Millie from the UK. This is Inspector Victor Spoiling, abbreviated in the ranks, though not within his hearing, to Spectre Spoiling. Tea, Victor?'

'I'm fine for now, thank you,' Victor answered as he shook hands with the others, before sitting at a chair offered by Worse.

Before resuming his own seat, Worse removed items from his pockets and backpack, placing them on the table in front of Spoiling, and naming them as he did so.

'Fiendisch's gun. Stronk's gun; he's through there,' Worse pointed to the rear wing. 'Fiendisch, you saw out front. Here's his wallet, keys, and mobile.' Worse held on to the last item. 'I was hoping I could look at this.'

Spoiling nodded. 'Twenty-four hours, and I learn what you learn.' He knew he had a better deal than if he sent it to his own IT squad.

'Now reassure me, Victor, you have kept up your fluency in Mandarin,' said Worse brightly as he repocketed Fiendisch's mobile.

'I feel a headache coming on.'

'What Nicholas has learned,' Worse continued, 'is that whatever was going on between here and the Humboldt, and he thinks it was some kind of virtual proceeds-of-crime stock exchange, the Chinese were in charge. Do you know of an Admiral Feng?'

'No,' replied Spoiling, 'but we were tracking a Chinese party called Zheng with connections to Fiendisch. We lost him two days ago, near your place, actually. You couldn't help us with our enquiries in that matter, could you, Worse?'

Spoiling spoke as if it were an afterthought, but in professional matters he was a master dissembler. Worse supposed that he had been connected with Zheng many hours before.

'He did drop in, but missed me and quickly left, I believe.' Suitably parsed, it was all true.

'Mm.' Spoiling looked at Worse with subtle suspicion. He was filing it away verbatim for re-examination.

'Nicholas was about to show us the operations centre. Will you join us?' Worse suggested innocently. 'We'll need those,' he added, pointing to Fiendisch's keys.

They all stood up, chairs scraping on the tiled floor. Millie had been looking tired, but the idea seemed to energize her. She was keen to see where her brother had been kept prisoner, to understand better his experience, and to cleanse her mind of imagery that had haunted her over the weeks of not knowing.

As they walked through the first office, Spoiling turned to study the lifeless portrait that was Stronk's face, neatly punctuated by a bloodless full stop on the forehead.

'Your work, I see.' Something held his interest, and he added, 'What was the last thing he saw, Worse?'

'He didn't share that confidence. Inconsiderate to the end, I thought.' Worse was disinclined to give an account of his flight across the room.

He became aware of Millie looking at him, but avoided her eye. Four men dead in the one night; for a mathematics don, that was unusual. She must have very mixed feelings about him. He knew he had mixed feelings about himself. Spoiling evidently sensed the tension, and understood it; he addressed Millie with a sort of emphatic kindness.

'Well done, you and Worse. You saved your brother's life.' He continued looking at her.

Millie looked at him, then back at Worse. She stepped across to Worse and put her arms around him.

'I can't thank you enough.'

She started crying softly. Worse was feeling emotional himself. It didn't help to have had no sleep. He put his arms around Millie's shoulders, closing his eyes against the start of his own tears. Now he could feel her shaking. Nicholas came up to them and placed his arms around both, remaining silent. Spoiling was looking away.

It was Worse who ended the embrace; there was someone he wanted to talk to. 'You three go ahead. I'll catch up.'

He took his mobile from a pocket and called Sigrid Blitt.

The **loopstrap** code in super-critical clock routines is still officially classified from the Cold War era. (In some quarters, Nicholas would be deemed a security risk for knowing its design.) Modern refinements built on solid-state laser hardware are used in top-secret military-precision (as opposed to commercial access) GPS software, in real-time missile interception platforms and, of course, in nuclear weaponry. Recent advances in clock design supporting cross-border superfast algorithmic stock trading do not use loopstrap techniques, but should be a cause of strategic concern: though protected by high order banking encryption, technical performance in this application is now dangerously close to military specification.

30. *FAMILLE OBLIGE*

When Worse joined the others, Nicholas was talking excitedly about the computing system and the trading platform that he was made to design, relating his discoveries and hypotheses regarding its criminality and disguise. The small space to which he had been confined only hours before was now presented with a slightly incongruous pride.

Millie was listening attentively, and proudly. Spoiling was listening attentively, and analytically. He had called in a software forensics team, but was not one to abnegate informed leadership of any investigation.

Worse looked around. You deserve to be proud, Nicholas, he thought, surviving this. And you, Millie, you should be proud, coming to find your brother.

Spoiling was quiet. Worse had seen it before. He would miss nothing that was said, but reserve questions until after the narrative had run its course. Worse himself was less restrained.

'Apart from Fiendisch and Stronk, did you see anyone else in the time you were here?'

'Only Vex, who came each day to cook and clean. I tried to get him to help me, get a message out, but he was even more scared of Stronk than I was.'

'No one else?'

'No. But I did hear someone. He was talking to Fiendisch. I could hear the voices, but not what was said. Stronk told me he was called Zheng, and that I wouldn't want to meet him. He just kept saying, "You don't want to meet Zheng." I suspect he was speaking for himself as well.'

'You never saw Charles Finistere?'

'No.'

'So there was no internet connection into this workspace?'

'No. If I needed outside sources, Fiendisch provided the information, and occasionally gave me supervised access.'

Spoiling had separated a little from the group, and was shuffling through stacks of papers, appearing not to be listening. He interrupted, without looking up.

'Where did that occur, the access?'

'Fiendisch would bring in his own laptop with wireless. None of the machines in here was enabled.'

Spoiling turned to face them. 'I think it would be fine if you all got away from here now. Go back to Perth. We will need statements in a few days. Thank you for your help, Nicholas. What caused the winery to explode, Worse?'

'There was some kind of spill. Gas leak. Bad electrics. A rogue spark. Who knows?'

'Mm. The fortuitous accompanies you closely, Worse, much as effect does cause, I always think. I trust the fire investigation will confirm your speculation. Are you fixed for transport?'

'If Nicholas can drive, we'll take my car. Millie and I need sleep.'

Spoiling walked out with them, locking the operations centre as they left. At the front door, he stopped to take in the scene. A fire team was still training hoses on the winery. Local police were guarding Fiendisch's body. A television news van was driving into the clearing.

'My team will be here shortly. I'll be in contact, Worse.'

Worse nodded as he and Spoiling shook hands. Spoiling turned to shake hands with Nicholas, and then with Millie. He had positioned himself so the others couldn't hear, and leaned forward to speak to her.

'Sometimes, events determine our lives. Then necessity determines sufficiency. You have found a good friend.'

He didn't wait for her response, but set off briskly toward the news crew. Millie, Nicholas and Worse walked around the destroyed winery to the access road, and along to Worse's car.

Worse and Millie slept for most of the drive home, while Nicholas found his way using the in-car navigation. When they reached the Grosvenor, Worse was awake, and gave instructions about where to park. He noted that Zheng's vehicle was no longer there.

He had invited Nicholas to stay with Millie in the spare apartment. Nicholas's own rental in Fremantle would be searched by police, in view of the break-ins, after which they would have clearance to return and collect personal possessions.

Nicholas was also given the use of a computer, and one of his first acts was to transfer his considerable account balances from Banco Ferende to one of the global majors with branches in the Ferendes. He also contacted his family, Rodney Thwistle, Edvard Tøssentern, and Paulo, and reconnected with his international software clients to explain his disappearance.

While he was doing this, Worse was in his workshop analysing Fiendisch's phone. He found numbers he recognized: Zheng, Ritchie, the winery fixed line and so on. But what was of most interest were two satellite numbers linked to devices both of which were currently located in the Ferendes. Worse was not immediately able to identify their account holders, but he logged the call history and set up a program to track their geographical movement. He wrote a short report of his findings for Spoiling.

Worse also put greater effort into identifying Charles Finistere. The address given in Securities Commission records was the same as that of Fiendisch, and there was very little else to discover. Directors' fees were deposited within the Humboldt, and the Humboldt seemed to have a very fluid interchange with accounts at Banco Ferende. Worse concluded that Finistere was a sleeping partner, and probably a fraudulent one, used to satisfy Australian fiduciary and domicile regulations. He informed Spoiling of this suspicion. In return, Spoiling reported that he had searched the Fiendisch house and there was no evidence of any other party having lived there. Also, two Chinese nationals had been detained trying to gain entry to the Humboldt at night. They were being questioned. Interviews of Vex and other winery staff had not been helpful.

Nicholas used his newly found freedom to investigate Fiendisch's project. His suspicions were largely confirmed. The software platform was in place to run a dual listing commodities market in Perth and Madregalo, using the Margaret River server. Some of the encryption was unfamiliar to him, and he consulted Worse. To his amazement, Worse had it deciphered inside half an hour.

'I've seen something very similar before,' Worse explained, without elaboration. It was a variant of the DPA method.

In response to Paulo's request of some weeks earlier, Nicholas also purchased high-resolution satellite imagery of the northern plain on Greater Ferende. The environmental devastation was shocking, and there was obvious evidence of mining in the path of deforestation.

It was clear to Worse that the Ferendes, a country to which he had never paid any attention, was at the forefront of events. And now that he knew about Banco Ferende, it was much easier to trace the deposits into Zheng's Hong Kong account. Their origin was a trust fund in Madregalo, and Worse set up a systematic attack to uncover its identity.

With regard to their personal safety, Worse felt that Nicholas and Millie were not at substantial risk, given that the local criminal apparatus had been dismantled. He was less confident for himself. He had been warned that the individual known as Admiral Feng would seek revenge for Zheng's disappearance, and might already have other agents in Perth. Worse would not accept personal risk that was indefinite in nature and duration. His recourse was to find Feng and mitigate it. He would go to Madregalo.

The others were pleased when he announced this. Millie had wanted to return to England via the Ferendes so that she could see Nicholas's work at the LDI station. All three therefore made joint arrangements to travel together, and Worse informed Spoiling of their plan. Nicholas discovered that Edvard and Anna had decided to revisit the station, and their flights from England were organized so that everyone could meet in Madregalo and travel overland together.

All these plans were in place within forty-eight hours of returning from the South-West. They had hardly left the Grosvenor, except to visit Nicholas's flat in Fremantle in order to collect his and Millie's belongings. On the way there, they drove past the Humboldt Bank. It looked sombre and lifeless. Worse thought about Fiendisch, and found his dislike for the person diluted by sadness. There had been a man of obvious intellect, who apparently managed to discover, or somehow acquire, the DPA. Worse would have enjoyed a conversation on the subject. Instead, they had talked like monsters, and Fiendisch was dead from it.

Millie and Nicholas were based in the spare apartment, but they socialized, had meals, and conducted all their business in Worse's side. On the afternoon before they were to fly out, Worse happened to hear the others in the lounge room, and left his bedroom to join them. He had been reading the chapter on criminal syndicates in Shin Wah's *A Scrutable History of China*, and wanted to pass it on to Nicholas.

As he entered the room, Millie stood up. She looked confronting, and directed her words at him with an uncharacteristic pressure of speech. She was clearly very upset.

'Nicholas knows nothing about that feud story, he swears. Why would you do that? What sort of person are you? You make stuff up, you hurt people, you kill people, you kill people without remorse. You are a ... a big hoodwinker.'

Worse stared at her, shocked. He felt the start of anger, but said nothing. He looked behind him for a chair, and moved to sit down. He had not expected to be attacked.

And he would not have expected his reaction, which was total capitulation to an exhaustion that suddenly possessed him. He wanted nothing more than to withdraw. A response that took form defensively—What do you know of my remorse?—was silenced in his mind by the reflexive: *What did he know of his own remorse?*

Fiendisch's words, 'I will kill the girl', had played in Worse's thoughts repeatedly. Each time he felt a dead chill, recomputed the wager, saw Fiendisch move his gun from Millie, and was weakened almost paralytic with relief.

Worse was staring absently at Millie, and she was glaring back, her face reddened. Nicholas had sat down. He looked confused and embarrassed. Worse forced himself out of passivity to speak.

It was unpremeditated, and he wasn't really sure where it came from.

'Emily, what is your experience of self-forgiveness?'

Millie stayed silent. Then she did what mathematicians throughout history have done when abandoned by their most obedient and persuading servant, deduction. She burst into tears. Nicholas jumped up and put his arms around her, just saying her name tenderly.

Worse stood up, said 'Excuse me', and walked through to his bedroom, still holding Shin Wah's *History*. He wanted to be away from her. He needed to talk to Sigrid. Most of all, he wanted to be asleep.

Two hours later, he was awakened by a gentle knock on his bedroom door.

'Come in.'

Worse was lying fully clothed on his bed, and sat up as Nicholas entered.

'We owe you an apology for earlier. Millie is beside herself over her outburst. She can't understand why she said those things. She knows, and I know, that we owe our lives to you. We can't overstate how grateful we are for your help, and your generosity.'

'Nicholas, neither of you owes me an apology. Millie is dealing with what she has seen. I understand that. I'm also dealing with it. Not very well, as it happens.'

Nicholas took this in but let it pass. He seated himself on the end of the bed.

'I need to talk to you,' he added, 'about that family story. The male line thing.'

Worse looked at him without responding, and Nicholas continued. 'I did tell Millie that I knew nothing about it, and I honestly believed that to be true. That's why she exploded at you. She thought you were playing some mind game. But I'm now having doubts. I think I was told something when I was about six. Six, Worse! He thought I was man enough to handle that gruesome stuff. As well as I remember, I was wide-awake for one terrifying night and then I put it completely out of my mind. I've never thought about it since, it was so repressed.'

Worse was sympathetic. 'Six does seem very unkind. Your father must have had a good reason to tell you then. Ensuring the story passed on.'

'And somehow it has. This afternoon, I've remembered a dream I had last night. The whole thing: fighting, exhaustion, blood. The vision of Jesus, the swints. It was as if I were there.'

'You were there, Nicholas, in the dream. That's exactly how the story does pass on.'

Nicholas appeared to process this. Then something occurred to him.

'How do you know our story? Only the family knows.'

'Two families.'

Nicholas stared at Worse. 'What are you saying? Who are you, really?'

'Richard Worse. Richard Magnacart Worse. Family motto for seven centuries, "*Famille Oblige*". Family crest, three swints. Same as yours from that day.'

Nicholas continued to look intently at Worse. 'It is *Famille Oblige*, yes.' He spoke quietly and seemed lost in thought for several seconds. 'I've never met a Magnacart before. I'd forgotten the name. You know, in all the circumstances of Stronk and so on, we never really introduced ourselves.' He held out his hand, then added, 'Is that why you helped?'

'*Famille Oblige*? Perhaps it was. I thought I helped because Millie asked.'

Nicholas nodded slowly, looking knowingly at Worse. 'Millie remembers that you offered.'

Worse showed no response. Nicholas continued. 'That's a nice connection, the motto. Can I tell Millie you're a Magnacart?'

'It won't be very meaningful to her, without the story.'

Nicholas ignored the implication. He stood up. 'When you're ready, come out for supper. Millie's been salve baking.'

31. PRINCE NEFARI

Madregalo, the historic and royal capital of the Ferendes, has more the character of a large town than a city. It nestles picturesquely into the bay, dominated from its higher reaches by the grand Palace L'Orphania. At night, that building's pink marble walls luminesce ethereally, long past the time when commoners below must see their way with very mundane and unpalatial electric lighting.

There is one long, timber pier leading into the bay, extended seaward with several pontoon sections. Tradition has it, and contemporary log charts support the belief, that it reaches to the exact point in the bay where HMS *King of Kent* dropped anchor in 1816. A light-rail tram carries tourists to a quaint, covered terminus at the end of the fixed portion. From there, even in good weather, only the brave venture forward on a pontoon walkway to capture the view of the settlement enjoyed by Captain Joseph and his party.

In Madregalo, there is none of the urban devastation of surrounding mountainsides, or high-rise construction on the waterfront, that blight so many cities of the developing world. That distinction belongs to La Ferste, the undisputed Ferende commercial and industrial capital. Situated forty kilometres to the east, it is built on land reclaimed from the Peril River delta. There are to be found the shipping port, the international airport, skyscrapers housing chain hotels and global corporations, and a night-life notorious even in Hong Kong.

But it is Madregalo where power resides, in the Parliament, in the Executive, and in those venerable institutions, such as Banco

Ferende and the Military Academy, that resisted relocation to the glitz of La Ferste. It is to this city-town with the great jetty and the historic waterfront that a visitor must come in search of influence or favour. And he will soon learn that success is not affirmed in the streets of the people, even though they house the tokens of a democratic state. For towering over every individual and every institution is the power of the Palace and its single resident: the absolute ruler of the Ferendes, Prince Nefari.

Prince Nefari the Beneficent, protector of the waters and the lands, seer, sage, superman, reputably descended from Rep'husela herself. Quite how a royal lineage could be traced to a virgin queen is not explained, and must never be questioned. Nor should comment be passed on the Prince personally, or royal consumption and display, or Palace interference in affairs of state, or the wider imbalance of Crown and Constitution. Even the most trusted audience in public will be thickened with informants, and transgressors are quickly made aware of the harshest law of *lèse-majesté* of any monarchy in the world.

And though the Parliament ostensibly forms a traditional cabinet government from elected representatives, important decisions are referred to the Palace and the Prince's Council of Secretaries. Some matters, such as international affairs, foreign investment, and control of the military, bypass the parliament completely. The original LDI submission to work in the Ferendes, for example, was negotiated directly between Tøssentern and a Secretary, with no input from the government.

Of course, that miscegenation of feudal monarchy and modern cosmopolitan society, being inherently unstable, requires power to maintain its uneasy equilibrium. Excessive power, not restricted to the ordinary instruments of fascist oppression: nepotism, censorship, sham judicial process, imprisonment and disappearance. Here is something far more awesome and effective: the Divine Right of the Royal Line of Rep'husela, enshrined in the Constitution, advertised by that unworldly physicality of L'Orphania, and instilled in the pliant infant psyche of every man and woman born to the Ferendes.

No wonder, then, that subservience is the norm, and the

Ferende *Book of Common Prayer* is a long entreaty not to be punished by Rep'husela, not to be plucked from the earth by her great servant condors, not to be dropped from the sky into the unforgiving Bergamot Sea.

But, as every tyrant in history can attest, not even fear of God will quell the dissidents and unbelievers. Along with secret police, prosperity is needed, and work, and promise of advancement, and pretence of freedom, so that every subject's mind is made too cluttered with the personal to be political. And so it was that Prince Nefari the Beneficent set about creating a fortune to be fabled in all Asia: for his nation, for his people, and above all for himself.

For the absolute ruler, there are no rules. For Prince Nefari, Banco Ferende was his financial fiefdom, and its covert pipeline to Western capital was the quiet, unprepossessing Humboldt Bank in Australia, managed by his ruthless Secretary, Karl Fiendisch; Fiendisch, together with a Securities Commission–conforming but elusive co-director named Charles Finistere, who was none other than Prince Nefari himself.

It was the brilliant Fiendisch who conceived the secret bourse for exchanging commodities, futures and risk notes beyond the law, who recruited the most talented software designers to develop and prove an efficient and impregnable trading platform, and who had acquired a legitimate Australian bank and a thriving vineyard to hide its purpose and deflect attention.

And it was Secretary Fiendisch who introduced the scheming Admiral Feng, bringing to the Palace a higher order of foreign tribute, sovereign wealth, and criminality. Duplicitous Feng, Janus Feng, sycophantic or condescending according to circumstance, comptroller of an organization feared throughout East Asia, seemingly with the assets of the mighty PLA at his disposal. And with the Admiral came Zheng, most trusted godson, special lieutenant to the Feng Tong and roving ambassador for enforcement, the first assigned whenever matters called for egregious brutality.

What a success the Feng connection had become. Fees and

other payments for logging concessions over the forests of the remote northern plain were swelling the Palace treasury, and so far none of the usual troublemakers in La Ferste had voiced objection. Now planning was in progress for a showcase motorway between that city and the capital. The shanty town of fishing families that founded Madregalo, and survived still on the city's western waterfront, would be razed and urbanized. Within that reclamation would also be located Feng's proposed casino, constructed and managed by Chinese interests, promising lucrative taxes and profits to the Crown. And, to the further glory of the Prince, Feng Tong would shortly guarantee selection of the Ferendes to host a nation-defining Olympic Games.

Only, recently there was trouble. Feng reported that his workforce at the logging operation had suffered repeated harassment from giant condors, which Prince Nefari privately took to be fanciful. Whatever the explanation, morale was poor and production suffering; the project could be abandoned. Next, Fiendisch had reported that his senior programmer at the Humboldt was compromised, and required quarantining. There was also a worrying link to another figure in Perth, in whom Feng Tong had taken great interest and considered sufficiently important to dispatch Zheng.

Then there was that curious, almost panicked call from Fiendisch reporting that the winery was on fire. Well, the wine business was peripheral; its loss was unfortunate but not fatal. But the Prince had found it impossible to bring reason and reassurance to the conversation. It was as if the ever-calculating, level-headed Fiendisch had suddenly lost his nerve, reading catastrophe into a string of essentially trivial incidents.

And now, it seems, catastrophe really had been unfolding. Feng's agents in Perth reported that the rogue programmer had escaped isolation, Fiendisch was dead, the Humboldt closed down with police and company regulators in control, and most mysterious of all, Zheng had disappeared. Their intelligence suggested that Feng Tong interests were now subject to a wide-ranging investigation headed by an Inspector Spoiling. Furthermore, the person principally assisting that task force and the figure most responsible for developments inimical to the organization was an individual named Worse. The agents were looking for him.

Worse and Nicholas reached the end of the fixed pier and turned to survey the city. Nicholas pointed to the western foreshore.

'That's the original fishing village that started the whole settlement of Madregalo. It was off there that some poor devil of a fisherman was half eaten by weaver fish early last century. Do you know about weaver fish?'

'No.'

'I'll let Edvard tell you about them; he's the world expert. Meanwhile, don't swim.'

Worse looked down into the water with added respect, more than for its depth. 'Anything else life-threatening that I should know about?'

'Apart from Prince Nefari and Admiral Feng? Only the killer condors that appear to materialize out of thin air.'

'Condors? I thought they belonged to the Americas.'

'This is the Asiatic variety. Edvard is the world expert on them as well. You'll see.'

They were to meet up with Tøssentern and Anna that evening. Nicholas, Millie and Worse, who was travelling as Richard Magnacart, had arrived that morning in La Ferste. After checking into their hotel, the two men drove across to Madregalo, where Nicholas was conducting an information tour for Worse's benefit. Later, they were to meet with some of Nicholas's friends to catch up on local news. Millie had been unwell, and stayed in La Ferste.

'Where we're standing, on this jetty, is the ceremonial capital of the Ferendes,' announced Nicholas authoritatively.

'I would have expected that to be the Palace,' observed Worse, his gaze lifting to the dominating façade of L'Orphania.

Nicholas looked around for others that might hear. 'No one goes to the Palace. That's why rumours abound. You know they say that the Prince keeps swints in cages. That would be the most irreligious act in Christendom, don't you think?'

'I'm sure there are many good souls in captivity.' Worse would not be drawn into relativism.

'Anyway,' continued Nicholas, 'this is the place where the Ferendes graduated from Protectorate to Republic. The Articles were signed in a wonderful Royal Gazebo, part of which is preserved as this.' Nicholas gestured at the terminus. 'There was a perfectly opulent royal tram carriage built for the occasion, and still used ceremonially from time to time, I believe.'

'You really do sound like a tour leader, Nicholas,' returned Worse, but he was enjoying the exposition. He added casually, 'What do you know about the Palace security?'

'Worse! Whatever you're thinking, stop there. Impenetrable. Don't even ask. That's a fast route to disappearance.'

'It was a perfectly innocent question, I thought,' said Worse.

'Well, innocence in Madregalo doesn't mean not guilty.'

Worse didn't respond. He was staring at the fishing village, and appeared to change the subject. 'Is there an heir to the throne here?'

'There are two siblings. The brother is Crown Prince Arnaba. Totally different. A scholar, by contrast; a theologian I think. He chooses to live in exile, and anonymity, not to avoid the people, it is said, but to escape his brother. The sister is Crown Princess Namok; married to Marshal Yiscosh, ex-Egyptologist, and now paramilitary strongman in charge of State security. My friends in the Democrasi call him King Nepotisti, which sounds suitably pharaonic, don't you think? They call her Runnin', and while the two of them live off a bottomless royal purse in La Ferste, she pretends to progressive, republican values. She's a shrill and shameless hypocrite, Worse; living privately like a spoilt princess, while at the same time she airs her cant in public at every opportunity, though I suspect most people by now recognize it for what it is.'

'Well, the older we get, the more discerning we become around that sort of thing. So, a regular messed-up family, then. Was he really an Egyptologist? They're generally likeable people. Apart from Napoléon, perhaps.'

'Only euphemistically. He traded stolen Old Kingdom artifacts to secretive Asian galleries and collectors. Worse, you need to realize there's a lot of euphemism in Ferende politics. It's virtually codified, it's politesse. The only effective counterforce is ridicule.'

Worse concealed his distaste, and looked along the pier. There was a tram coming. 'Let's ride back.' Very quietly, he added, 'And revolution, surely.'

As they walked across to the terminus, Worse looked out to sea. The cruising, industrial and naval docks were in La Ferste, and only one ship was anchored off Madregalo. It was a Chinese flagged destroyer. Nicholas noted Worse's interest.

'That's quite a statement, mooring off here,' he said. 'The locals are left in no doubt as to who has influence, who has power. My friends would find that intimidatory. The Chinese will call it a goodwill visit.'

Worse made no response, but took from a jacket pocket some compact binoculars and studied the vessel for a full minute. Eventually, Nicholas spoke.

'Worse, in Madregalo you need to be careful where you rest your gaze. There is, you know, an invidious Internal Security Act. Paragraph 51; also called the Vanishing Act. No one will tell you they've actually seen it, the irony being it has to do with disappearing subjects. But there is a very visible Secretary, named Madam Kohl, who oversees it. Try to avoid her, Worse, and remember that you're not the same free agent who left Perth.'

'I'm sure that's good advice, Nicholas,' said Worse absently, folding the binoculars.

As they rode the less-than-opulent public tram back to land, Worse noticed work teams setting up banners and decorations along the jetty.

'Is all this regalia normal, or is there some festival about to happen?'

'I don't know,' said Nicholas. 'We'll ask this afternoon.'

Apart from its connection with acquisitive Egyptology, the name **Napoléon Bonaparte** appeared in the context of a recent Cambridge philosophy paper. Candidates were required to present four deconstructions (using, respectively, figmentation theory, credule analysis, Thortelmann path enumeration, and the post-subtlety paradigm) of the following expert statement:

Many people assume that the Arc de Triomphe was built from the ground up. This is only half true, as the actual order of proceeding was to build it up on one side, across the top, and down to the ground on the other side. (The alarm and ridicule it was feared this might engender were abated by concealing works from the public behind enormous canvas screens, and this explains why no contemporary etchings exist depicting accurately the progress of construction. Those that purport to be so are the wholly predictable fantasies of illustrators allowed no actual viewing.) There was a sound practical reason for this. For Parisian engineers of the early 1800s, it gave confidence that in the future one or other vertical support could be removed, in turn (for restoration, say, or affixing revisionist iconography, or even to accommodate extravagantly broad Napoleonic parades), without risk of the whole structure collapsing. Almost two centuries of continuous good standing has proved their *méthode expérimentale* inspired. (Lord Enright, *Arch and Lintel.*)

32. ADMIRAL FENG

They took the tram to its upper terminus, just outside the Palace entry, and walked back down Ahorte, the beautiful tramway boulevard connecting the Palace to the pier, as far as the Kardia, the main square of Madregalo. Nicholas secured an outdoor table at a café, while Worse found a tourist shop. He returned with a map of the city and sat down, unfolding it to study the central streets. Nicholas ordered coffees. Worse spoke without looking up from the map.

'What did you decide to say to Millie about the families?'

'I have told her the story, as well as I remember.'

'We remember the vivid.'

Nicholas was left to interpret this as approval. When the waiter reappeared with their order, Worse refolded his map with conspicuous ineptitude and asked innocently about the festivities in town.

'Tomorrow is the biggest day for Madregalo, for the Ferendes. It is the signing of the treaty, the great peace and cooperation pact with the Envoy. The Entente.'

'Envoy?'

'Admiral Feng, the Chinese Envoy. The Ferendes will be rich, and protected by our great friend, the People's Republic. Tomorrow, I will take my son to watch our biggest day. They will have the ceremony on the pier.'

When the waiter had moved away, Nicholas and Worse exchanged looks. Worse placed the map on the table and leaned over, speaking quietly.

'That was a well-rehearsed enthusiasm. Lacking something, though, didn't you think?'

'Authenticity,' agreed Nicholas.

'Joy,' added Worse. He looked around. Work teams were in the square, erecting enormous portraits of Prince Nefari and Admiral Feng, along with rows of flags of the two nations. 'It's depressing how some things never change. Hegemony, exploitation, empire.'

'Anyway, Feng's not a diplomat, he's a criminal,' said Nicholas, lowering his voice when the waiter came close.

'He may be both.'

As Worse reached for his coffee, they heard sirens approaching. A police car followed by a black limousine entered the Kardia from the south on Ahorte, and stopped about fifteen metres from their café. The occupant of the limousine opened the tinted rear window and surveyed the activities in the square.

'Admiral Feng,' their waiter announced. 'He will be visiting the Palace.'

Feng's gaze rested approvingly on his own portrait before glancing at the café, where he found his eyes locked on the uncompromising stare of Worse.

'Look down at the map, Nicholas,' Worse instructed his companion sharply. His own face was partly concealed by the coffee cup, held before his mouth with two hands, elbows resting on the table. Feng sat forward slightly, as if to be absolutely sure of the insolence he was witnessing. Worse's stare didn't falter. The waiter, unnerved by the Admiral's apparent attention, retreated to the kitchen. Half a minute later, Feng's window closed, the siren restarted, and the motorcade resumed its course.

'Through no fault of my own, I seem to have come to the Admiral's notice,' observed Worse drily.

'I thought the Zheng visit presaged that fairly convincingly. What happened to Zheng, by the way?'

'Not entirely sure. Dropped out of sight, quicker than he came.'

Worse reached into his bag for his laptop and opened it on his knee. The locations of the two satellite phones identified from Fiendisch's call history were converging, and he was now sure which party attached to each. It didn't surprise him to confirm that the first call Fiendisch had made when the winery exploded was to Feng, not Nefari. He took up his mobile and dialled Nefari. It was about thirty seconds before the ringtone sounded, at which time it was immediately answered without greeting. Worse guessed that it was a personal handset, and didn't waste time with niceties.

'Listen carefully, Nefari. Feng isn't just ripping up forests in the north for timber. He's mining. He's shipping out rare earths worth a fortune monetarily and strategically. That's the mineral wealth of your people, and he's not paying for it. Go up to the plain and see for yourself. There're also massive hydrocarbon prospects offshore. Your shore. Feng will pump it dry to the PRC. Don't sign the Entente tomorrow.'

'Who is this?'

'Tell Feng that ugly godson met certain death. Good, there's Feng at the Palace door now.'

'Zheng is dead?'

Worse ended the call. Nicholas had gone into the café to pay their bill, and returned in time to hear the last few words. He thought Worse was joking at his expense.

'Who was that? Prince Nefari himself, I suppose. On speaking terms, are you?'

'I did most of the talking,' Worse said.

Nicholas's smile vanished. 'Jesus, Worse. What have you done?' He looked around anxiously. 'This is a police state, for Christ's sake. We had better get moving.'

Worse folded his laptop and returned it to his backpack, along with the map. Then, with his hands concealed within the pack, he removed the SIM card from his mobile, replacing it with another.

'Sure,' he said belatedly, and stood up.

Across the square from their café, on its northern perimeter, was the historic main branch of Banco Ferende, its façade now partly obscured by national flags. Nicholas pointed it out to Worse, almost ruefully. It had served him well when he lived at the LDI station, and he liked its manager. He decided that today he would not pay his respects as he might normally have done when in the city. Even though Nicholas felt certain that Mr Denari could not be corrupt, the bank itself was demonstrably manipulated by the Prince and Feng Tong.

There was still half an hour before they were to meet Nicholas's contacts, in a church a short distance to the east. By now, Worse's insouciance had calmed Nicholas, and he was keen to show his friend something on the way. He led Worse across the square.

The centre of the Kardia was dominated by a beautiful fountain, sculpted in glass. From some distance, Worse thought he was looking at a large, rather featureless semi-transparent ice cube with water running down its sides into a circular pool. But as he approached, he could discern its finer form, that the apparent block was a three-dimensional tapestry of fish interwoven most ingeniously.

Encircling the pool were park benches made of stainless steel and heavy cast glass, and several people were sitting, eating snack lunches, reading, or just looking.

'Weaver fish,' said Nicholas quietly.

Worse said nothing. He walked a short distance around the pool, to where there was a vacant seat, but remained standing, staring at the sculpture. Although the object was in front of him, he was trying to recompose its geometry in his mind, trying to understand it, understand how the artist could have made something so beautiful, so impossible, but solid and real.

Nicholas followed Worse around, sitting down behind him, observing his friend with more interest than he had for the fountain. They were like that for ten minutes, when Worse turned to him.

'You must tell me about weaver fish, Nicholas.'

Nicholas stood up as Worse set off distractedly in the direction of St Alonzo's. Halfway across the open space, Nicholas received a call from his friends. They were unable to meet after all, and were reluctant to talk on the phone. He reported this to Worse, whose only response was to change direction, heading for where they had parked the rental car.

Worse was not the first to be entranced by **Otavio Fitrina**'s glass fountain. Computer simulations have determined the optimal 'crystalline' structure of a three-dimensional woven array of weaver fish to be a rectangular prism, and the sculptor has chosen the cube. The secret to the quite magical interior detail is that it was cast sequentially in cubic laminations (there are sixteen). The glass used in each successive casting was composed to have a lower melting point than the previous layer, which was tempered and pre-cooled. In this way, sculptural detail was preserved throughout the solid form. During manufacture, the progressively enlarging core was centred on a tubular titanium mandrel, which now functions as the fountain water conduit.

There is a small but erudite literature on the flotation physics of the weaver fish superstructure, and how it might be supported. Those fish above the water's surface lose buoyancy, and it is hypothesized that their weight must be balanced by a subsurface platform of weaver fish arrayed to swim (albeit stationary) uniformly upward, and so precisely numbered as to satisfy equilibrium of forces. Fitrina has portrayed this base layer of vertically columned fish, though it is difficult to discern beneath the water.

Visitors are advised that the fountain is the most frequently, but most incompetently, photographed attraction in Madregalo, and are urged to purchase one of the beautiful professional images offered commercially, even as postcards. These were obtained using specialized strobe lamp trans-illumination and a research-quality light-field camera, where the image is resynthesized digitally in post-production. The technique reproduces extraordinarily the intricacy of weaver fish intercalation deep within the sculpture.

You may notice that the fountain water is very slightly purplish, and that seagulls, which are generally a nuisance in the square, never settle in the surrounding pool. The explanation is given that weaver fish, by their nature barely visible, inhabit its depths. Whatever the truth of this, the possibility has certainly deterred vandals.

33. LA FERSTE

Worse asked Nicholas to do the driving to La Ferste. They were both quiet. The forty-kilometre drive was slowed by roadworks and survey teams planning the new motorway, and in places the temporary detour loops were barely passable. Half an hour into the journey, Worse took his mobile from the backpack and pressed a number. Names were not exchanged.

'I can't make my report until I get some help with punctuation,' said Worse. 'Can you recommend a grammarian in these parts?'

'I expected you to ask before you left, and I have a name right here. He's a philatelist, but a most accomplished apostrophist as well. You will find him excellent.'

'He wouldn't like Verita's, would he? How will I know him?'

'By his incomparable grammar. And he speaks ... elliptically. I will tell him to expect you.'

Worse wrote down some details, finishing the call with, 'Thank you.' He then leaned forward to program an address into the car's GPS. Nicholas contained his curiosity only to that point.

'What was that about? I can help with grammar, for heaven's sake.'

'Not this variety. Special punctuator with remote full stopping. Victor is helping. Do you mind following the instructions?' Worse leaned back in his seat and closed his eyes. It wasn't difficult for Nicholas to decode.

'Jesus, Worse. Do we need that sort of thing here? You can't seriously be thinking of, you know, the Prince.'

'We are thinking seriously of everything, Nicholas.'

Worse hadn't opened his eyes. He was quiet for a full minute, then added, 'Feng is on top. Feng runs Nefari and Nefari runs

Banco Ferende. Feng ran Fiendisch and Fiendisch ran the Humboldt. Feng ran Fiendisch and Fiendisch ran his team of killers, Stronk and the other two. Feng ran Zheng. Feng runs the northern operation. Feng will run the Entente.'

Worse was quiet for another minute, then spoke again. 'So, Feng ordered me dead. Feng ordered you dead. Feng ordered Millie dead. Feng is the one. Don't waste sympathy on him.'

Nicholas didn't respond, and the only voice in the car for the next hour was synthesized in the satnav, guiding them onto the Marshal Yiscosh Expressway. The address was on the other side of the city centre, over the Peril River, and they crossed on the spectacular CoshEx suspension bridge. When Nicholas slowed at the east-side toll plaza, Worse woke up.

'When you get there, drive past while I have a look. We'll park in the next block. You should wait in the car and I'll walk back.'

No more was said. Worse didn't catch sight of the address as they passed, but he had a street number to identify it, and set off along the footpath. It was a good area of town, with several antique map shops, philatelists, coin and medallion traders, and rare-book sellers. Normally, Worse would have enjoyed browsing in all of them, and perusing his prize purchases in one of the cafés that he passed.

He pushed open the door of No 303. A short, white-haired, bespectacled man was completing a transaction with a customer. Worse looked at some sheets of historic Ferende stamps, many with depictions of a chariot seemingly drawn by condors in a two-by-two harness. He was studying a framed etching of Madregalo from the sea, dated 1916, when the owner approached him.

'Can I help you?'

'My friend said that you might assist me with stationery, that sort of thing.'

'What is your friend's name?'

Worse stayed silent, looking at the man as if there hadn't been a question.

'What is your friend's ... affliction?'

'Headaches,' Worse replied without hesitation. The other smiled slightly.

'How are his headaches, poor man?'

'Bad. Every time I speak with him, he's getting one.'

'Ah. He must find you ... perplexing.' It was Worse's turn to smile.

The owner latched the door to the street, and invited Worse into a rear room, instructing him to stay there while he disappeared down a hallway. He returned with a parcel in plain paper, and handed it to Worse, gesturing for him to sit down in an armchair. Before sitting, Worse held the package for several seconds, as if appraising its contents by weight. He then sat down and unfolded the paper carefully. Under the paper was a new oilcloth wrapping, which Worse unwound like swaddling, all the time feeling the weight, feeling the balance as he held it. He knew exactly what was in his hands before seeing it, and was pleased. It was his favourite weapon, a Totengraber 9 with integrated Prussica sight; like Zheng's, but a model variant.

'Your friend chose.'

'He is a good friend.'

Worse opened the breach and held the barrel to the light. He removed the ammunition clip and checked it was full. With the magazine empty he squeezed the trigger, listening and feeling, his eyes closed in concentration. It released with the purest German accent that only a Totengraber could sound. Then he held it to the light again, backwards, squinting to compare the diffraction symmetries in the barrel and the sight.

'Not many ... do that.'

Worse acknowledged the comment with the slightest tilt of his head, and brought the weapon close to his nose; he was smelling the metal, the oils, and for residue. Satisfied, he held the clip up questioningly.

'Only one. Your friend said you use ... punctuation ... sparingly.'

Worse smiled as he reassembled the pistol and wrapped it. 'How much do I owe you?'

'Your friend paid.'

Worse stared at him, then put the package in his backpack. Standing up, he offered his hand, which the other took, before leading Worse back into the shop and unlatching the outer door.

'Wait,' he said to Worse, and stepped across the shop to collect the Madregalo etching. At the counter, he wrapped it in tissue paper and placed it in a thin brown carry bag.

'This is ... from me,' he said, handing it to Worse.

Worse stared at him again. It was rare to meet a man and learn almost nothing about him, except that he was good.

'Thank you.'

Worse stepped onto the street and set off quickly toward the car. Nicholas saw him in a mirror and unlocked the car as he approached.

'Successful?' Nicholas looked doubtfully at the carry bag as Worse settled into the passenger seat.

'Yes. It's a very fine etching of Madregalo, dated 1916.'

'Tøssentern will enjoy looking at that,' said Nicholas. He started the engine and pulled out into the traffic.

At the entrance to their hotel, a valet took their car. Nicholas went up to his room, which he was sharing with Millie. Worse seated himself in the lobby to observe comings and goings for a while. Satisfied that they had not been followed, at least into the hotel, he went to the elevator station.

When he rang Nicholas's room bell, he was pleased to see Millie open the door—at least she was well enough to do that. She invited him in and closed it behind him.

'Nicholas is having a shower. Would you like some tea?'

'Yes, thank you. But how are you? Did you get a good rest?' It was really to make that enquiry that Worse had come to her room.

'I feel completely fine. Whatever it was, gone.' Millie made a dismissal gesture with her hand as she walked into a kitchenette to make tea.

'Has Nicholas told you about our day?'

'Some. Not all, I'm sure. I want to see the fountain that held you in thrall.'

Worse smiled at the language she, or Nicholas, used to describe him.

'I think you will be held in thrall, too. It's very subtle, which I know to be your preference.'

'And the treaty thing tomorrow. Are we going?'

'Definitely,' said Worse. 'Any news of the others?'

'Edvard phoned from Hong Kong this morning. Their

connection looks good. They should be landing about now. We're planning to have dinner together, just in the hotel. Is that okay for you?'

'Absolutely. Thank you,' Worse added as Millie handed him tea. He almost dropped it in surprise as she reached up to kiss him on the cheek.

'Let's sit in there.' Millie led the way into the entry sitting area. She pointed to Worse's carry bag.

'What have you got there?'

Worse took the framed etching and slipped it out of its tissue wrapping. He handed it to Millie.

'I found it in a philately shop.'

'It's very large for a postage stamp,' was her first comment. 'It's charming. Is this where you were today?' She was examining it minutely.

'It is where we were today, nearly a century removed.'

Worse finished his tea, and realized he was quite tired.

'I'm going to rest for a while. What time were you thinking for dinner?'

'Say, seven? Nicholas and I thought we should do it as room service. It will be more private. They can set up for five people in here.'

'That's a good idea. I'll be back at seven unless I hear otherwise. Thanks for the tea.' Worse stood up, and his voice changed in tone. 'Millie, make sure you use the door lens before opening, please.'

'I will.'

To emphasize her compliance, she used the lens before opening the door to let him out.

A few hours later, at seven o'clock, she opened it again, to let Worse in. Nicholas joined her at the door to welcome him.

Room service had provided an attractive table setting, and brought in comfortable dining chairs. Tøssentern and Anna were already seated, and both stood as Worse entered. Nicholas introduced them, invited everyone to sit, and offered drinks. Worse had been carrying his backpack in one hand, and he placed it on the floor to one side before taking the vacant space next to Anna. She smiled at him as he sat, but said nothing. Tøssentern addressed Worse.

'We've been told about some remarkable adventures in Perth, Worse. We clearly have you to thank for saving these two wonderful people.'

The others joined in a chorus of appreciation. Worse looked across the table to find Millie giving him a joyful smile.

'Everyone played important parts,' Worse said quietly, and conspicuously altered his posture as if that might change the subject. Anna sensed its meaning.

'Have you been to the Ferendes before, Richard?'

Worse was slightly startled; only Sigrid called him Richard. He didn't mind, but wondered about its purpose. Nicholas had presumably explained that he was travelling as Richard Magnacart, and he supposed that Anna, quite reasonably, was acknowledging that identity. (Millie, too, had entered the Ferendes on false papers; concerned for her safety, Worse had provided a passport in the name of Millicent Ropey.)

'No. I might say, though, that I have been well inducted by Nicholas during twelve hours of cultural immersion.'

'You have an excellent tutor. Nicholas knows more than any of us about this mysterious place,' offered Tøssentern.

Anna had continued to hold Worse's attention during this interruption, and spoke again. 'I hope you saw the Fitrina fountain.'

'I am told a witness account has it that I was in thrall.' Worse looked from Anna to Nicholas, and back. Anna smiled.

'Not surprisingly. Do you know about its fabrication?'

'Nicholas explained it a little. An ensemble cast, you might call it.'

Anna smiled again. Tøssentern leaned forward.

'Or matryoshki perhaps, in glass. Extraordinary.'

The others were quiet, accommodating this new image to the object. It was almost impossible not to be drawn into the abstraction, to bring metaphor to, and take metaphor from, Fitrina's masterpiece. Nicholas was the next to speak.

'They say there is an invisible hollow network, like a maze, throughout the casting and that if you could find the entry or exit and pump coloured dye into it you would see writing and it would be the magical words that let you escape from inside, escape from the weaver fish.'

'So Fitrina cast a spell. Surely that's apocryphal,' rejoined Anna.

Worse appreciated the play; it was something that Sigrid might have said. In fact, Anna reminded him of Sigrid in many ways.

'Invisible within glass. How are we to trust our senses?' mused Tøssentern.

It was Anna who had raised the subject of the fountain and, as the others talked, its metaphoric reach was taking form for her. Those troubling meditations during dinner with the two Penelopes had left her seeing Thornton's greenhouse differently. It was a built emblem of the forced cohabitation of opposites, like winter and summer, the expressed and the private, the fictitious and the real. And glass, that most illusory of materials essential to its making, far from contributing clarity, gave concealment to the paradox.

And here was Fitrina's brilliance, nesting glass inside glass, hiding conceit within conceit, refracting fable into fable; complete with the promise of some authorial thread coursing through, to make sense of it all.

Anna thought of something else that had troubled her from that evening in Chaucer Road. It might also be sculptural, made layer on layer: Edvard's interminable progression of masquerades spilling forward into the figment, or the person, of Barnabas Bending. Tøssentern was speaking again.

'By the way, Worse, I think you know Rodney Thwistle. He was very keen for me to give you his regards. Whenever your name comes up, he goes into a sort of fugue state and talks about pixelation, for some reason.'

'The defective pixelation algorithm. We had a short correspondence on the subject, years ago. So he's still worrying about it. That's surprising.'

Worse sounded sympathetic. He liked Thwistle, and made an instant judgement. After all, even equipped with the algorithm, decryption required information about the error statistics. And it was only a matter of time before someone else discovered it. Fiendisch apparently had, or was very close.

'When you next see him, please pass on my regards, and say that I have a solution for the DPA that he is welcome to study. Only, he will need to come to Perth, make a holiday of it.' Worse knew this was a mischievous offer.

'But Rodney has never been further than Oxford!' Anna was reporting the legend that they all had heard.

'Yes, well. I'm not emailing it. And I'm not publishing it. He can weigh up the choice of lifelong fugue states against unthinkable travel to a beautiful city, including an escorted side-trip to a famous wine region. My expense,' added Worse with a flourish of munificence.

Tøssentern looked at Worse with enormous respect. Within memory, no one had been able to entice RT to venture further than a genteel bicycle ride from Nazarene College, but this might very well work.

'I will deliver that ultimatum with the greatest sensitivity.' Tøssentern could hardly contain his anticipation. Anna was smiling. PH-D would assist in this campaign, she was sure.

'Somehow, I feel cheated of the Margaret River experience,' said Nicholas with good-natured complaint, as he refilled wine glasses. 'Bound and gagged, imprisoned, only Vex and Bad Warden Stronk for company.'

'What about me? Sped through town in the dead of night, no wine, no food, no rest.' Millie also had a case for compensation.

'Well, I suppose it's only fair that you two come back as well, and we'll try to do the wine tour more conventionally. No explosions, for example,' said Worse.

'Explosions? We haven't heard about those,' said Anna with interest.

'Oh, Millie blew up a winery. Total write-off. She knows she mustn't do it again,' Worse said.

'There was also an exploding car, remember. Your doing, entirely,' said Millie.

'My God, that does sound fun. I suppose I will need to moderate my travel pitch to Rodney,' calculated Tøssentern aloud. 'Explosions, he may not wish for.'

'You two might think about a holiday there as well.' Worse directed the suggestion to Anna.

'Perhaps we will.'

Anna had developed the habit of measuring alternatives according to how they might impact on Edvard's depression. At the moment, she felt good. She had known all along that Edvard would return to the Ferendes at some point. He was driven to do so, and it could well be integral to his recovery. Now it had happened, she was completely sure that she had made the right decision in accompanying him.

The last visit to Mingle Lane had presented an unexpected development. As Edvard was leaving, he sheltered briefly from the weather in the entry to the professional suites. There he studied for the first time a series of framed architectural drawings adorning the walls, and was shocked to discover the history of Clement House. As a child, he had heard the name Oriel Gardens in hushed tones, but never had any idea of its location. The realization that he had been entering that building week after week, unaware that a few floors above was the room where his stepsister had died, was unbearable. He had told Anna that he could not return, and she had been trying to make alternative arrangements for Barbara Bokardo to consult with him elsewhere.

But now they were here, and many things had changed for the better. Nicholas had come back as part of the LDI team. The 'Chinese problem' in the north for which Edvard felt responsible had proven to be part of a much larger canvas, drawing in help from others including, it seemed, investigators in Australia. Moreover, for the present at least, these developments appeared to have displaced Edvard's fixation on locating the wreckage of *Abel* to examine its fish traps. Finally, there was this man sitting beside her, Worse. He seemed like a valuable partner in their company.

While she was absorbed in these thoughts, Tøssentern was giving Worse a very brief account of their discoveries concerning the Asiatic condor, as well as an internet address for his Lindenblüten lecture on the weaver fish, for Worse to access at his own convenience.

The conversation was interrupted by room-service maids

arriving with fresh coffee. When the staff had left, Anna asked about plans for the next day. Nicholas had been told by the café manager in the Kardia that the signing on the pier was scheduled for two o'clock in the afternoon, but there would be hours of celebration leading up to it. Everyone expected large crowds in Madregalo. After a discussion that seemed to lack resolution, Worse decided to take control.

'I suggest that we leave here at half past six, all in the one car, Nicholas driving. We find a comfortable café on the waterfront with a good view of the pier, close to Ahorte, and base ourselves there for the day. Breakfast, lunch, gossip, binoculars, books, mobiles, hats, insect repellent, maps, medications, walking shoes. We meet in this room at six-fifteen and go down together. I'll have the car brought around ahead of time.'

To the others, Worse's suggestion sounded more like an instruction. Four faces were watching him silently, conveying, 'Really? That early?'

Worse glanced around the table with an implicit definiteness that replied 'Really. That early.' The result was a general murmur of agreement, and a reluctant realization that this should not be a late night.

34. *KENIJO*

The following day had been declared a national holiday by the Palace, but La Ferste might well have been another country. Taking road traffic as a surrogate measure, observance in the economic capital seemed negligible. La Ferste was getting on with profitable business, leaving the ceremonial, the anachronistic and the irrelevant to its monarchist sister, Madregalo.

But when they reached the start of the dilapidated intercity highway, it was clear that driving conditions were worse than on the previous day. Evidently, many of those who considered themselves too cosmopolitan to be interested were drawn to the spectacle in Madregalo, after all.

Progress was slow, and it was after eight o'clock when Nicholas finally parked the car close to where he and Worse had left it the previous day. Worse had memorized his map, and led the way through backstreets to the pier. He was deliberately avoiding the Kardia, because he expected it to be crowded and have excessive security, and because he wanted Millie to see the fountain when there was more time to appreciate it.

When they entered the southern end of Ahorte, Worse headed to the start of the pier. There was a tram station and, on the west side, an adjoining restaurant called Felicity's that he had noted the previous day. He arrived first, as the others had fallen behind, and was fortunate to commandeer a table, open to the beach, that could accommodate five. When they caught up, muttering things like 'single-minded' and 'cracking pace', they finally felt well rewarded for the early start. Before them was an uninterrupted view of the pier and the lower section of Ahorte, where the royal tram would appear on its journey to the signing ceremony.

The other tables were all taken. Everywhere, the Ferende flag was flying, hanging, draped or spread, and Ferende national colours decorated most available surfaces, including children's foreheads. The menu was special for the day, and music and commentary were provided by a Ferent language radio station.

They ordered breakfast, and settled in to enjoy the day. Worse, seated between Anna and Millie, took out binoculars to scan meticulously everything within range, including the destroyer in the bay.

Breakfast was served, then cleared. The others variously read, watched, chatted, ordered coffees, drank them, and ordered more. The restaurant manager, who called himself Mr Felicity, was delighted to find in Tøssentern a foreigner who could speak fluent Ferent, including his childhood dialect. He presented Tøssentern with a glossy Order of Ceremony, declaring it would become a valuable souvenir. It certainly assisted in knowing what to expect as the day progressed, and provided a summary in grand, sweeping statements of what the Entente Ferende–Chinoise would bring to the people. Though not, as Nicholas discreetly pointed out, what it would take from them.

At eleven o'clock, the public tram service stopped. At twelve, a regiment of Palace guards marched down Ahorte and on to the pier, depositing members to each side at five-metre intervals all the way to the Gazebo. They were to stand at attention for another four hours.

It had rained in the night, but the sky was now clear. During the morning an atypical breeze started, which they first noticed when needing to batten down anything that could be blown from their table. Its effect was to make the bay choppy and the water look grey. Tøssentern and Anna were pleased to be wearing their Reckles hats.

The next spectacle was a military band, which they could hear on Ahorte before it came into view. It continued down the pier, taking up station at the Gazebo. At that distance, and with the breeze, Worse was thankful that their music hardly intruded on his thoughts.

Those thoughts were on Feng.

He had Feng's satellite phone number, and if Spoiling's

representations came through, he could soon have transcripts from the Signals Directorate. He knew where Feng travelled, he had seen his face, he knew what his business was, he knew the identity of his closest criminal accomplice, Nefari. He had Nefari's number, he knew where he lived, he knew where he travelled, he had spoken to him directly. And through Nefari he had baited Feng. The bait was Zheng.

What would Feng make of the words 'met certain death'? The obtuseness would keep coming back to him, distract him, cause errors. It would eat away his certitude like a strong acid. And that acid Worse could replenish at will. Altogether, he felt very strategically placed.

Worse was convinced that this so-called Entente was in reality a business plan joining the corrupt Nefari to the criminal Feng. Without Feng, Nefari would fail. He had already lost Fiendisch and the whole extravagant scheme at the Humboldt. He would soon lose control of Banco Ferende as international regulators forced audit closures.

It didn't matter, then, if the Entente were signed or not; without Feng, it would lose meaning. The inference comforted Worse. It removed an urgency to interfere in the day's proceedings. Equally, it established Feng as the party to eliminate. And, for this, Worse had the means. It was just like Zheng's.

While he was meditating on Feng, Worse had opened his laptop and was tracking the satellite phones. He expected that the two principals in this charade would remain readily contactable between themselves; that was a basic rule for colluding parties. He wasn't surprised, therefore, to find Nefari's moving slowly down Ahorte, and Feng's out on the bay, where the destroyer was moored. This was consistent with information in the Order of Ceremony, where it was stated that Prince Nefari would take the royal tram to the ceremonial Gazebo, where he would receive the honourable Chinese Envoy, Admiral Feng, who would arrive by launch from the 'Friend Ship' moored in the bay.

Two minutes before Nefari's carriage came into view, Worse informed his friends that the Prince would appear in two minutes. Nicholas and Millie showed no surprise at this precision forecast.

Nicholas had described the royal tram as opulent, and so

it proved. Smaller than a public carriage, it was canopied at one end and open at the other. Prince Nefari was seated on an elevated golden throne at the open end, facing back toward the land. Beside him, on running boards, were footmen in gold, red and brilliant blue costume. The carriage was swathed in gold and silver, with richly coloured silks threaded with precious metals and gemstones. The Prince wore a white naval dress uniform encrusted with medals, over which was draped a long cape checked in two tones of royal blue, and edged in ermine. He might well have been a pharaoh. As the carriage progressed along the pier, the band played a procession piece that gradually built in volume and tempo to a royal fanfare audible well beyond Felicity's.

The program given to Tøssentern described what was to happen next. Protocol required that the Prince be at the Gazebo first, facing the city, and that the supplicant Envoy then approach from the sea. He would be escorted from his launch to the foot of the throne, and the documents signed on a jewelled hand plate supported by Palace Secretaries.

Worse looked at the destroyer through binoculars. The ceremonial open launch was afloat under davits at the stern, and was soon underway. As it neared, he could make out a figure, dressed in naval uniform, standing on deck, using the bow rail for support. Worse glanced at his laptop screen; Feng was carrying his satellite phone. It was almost tempting to call him and mention Zheng.

The launch was now passing the pontoon tip of the pier on the west side, still tossing a little in the choppy water. Worse was scanning through binoculars from the pier to the launch when he heard Anna cry out, 'Edvard, look.'

She was pointing outwards, upwards. Worse's eye followed the line, but he saw nothing. Then he caught it; a transient patch of darkness in the sky, vanishing before he was sure it was real. There it was again, just for an instant, hundreds of metres on, higher. This time, the others all saw it. Anna sensed what it was. Tøssentern knew beyond doubt. He leaned in front of Anna to whisper to Worse.

'Condor.'

Worse listened without taking his eyes off the scene; he was scanning the sky, ready for the next apparition. And when it came, it was very, very different. Far distant from the last appearance, completely out of nowhere, four enormous condors materialized in the sky high above the pontoons. First they flew upwards, catching the breeze, maintaining a perfect two-by-two formation as if joined in harness. From there they swept down westwards across the bay, gaining incredible speed in the dive, then pulled up to their previous height, repeating the manoeuvre eastwards.

The restaurant had fallen silent, the radio turned off. Worse briefly raised his binoculars to look at Nefari and Feng. Neither seemed aware of what was happening. He looked back at the condors. They were high in the air on the other side of the pier, turning. Even at the greater distance, they looked larger. Still in perfect formation, they dived. This time, it was a deeper, faster descent, and headed, it seemed, straight for the royal carriage. The Prince, oblivious, continued staring vacantly at his subjects on the land.

But the condors didn't attack the Prince. Instead, they dived beneath the carriage, beneath the pier, vanishing from sight for just a moment. But what emerged from under the pier on their own side caused even Worse to catch his breath. Not four condors, but one. One gigantic bird that flapped its wings powerfully to pull up from the water, gaining height, retracing the path of the previous four.

It wasn't clear if the Prince had caught sight of it, but several footmen on the pier were panicking, some running back toward land. Feng had certainly seen it, abandoning his sedate stance at the bow and gesticulating to his helmsman in the stern. Worse saw the launch begin to go about, its bow and stern waves whitening.

When that single monstrous condor had reached its chosen height it turned, wings spread. There was an instant when the sun caught its plumage at such an angle that to those in the restaurant it looked sheer gold, but in the dive the sinister, iridescent black returned. This time it was further out, sweeping across the pontoons to rise again high in the eastern sky.

It was almost possible to imagine its presence as benign. The great, mythical bird that lived in the Ferende unconscious coming out to celebrate, performing a people's exhibition in the way an air-show flyover would serve in similar circumstances. But for those who had seen it from the pier, it was anything but propitious. They were fleeing.

From the east it came, falling faster than seemed possible, headed for the pier. The Prince stood, turning to see what was disrupting the ceremony, why his guards, footmen and Secretaries, even his carriage driver, had sacrificed decorum and run to land. He found himself alone on the pier. He would have seen a fast-moving shadow on the water, then looked upwards for just a moment's comprehension of its cause: the black, faceless messenger of Rep'husela streaking directly to him.

And suddenly that imperious, solitary figure, dressed lavishly in medallioned white, royal blue and silvered ermine, was blackened out of sight, enclosed in seething plumage with great wings beating on the side. The massive creature then half flew, half dragged itself from the carriage to the pier's edge, plunging over, making flight just above the water.

The bay was glassy calm now, despite the breeze, and for a moment condor and reflection were almost joined in doubled size. It seemed to struggle there, low across the water, until it caught the wind for lift and pulled away, gaining height to the west. Prince Nefari the Beneficent was on his mythic journey to the Bergamot Sea.

Worse followed the condor's flight for a few seconds, then lowered his glasses to Feng. The launch had failed to go about, and was now side-on to the shore, bow pointing to the empty throne, the sea churning off the stern. To Worse, it looked high in the water, and wasn't making headway, as if fouled on some underwater snag. Feng was clearly shouting at the helmsman, raising his arms threateningly, striding the deck end to end. But when he next reached the bow, the vessel lurched stern up, as if extraordinarily unbalanced by his weight. The propeller was lifted half above the surface, raising a disc of sparkling water that drenched the sailor and spilled down the deck. Feng, imagining he could re-trim the boat, tried to make his way aft, clutching the handrail, but the combination of dress shoes and steep, slippery deck worked against him.

The boat was now pitched dangerously, the stern fully out of the water, the bow under. The helmsman could do nothing to regain control, and was hanging on for his life. Worse wondered why the boat wasn't sinking: at that angle it should slip straight in. Perhaps the same snag was somehow supporting it. He lowered his glasses briefly to seek the opinion of Tøssentern, who was observing events through his own binoculars. At that very moment, Tøssentern spoke quietly to Anna, and Worse heard it.

'Weaver fish.'

Behind Tøssentern stood Mr Felicity, ashen faced, staring out to sea and repeating softly, mantra-like, *'Kenijo, kenijo.'*

Worse looked back at the launch. The sailor aft was still clinging on. So was Feng, just forward of midships, but now he seemed to be dancing, skipping from foot to foot as if the deck were on fire.

Something else was happening. Worse adjusted focus carefully, but couldn't improve the clarity. The gunwale beside Feng had lost definition, looking strangely glassy. Within another minute, the deck itself was out of focus. Feng stopped jumping, his once immaculate white trousers tinged with purple. One hand still grasped the rail, the other flicked wildly at his legs as a watery, refractive film seemed to cover him from below.

Worse strained to see. He steadied the binoculars with his elbows on the table, screwed the barrel back a fraction, and found the focal plane. The sea around the launch was carpeted with interlinking fish, almost invisible but for their movement as they organized. Towards the bow, where Feng was caught, that woven surface curved upwards, high above the deck. Weaver fish were joining at the base, insinuating themselves into a solid tapestry, widening it, strengthening it from beneath, pushing their woven tower upwards with amazing speed, now almost to a man's height.

Feng's last movement was to raise his second hand to grasp the rail beside the first. He was leaning over, staring at the land. Worse felt personally transfixed, as if some superhuman vision had locked their gaze once more. This, it seemed, was the bringing to account, and the *coup de grâce* would be Worse's favourite—incomprehension.

'Zheng,' he mouthed beneath the binoculars, 'Zheng met certain death.'

Feng's countenance instantly changed, to hatred fixed on Worse. His mouth opened to form a curse. Before it could be voiced, the topmost weaver fish pushed higher, interlocking rapidly at their apex to envelop him entirely.

The genius of the structure was now more evident, how it was propagated upward, how it could be stable two metres above the water. To Worse, it was more intriguing than the sculpture in the Kardia. This was not assembled over months in a precision foundry, this was not the patient labour of a master craftsman. Here, the geometry was living, dynamic and imperfect, and its artistry and cleverness and orchestration belonged to the weaver fish alone.

And Feng, that figure fixed within, motionless, diffuse and indistinct as if set in aspic or imprisoned in Fitrina's casting, continued looking at the land. The tapestry around his face first swelled with reinforcement, then tightened like a wringer. The man inside diminished, becoming faint and shrunken as his substance seemed to dissipate. Seconds later, the aspic curtain fell away, peeling downwards as the weaver fish retreated and slipped beneath the water.

For a moment Feng still stood, still grasped the rail, still stared at Worse. Then he toppled forward, *rinlin* face, *rinlin* hands, and crumpled Admiral's suit, into the bay.

The carpet on the sea was gone, the former swell and chop returned, the deck and gunwale regained their natural sharpness, the bow lifted, and the hull set properly in the water. The sailor at the stern was spared.

The restaurant was deathly quiet. They had witnessed two grotesque, mythically charged attacks that, for the Ferende people, were surely not random. Mr Felicity began to speak, in Ferent, his voice picking up in volume and emotion.

'It is a Ferende prayer, the *Enorem*; very ancient, catechismal,' advised Tøssentern quietly. 'Now he is asking Rep'husela to show mercy on Madregalo, to cleanse,' he hesitated in translation, 'more to bless, this bay. He is asking that the spirits of the Prince and the foreigner not inhabit the bay. And, believe it or not, that his business not suffer. Now he is asking everyone to leave. He is apologizing.'

Worse was the first to stand up, collecting his things, and leave payment. The others followed. As they made their way between the tables, Tøssentern approached Mr Felicity, who looked stricken, and quite solemnly offered his hand, speaking to him in Ferent. In return, Mr Felicity briefly hugged Tøssentern, and cried.

They felt rather stricken themselves. Worse glanced back at the pier as he led the way up Ahorte. The royal carriage, symbol of absolute rule only minutes before, looked shabby from this distance, like a fairground replica, its silks and canopy fluttering for attention. And that magnificent throne, more desolate than empty, lay fallow in its pointless ostentation, now projecting excess, absurdity, and downfall.

Worse wanted to find somewhere to regroup, away from the bay, where they could consult and process what they had seen. In the Kardia, he secured the same café table that Nicholas and he had occupied the previous day.

Customers were few, and waiters seemed reluctant to serve outside. Many shops, normally crowded with tourists, had hastily closed, and the Kardia was almost vacant, offering an uninterrupted view to the fountain. There were many more military uniforms in evidence than was usual. The ceremonial Palace guards in their brilliant blue capes, who had earlier lined the tramway, appeared to have lost all discipline and were standing around in agitated, talkative groups, their automatic weapons shouldered carelessly. News that there was no longer a monarch to protect seemed to have left them purposeless.

'What do you think will happen, Nicholas?' It was Anna who asked. She was looking up at the façade of the Palace, already flaunting its cosmetic radiance stolen from the afternoon light.

Nicholas had spent the walk up Ahorte considering that question, particularly the implications for their LDI station. He was optimistic.

'I expect there will be a mixture of shock and celebration. The

Prime Minister will declare a period of mourning. The constitution will require that Crown Prince Arnaba return from wherever he is. The induction of Secretaries is for the life of the monarch, so they should lose power. That means there is an opportunity, which won't be lost on my Madregalo friends, to reassert the authority of Parliament. La Ferste will carry on as usual. And the Entente? Sunk without trace along with the Admiral, I would have thought. Feng Tong is decapitated; that will seriously impact on the northern exploitation. Remember, these were not ordinary deaths. These were totemic deaths. They're loaded with significance that will work against Chinese interests for generations. You can be sure that any part the People's Republic officially or unofficially played in the bogus pact will be hastily expunged from the record, the associations are so negative now.'

'Quite the Entente Fatale, as it turned out,' observed Tøssentern, who had otherwise been silent.

'I think there's something else we should talk about,' continued Nicholas. 'Our condor paper.'

'Go on, Nicholas,' said Tøssentern.

'Well, after seeing what happened today, that apparent intentionality, its sentience as a bird, it seems to me that we know a lot about the aggregation of *Phulex* but nothing about the coherence, the emergent nature, of the condor that results. I just wonder, particularly given its cultural significance, how responsible it is to publish the first with no understanding of the second.'

'You're right, of course,' said Tøssentern. 'Anna? If Paulo and Walter agree, are we all happy for an indefinite stay of publication?'

While she was listening to Nicholas, Anna had been looking at Edvard. He had come back to the Ferendes with a purpose, in search of release and reintegration that no amount of therapy in Mingle Lane could provide. She had come to realize that the idea of locating *Abel* was only partly a quest for the weaver fish, about validating a passion that had nearly taken his life and left his psyche damaged.

There was another meaning. For the Resurrect from Copio sitting beside her, *Abel* was the point of departure, and his quest was very different. It was a going back to be well, to being at peace again in silence, to being the Edvard Tøssentern of before.

This day had changed everything. And miraculously, they had been there. All the tenuous history, mythology, conjecture and imagination investing the weaver fish had been summarily shaken and resettled into witnessed fact.

Of course, notwithstanding its drama, the event would bring no scientific advance, no taxonomic triumph, no fame to naturalists. But for the Ferende people there was something far more important. The weaver fish, visitant protector and keeper of conscience for their nation, had accorded them not a sighting but a benediction, received by every individual as their word.

And now, perhaps, Edvard would remember, and be free to deconflate the word and thing, the idea and the act. Then, finally, he might abandon *Abel* and return to his first love, which was language, and that would complete his healing.

For Anna, too, there had been a blessing taken from this place, though not today; and nor was it a word. It was a secret, held in trust, and carried on her person all these months.

She felt inside her pocket for Edvard's watch, and held it out before him. Edvard took it slowly from her hand — it was a token and an act of returning for them both. Yet to Anna there was more: a communion of their strengths, which in its solemnness and touch was like renewing a betrothal.

> Now quietly kiss, while the scholar keeps
> vigil, and the sorcerer sleeps.

Those lines of rite from Satroit, once dangerous and distancing, seemed now to belong. She placed an arm around Edvard's shoulder, and drew him closer. Yes, she too was optimistic.

Worse and Millie had been consulting a map and talking quietly on their side of the table. At this point Worse stood up abruptly, saying, 'Excuse us for a few minutes.' Nicholas supposed they were going to the fountain, and was slightly surprised to see them cross the square and disappear into a narrow street. He had wondered a few times if a romantic connection might be developing. He wouldn't mind. He liked Worse, of course. And a Magnacart–Misgivingston union would be nicely apposite; historical, in fact.

They had been planning how to get to the LDI station without inconveniencing Paulo to collect them. Nicholas offered to charter a four-wheel drive bus and driver for the transfer from La Ferste the following day. He had taken his mobile from a pocket to make arrangements when he received a text message from Worse.

Look at palace.

He passed his phone to the others, saying quietly, 'It's from Worse.' From where they were sitting, it was easy to turn in their chairs for a view of the overbearing walls of L'Orphania, unobstructed by the café awning sheltering their table. They watched expectantly for a minute or so. Tøssentern and Anna, who were not yet well acquainted with Worse, had no idea of what might happen. Nicholas, knowing Worse, thought it could be anything.

Suddenly, above the Palace, there appeared a dense black cloud that billowed and spread, expanding rapidly to momentarily half darken the sun, and seemingly fed from a choking black geyser erupting from the roof. Nicholas was shocked. *Jesus, Worse*, he was thinking, *what have you done?* His eyes fell to the lower walls, anticipating flames and explosions to account for the smoke. *Jesus, Worse, we're in big trouble.*

But when he looked back to the roof, the geyser had ceased, and what he had thought was a cloud of smoke had separated into discrete, floating cinders.

'Swints,' he almost shouted. 'The swints are free!'

And as they watched, those graced and gilding birds circled the Palace once for orientation and once for salutation, then set their tidings course north-west to a haven most had never seen: a consecrated English belfry in a hidden-away village called Postlepilty.

THE END

O Lord.

I have deceived; how so am I rational?

That my faith is come by the misery of swints, and my Evensong a raven call? That my testimony is clothed in a Parsan word, or the sayings of a mute man, or the silence between them?

My son.

Reason and unreason are one, as are truth and deception one, like glass beneath water and above.

If I speak of two things, prayer and pestilence, these are made of one voice and borne on one breath.

Both are sounds on the wind. They are equal-blinded in the sun; nor by my hand do they differ in darkness.

Each is a vessel, sent forth, but the two are a fleet. Together they hold meaning or together they founder.

When one is pure the other is pure, for then is my voice pure. But if I am mute in one, I am mute in the other.

Wherefore my words are one word, as my silence is one silence.

Then also my word and my silence are one.

For each is the other's keeper, as two watchmen of the fleet are watchful for both, and call aloud the sounding, or strike their bells at night-sea figmentations.

My word and my silence are like the warp and the weft. Without one, there is not the other, and I am unclothed; but when I have both, my garment is woven, as your testimony also is woven.

My word and my silence are each embraced, one in the other, as lovers in arms are both holding and held.

My word and my silence cannot be parted. Where the parchment is bare we see what is written, and by all that is covered we see what is not.

Even then, the two will come forward in taken turn, as do ships in the weather, or lovers repose, or the parchment is lighted, or the threads of the weaving are brought into view.

Now what I sent forth is a vessel of word and a vessel of silence, and you have received them.

So too is the prophecy of the Syllabine this word and this silence, yet the Roman listens in wonderment.

Leonardo di Boccardo
Conversazioni e Silenzio

INDEX OF FIRST AND FINAL MENTIONS

NOTES AND ACKNOWLEDGEMENTS

I thank the Office of the Trustees in Perpetuity *Reliquiae di Boccardo* in Florence, for permission to use materials in approved translation (by Lord Enright, with permission, and this author), including the unattributed epigram pair in Chapter 28. Negotiations were conducted through the London Trustee, Dr Barbara Bokardo, to whom I am greatly indebted.

I am grateful to the Libraire Satroit in Istanbul for allowing quotations from 'The Guardianship of the Holy Land' and 'The Betrothal'. Permission to reproduce 'A Suitor's Reverie' was not sought as the Institute formally renounces this work, though the authorship is beyond question. The translation given is by the present author.

I thank Dr Edvard Tøssentern, the President of the Lindenblüten Society and the Syndics of Nazarene College, Cambridge, for permission to edit and publish the material of Chapter 1. The examination question (Chapter 31) was provided by the office of the Rede Professor of Logic in Nazarene College, and is reproduced also with approval of the College Syndics.

The content of Chapters 3 and 4 is reproduced with the permission of *Aviation Reviews* and Dr Anna Camenes (Chapter 3). I am grateful to Dr Camenes for sharing her ideas, both proven and speculative, on seki fruit. I likewise thank Dr Camenes and Dr Sigrid Blitt for assisting my understanding of credule theory and sekitriptyline pharmacology.

The anonymous Obituary of Chapter 5, the postscript by Professor Pioniv, the Review content of Chapter 10, the editorial Letter and Reply of Chapter 11, and the Editor's Note in Chapter 12 are reproduced with the permission of the publisher of the *London Tribune*. I am pleased to report that, following an unexplained absence, Simon Vestry has returned to the review pages of that august newspaper. Readers who have tired of weaver fish reportings and the documentary genre in general might enjoy his re-inaugural critical essay, entitled 'In a regime of impossible truths, fiction is stranger than fiction'.

The email of Chapter 6 is reproduced by courtesy of Dr Linda Feckles, with the caveat that certain engineering concepts contained therein are protected by patent.

Discoveries concerning the Asiatic condor are presented without material input from the stated principal investigators. The author has ascertained facts as accurately as circumstances allow, and is confident of committing no serious error; the test of this must await peer-reviewed publication of the scientific data.

My attempts to correspond with Rev Barnabas Bending have been unsuccessful, despite repeated assurances from his curate that this would be welcomed. I am informed that the Postlepilty Symposia have been discontinued.

Readers interested in knowing more about swint ethology or physiology should note that the species designation *transmuta* in place of *tinctoria* appears commonly in the North American academic literature. An entertaining place to start is T Thurdleigh's 'Prime factorization of avian flock counts' in *J. Numerical Ornith.*, and the references therein.

I regret to inform the reader that certain perfectly benign comments made by Dr Rodney Thwistle (recounted in Chapter 13) were overheard and misunderstood by a humourless drinks waiter, and a fatuous complaint lodged. Nazarene College is currently deeply divided between accusers and defenders, with a passion of enmities not seen since the Interregnum of the 1870s. The antagonists believe they differ on nothing less than what constitutes civilization; but in essence the central argument is whether irony is a human right. Thwistle is holidaying in Margaret River.

I am grateful to Dr Penelope Loom and Vissy Mofo (Captain Hate) for sharing their personal recollections of the dinner party in Chaucer Road (Chapter 15), and for permission to reproduce his letter and the poem 'Z-words in Latin', as well as the soliloquy of the Cycladic figurine (about which he advises some technical reservations).

I thank Dr Penelope Hyffen-Dascher, who also contributed her version of conversations reproduced in Chapter 15. Any inaccuracies in the account of that event remain the responsibility of this author. I am further grateful to Dr Hyffen-Dascher for providing an introduction to UITA Press.

I have been unable to contact Professor Lecémot or his agent, despite all reasonable efforts including a personal survey of the Paris Métro. His letter is deemed crucial in elucidating other matters and is reproduced here without permission, in good faith, and without prejudice.

I am indebted to Sir Peter Magnacart, who generously shared the private family feud story with this outsider, and provided access to archival material, including a priceless Codex with commentaries on the Pontage chronicle commissioned by the Magnacart family in the sixteenth century. The earliest history of Mingle Common (Notes to Chapter 23) was sourced partly from this document.

The description, address and occupation of the unnamed philatelist in La Ferste have been fictionalized for that person's safety. Likewise, identifying details of certain other individuals have been altered in the interests of privacy, security, or protection from criminal proceedings. No imputation relating to any other person, or any other business or property (similar or otherwise) should be made from the facts stated concerning Humboldt Bank, Verita's Wines, or their related entities as here described, or the premises and activities of the place and business named as Grosvenor Apartments.

I thank Inspector Victor Spoiling for explaining aspects of forensic chemistry and police procedures, and for some informal and most ethical conversations regarding the person identified in this work as Richard Worse.

I am instructed to make clear that Dr Sigrid Blitt and Dr Emily Misgivingston provided no information regarding the identity or character of Richard Worse. Nevertheless I remain grateful, as what was not forthcoming proved most enlightening. My one question to him, kindly forwarded by Dr Blitt, as to whether he tracked Prince Nefari's satellite phone to a point in the Bergamot Sea, has not been answered.

I thank Abbess Magdalena Letterby on a thorough (if divinely insisted) reading of the manuscript, for clarifying several authorship anomalies, and for her very generous contribution in a foreword. I was astonished to discover that she is an accomplished pistolier and familiar with the Prussica gunsight; thereafter, on certain matters, I ensured that we spoke around corners.

And now, to Edvard Tøssentern: Without you, this history could not have been told. Indeed, without you, it would never have happened, and I owe you every gratitude.

And to the reader: When recounting events in the Ferendes, I have occasionally been questioned on the matter of veracity. I wish to place on record that all facts have been meticulously checked and witness statements where possible corroborated, with rigorous observance of the public's right to be truthfully informed and my own professional responsibility as an historian. Where I could only speculate on proceedings, this has been clearly stated and, I believe, argued impartially.

In assembling the material for this work, and attempting to make sense of it, I have been encouraged by a special group of individuals who are good writers, good listeners, and good friends, and I thank them.

I wish also to express my appreciation and admiration for the work of Alison Pilcrow, of UITA, who edited the manuscript. I am unable to explain how her addendum to Chapter 15 increases transparency.

I am grateful to all who have been my teachers.

Finally, to my family and dearest friends: I thank you for every affection, and for your interest and belief.

TRAVEL ADVISORY AND DISCLAIMER

At the time of writing, the Ferendes is in political turmoil with a vicious power struggle between the Yiscosh military and the Democrasi. Foreign legations in Madregalo have been downgraded or closed, and offer no guarantee of assistance to nationals. International air travel through La Ferste is severely disrupted, and freedom of movement within the country is not assured. There are reports of visitors fleeing to the western plateau and being airlifted out. Expatriates who remain are strongly advised to avoid Madregalo's historic Kardia, where Fitrina's fountain has become the symbolic heart of the revolution—enlisting freedom fighters are ceremonially baptized in its water. Only streets distant, a police battalion encircles the vacant L'Orphania. The dangers are compounded by an escalating geopolitical polarization in the South China Sea, with a real prospect of regional war. This author can only stress the consensus diplomatic advice that non-essential travel to the Ferendes be delayed or cancelled. In particular, for reasons that must be clear, holders of Australian passports should not visit under any circumstances until further notice. In no way should the content of this work be viewed as an invitation, recommendation, encouragement, persuasion, inducement, incitement, or in any other way interpreted to suggest that any person, for any purpose whatsoever, travel to the Republic of Ferendes.

ABOUT THE AUTHOR

A B C Darian is an historian, and believed to be Timothy Bystander, who was exposed as the late Daniel Halfpenny, who is survived by the alias Robert Edeson, a graduate of the universities of Western Australia and of Cambridge, who is conjectured to be Magdalena Letterby, but she is almost certainly A B C Darian.

An Aardvark Bureau Book
An imprint of Gallic Books

First published by Fremantle Press, Australia in 2014
Copyright © Robert Edeson, 2014

First published in Great Britain in 2016 by
Aardvark Bureau, 59 Ebury Street, London, SW1W 0NZ

A CIP record for this book is available from the British Library
ISBN 978-1-910709-14-6

Printed in the UK by CPI Group (UK) Ltd, Croydon, CR0 4YY
2 4 6 8 10 9 7 5 3 1